COLD

Bond jinked the chopper in the other direction, still climbing, but coming dangerously close to the top of the trees. Then he was free and away, though he guessed not for long. In every direction he saw rock, stone and mountain: a whole landscape of peaks and troughs, some of the peaks still bearing traces of snow from the previous winter.

Grabbing at the headset which he had knocked off the seat in his rush to get in, Bond jammed it around his ears, adjusting it as he climbed towards the nearest series of brutal, belligerent and threatening pinnacles and sheer drops. As he turned, a staccato series of beeps sounded in the earphones and he saw a square red light begin to pulse to his left, warning him that a rocket had already locked on to him. He hit the chaff and flare releases – two fist-sized knobs which would shoot a series of flares and large magnetic confetti to his rear in an attempt to confuse the incoming 57-mm rocket. At the same time he pulled up to a near vertical climb, felt the Cobra sway and buck, then bump heavily as the rocket passed him only a few feet away . . .

Other James Bond Books by John Gardner

Licence Renewed
For Special Services
Icebreaker
Role of Honour
Nobody Lives Forever
No Deals, Mr Bond
Scorpius
Win Lose or Die
Brokenclaw
The Man from Barbarossa
Death is Forever
Sea Fire

Licence to Kill
(based on the 1989 film written by Michael G. Wilson
and Richard Maibaum)

Goldeneye
(Based on the screenplay by Jeffrey Caine and Bruce Feirstein
Story by Michael France)

Also by John Gardner

The Nostradamus Traitor   The Garden of Weapons
The Quiet Dogs   The Werewolf Trace   The Dancing Dodo
Flamingo   The Secret Generations   The Secret Houses
The Secret Families   Maestro   Confessor

About the author

John Gardner was educated in Berkshire and at St John's College
Cambridge. Before becoming a novelist he had many fascinating
occupations and was, variously a Royal Marine officer, a stage
magician, theatre critic, reviewer and journalist.

Ian Fleming's

JAMES BOND

in

John Gardner's

COLD

CORONET BOOKS
Hodder and Stoughton

First published in Great Britain in 1996 by Hodder and Stoughton
A division of Hodder Headline PLC

First published in paperback in 1996 by Hodder and Stoughton
A Coronet Paperback

10 9 8 7 6

A CIP catalogue record for this title is
available from the British Library

ISBN 0 340 65766 9

Typeset by
Letterpart Limited, Reigate, Surrey

Printed and bound in Great Britain

Hodder and Stoughton
A division of Hodder Headline PLC
338 Euston Road
London NW1 3BH

This book is dedicated to the executives and staff of
Glidrose Publications (the owners of the
James Bond Literary Copyright)
who had confidence in me
when choosing a successor to the late Ian Fleming
and have given me so much assistance and help
over the past sixteen years.

Contents

BOOK ONE – COLD FRONT

1	Disaster	3
2	Bait?	15
3	Voice Mail	25
4	A Chill Down the Spine	35
5	Conjunction	47
6	Cold Comfort	57
7	A Judas Kiss?	71
8	At the Villa Tempesta	81
9	If You Can't Beat 'Em	95
10	Kidnap	111
11	Graveyard	121
12	The High Road	131
13	Water Carnival	141
14	Interlude	153

BOOK TWO – COLD CONSPIRACY

15	A Voice from the Past	167
16	Need-To-Know	175
17	In Room 504	187

18	The Unravelling	197
19	Lazarus	207
20	A Close Call	217
21	Antifreeze	227
22	Die Like a Gentleman	235
23	Wedding Bells	245
24	A Day of Days	255
25	Clay Pigeon	265
26	Facing the Music	275

BOOK ONE

Cold Front

1

Disaster

ZULU TIME IS the military term for Greenwich Mean Time. It is Zulu Time which is used by NATO and Coalition Forces, the world over, when operating in the field and it pays no attention to things like Daylight Savings Time. It is the time also used by the Secret Intelligence Service, and on that evening it was just after 17.00 hours Zulu Time (5 p.m. to us lesser mortals) on Tuesday, 20th March when the disaster occurred.

In the tall anonymous building overlooking Regent's Park one shift of secretaries and deskbound officers was preparing for the end of the day's work. James Bond, irritable as ever when he was out of the field, was just putting his signature to the last page of a memo when the red telephone, his direct line to M's office, started to ring.

Later, he recalled feeling a second of dread for some unaccountable reason.

'Bond,' he said into the mouthpiece.

At the other end, M's PA, the faithful Moneypenny, sounded shaken and in tears. 'Bradbury Airlines flight to Dulles. Blew up on landing. James, I . . . I had a friend on board. I . . . Please get up here.'

M had a videotape running when a red-eyed Moneypenny buzzed him through: the video, soon to be seen all over the

3

world, captured by a major network for a two minute spot with a sale to CNN, showed the arrival of Bradbury Airlines' inaugural flight into Washington Dulles International, some forty minutes' drive from the centre of Washington DC. Stark, horrible and shattering in its dreadful images.

The Boeing 747–400, which was Flight BD 299, came sweeping in over the trees for the flare and touched down, the black, white and gold livery of Bradbury Airlines glinting as it caught the sun – a picture perfect landing on a picture perfect day.

The main gear caressed the runway, then came the dreadful sight. First a plume of fire and smoke seemed to break from the aircraft, just behind the flight deck. The flame swung back and a second explosion ripped through the cabin, close to the wing roots, then a final blast just forward of the tail. One wing sheared off completely; the remainder of the Boeing careered down the runway like some obscene firework, scattering fragments of burning wreckage and people as it went.

Bond realized that he had stopped breathing during these appalling few seconds, and knew he was standing grey-faced as M looked away from the screen. 'How d'you think they did that, James?' His voice shook with a mixture of anger and shock, but it turned Bond's mind inside out. Looking at his old Chief he thought he could detect a glistening of the eyes that betokened tears.

'How . . .?'

'Watch it again.' M rewound the tape and played it back in slow motion, keeping up a running commentary that made Bond think of the fractured voice of the film news commentator, heard so many times, on the surviving graphic footage which chronicled the final moments of the airship *Hindenburg* in 1937 – 'His gear touches down . . . God, look at it . . . the gear touches and there goes the first explosion, abaft the flight deck . . . Oh, God, James, it hasn't moved its own length before the main cabin explodes . . . The port wing crumples . . . Fire . . . Then the explosion for'ard of the tail.'

In the back of his mind, Bond calculated the fact that the loss of life in the *Hindenburg* disaster was, amazingly, thirty-six out of ninety-two passengers and crew. What he had just witnessed would have blown apart or incinerated almost four hundred people. He was shocked and sickened by this obvious act of wanton carnage.

'So, how, James? If it was your job, how would you have done it?'

Bond shook his head. 'From Heathrow? It's not possible. Security's tied up tighter than a champagne cork.'

'So, how would *you* have got around that? Somebody did.' The old man sounded angry and stunned.

'I'd want . . .' Bond began, then the intercom buzzed on M's desk and Moneypenny's voice came through. 'I have the list you wanted, sir.'

M told her to bring it in, and Bond noted her eyes were still red, her manner, if anything, even more subdued.

'Poor girl.' M scanned the papers she had brought to him once she was out of the room again. 'An old friend of hers was one of the senior flight attendants on BD 299.' He paused as though about to say something else, then seemed to change his mind. 'You were telling me how you'd have rigged up explosives like that, James.'

His use of Bond's given name instead of the peremptory 007 signalled that he was in an almost fatherly mood. It also indicated his level of trust.

'I'd need to know how long the aircraft was actually on the ground between flights. Where it had come from on its last

5

assignment. Who did the maintenance. All the usual things.'

'Walking back the cat?' M seemed to be proud of his knowledge of arcane terms.

'That's what I understand the Americans call it, sir.'

Almost immediately, M's mood changed from the whimsical back to the serious area of the disaster. 'And if you were the mad bomber, how would you fix it?'

'The first one I'd say was in the lavatories just behind the flight deck. I suspect the one in the rear would be similar, while the explosion from midships would have been set in the crew station and galley between business class and economy. Unless Bradbury's people had a new configuration on their 747s.'

'Unlikely, even though the aircraft are new. Bradbury only bought two, I gather. His entire fleet consists of a couple of 747s, five 737s, two Learjets, a pair of Airbus 340s and four Shorts 360s for commuter flights in the UK.'

'Well, that's where I would plant the explosives; my best guess would be that's where they were.'

'And the method of detonation?'

Bond frowned. 'Could be a button right there at Dulles . . .'

'By a button, you mean remote control?'

He nodded and M quietly asked him to say the word – 'Yes or no, James.'

'This being taped, sir?'

'Yes.' Matter-of-fact, as though it were the most normal thing in the world. 'Go on, what other method?'

'The explosions detonated at the moment the gear touched the runway. I'd say some kind of trigger mechanism, like a very sophisticated mercury switch, phased to activate the bombs when the wheels bumped the runway at Dulles.'

'And what would you use? What kind of explosives?'

'Any good plastique. Semtex, C4, whatever. But there's

something else bugging me, sir. Nobody's mentioned that Harley Bradbury was on the flight.'

'He wasn't.'

'Why not? The man's a great self-promoter. He's made a point of being on every inaugural flight since they first started flying.'

Harley Bradbury was a prime example of the self-made British multi-millionaire. At the age of forty-two, he seemed to have come from nowhere. In fact he had come from buying up remaindered books at a fraction of their cost, supplying them to libraries – both public and private – before his first major purchase, a small publishing house, which he saved from extinction by borrowing heavily. That was in 1982. By 1990 he owned three publishing houses, a chain of shops selling music CDs, a recording company and an airline. Bradbury was one of the big success stories of the '80s, matched only by Richard Branson of *Virgin* fame. He had won the Heathrow-Dulles route against many attempts to block it. This was to have been a big day for Bradbury.

'Why not?' Bond repeated. 'Why wasn't he on board?'

'Last-minute change of plan. It appears that he was called to his headquarters for some important meeting only a few hours before 299 was due to leave. Flew up in one of his line's Shorts 360s.'

'The Bradbury Air HQ?'

M nodded. 'Birmingham. That's where he keeps the fleet.'

'Lower airport charges?'

'No room at Heathrow.'

After a short pause, Bond asked if there was anything M wanted him to do.

There was a silence while both men seemed to stare into space, the dreadful image of the aircraft touching down and then exploding playing again and again in their minds.

'Initially, I thought you could check up on Bradbury and those who helped fund the airline, from this end.' M cleared his throat, shaking his head as if to rid it of the pictures of disaster. 'Changed my mind. All the scavengers are dashing to DC – to Dulles.' M glanced again at the papers Moneypenny had brought in. 'The NTSB Go-Team are already there, as are the FAA, representatives from Boeing and ALPA. The FBI also has a team, of course.' The NTSB was the American National Transport Safety Board. The organization always had what they called a Go-Team ready for any major disaster. FAA was the Federal Aviation Administration; while ALPA – the Airline Pilots' Association – always had a representative at a serious crash site.

'As the flight originated here, and it's a British airline,' M continued, 'people're assembling here to join the fray.'

'Who in particular?'

'Well, Bradbury himself with a couple of his senior people. A team from Farnborough, naturally, and a pair of people from our sister service, because it appears to be terrorist-related.' By Farnborough, M meant the Aircraft Research Establishment, that extraordinary team of aeronautical scientists who time and again had pieced together the reason for aircraft crashes. The ARE had been mainly responsible for tracking down the makers and planters of the bomb that had blown Pan Am 103 out of the sky over Lockerbie, Scotland, in 1988. Their sister service was, of course, the Security Service, often referred to as MI5.

'There'll also be a member of the British Airline Pilots' Association . . .'

'And, presumably someone from our own department just to balance out the folk from "Five." '

'Naturally.'

'And I'm the first choice?'

'You were.' M looked up from under his grey bushy eyebrows. 'Now there might be problems concerning that.'

'Problems?'

'Brace yourself, James. Moneypenny's not the only one to have lost a friend in this disaster. An old close companion of yours has also perished.'

Bond did not flinch. 'Who?'

M sighed. 'She still clung to her minor title and name even though her husband's long dead. Tempesta. Sukie Tempesta.'

The shock hit Bond in an amalgam of sudden sorrow and disbelief. The *Principessa* Sukie Tempesta dead. He had shared much danger with this golden girl, much danger and a lot of loving as well. In his mind he saw her very clearly: the mane of red hair and her habit of blowing the odd unruly strand out of her face, away from her brown, violet-flecked eyes. Like anybody hearing of a sudden death, he could not believe it and a jumble of thoughts crowded his mind.

Her maiden name had been Susan Destry. He recalled some raunchy pillow talk, her laugh and the words, 'Destry rides again.' A convent educated girl, she had answered an ad on a kind of whim and so became nanny to the grandchildren of *Principe* Pasquale Tempesta, sire of an old and respected Italian family, who was over eighty years of age when she married him. 'A marriage of convenience,' Sukie had called it, and the entire tribe had been anxious for the wedding to take place. Anything that would keep the old man happy. When Bond first met her there had been danger and violence, played out over several weeks of turmoil.

He could see her quite clearly now, the slim figure with drop-dead legs and a quirky sense of humour. Dead? Sukie Tempesta dead? It did not seem possible.

He realized that M was looking at him with the eyes of an inquisitor. 'I would have liked you on this one, James,' he said finally, 'but I fear you may be too personally involved.'

'Don't worry, sir. If Sukie was killed in this horror, it will make me even more determined.'

'Yes, but can you remain detached? You, of all people, know the problems that come with personal vendettas.'

'I'll be fine, sir.' Even as he spoke, Bond asked himself if he were being honest.

'Good man. Let me make some calls. After that I'll be able to brief you thoroughly.'

He waited for his old chief to work the phones, as they called it, and half an hour later he was being instructed on the situation he would have to face. An Air Transport Command VC-10 was to leave Lyneham that evening with a number of other people, flying straight to the crash site at Dulles International. Towards the end of the briefing M said they were also giving Bradbury and his own team a lift. 'They're my only definite no as far as contracts're concerned,' he told Bond. 'I don't want us getting our wires crossed with the Security Service. So keep your distance from Bradbury and his people. Understand?'

Bond nodded, and when the briefing was over, he left the building, went back to his flat off the King's Road, packed a bag, readied a briefcase and waited to be picked up by one of the SIS cars that would drive him to Wiltshire and Lyneham.

Later that night he boarded the old VC-10 – still the Royal Air Force's main transport aircraft – settled himself in a seat towards the rear and promptly fell asleep.

He was wakened by a WRAF flight attendant offering him breakfast and saying they would be landing within an hour. During the meal he looked around, identifying his fellow travellers: a pair of men who had the look of specialists about them – obviously the couple from the Aircraft Research Establishment; a man and woman, sitting a few rows in front of him, both of whom merged into the background like chameleons, certainly the Security Service; one tall, big, silver-haired and clear-eyed man, undoubtedly from BALPA; and right forward, the unmistakable form of Harley Bradbury, accompanied by a knot of four PAs and secretaries, plus the VP of Bradbury Air. The group appeared to be hunched together, as though discussing the way in which they would be dealing with the catastrophe. It would mean certain financial disaster for Bradbury, Bond knew, and was quite pleased that M had given him the hands-off order concerning that particular group. Bond liked money-men about as much as he liked politicians, who were pretty well off his scale of people to be trusted.

As they swept down at Dulles, he was able to catch a short glimpse of the wreckage beside the runway, with people in overalls moving around it and the usual post-crash vehicles lined up at strategic points along the site.

The aircraft finally came to rest, parked on the far side of the midfield terminal from which the clumsy 'people mover lounges' ploughed to and fro to the main terminal buildings. Two sets of mobile stairs were driven into place and, seconds later, two men came up and into the main cabin.

One was from the British Embassy, the other did not specify his position, but had about him the look of a man of authority. Bond put him down as probably the overall leader of the crash investigation team. Both were businesslike and brisk. All customs and immigration inspections were being waived; out of deference to some of those on board, they were parked at a point where neither press nor public could see faces or take photographs. Those who had no immediate business at the crash site would be bused out to a hotel some ten minutes from the airport. The team from ARE and Mr Bradbury's group would be taken straight out to the scene of the disaster. There would be a general briefing and a sharing of information at three-thirty that afternoon in the hotel.

Bond, the representative from BALPA, and the couple from the Security Service were bundled down the rear stairway and into a crew bus which drew away quickly, heading for the airport exit. Bond gave the people from MI5 what he considered to be a disarming smile and introduced himself, holding out his hand. 'Boldman,' he announced. 'James Boldman.'

'Yes, we know.' The man gave him a half-hearted handshake, while the woman merely smiled and said, 'Mr and Mrs Smith. John and Pam Smith.' She had lank off-blonde hair and wore outdated granny glasses, her ankle-length shapeless dress covered by a black coat that looked as though it had come from an Oxfam shop, the shoulders spotted with dandruff.

The BALPA captain nodded at them in turn, saying that he was 'Mercer, Edward Mercer.'

'One big happy family,' mused John Smith as the driver honked his horn loudly at a tourist-driven car that suddenly swerved in front of them.

At the hotel, Bond held back to let the others check in first so that the registration desk was clear before he took out one of his Boldman identity credit cards and filled in the form.

'There's a long fax for you, sir.' The young attractive black girl who was on the desk pushed an envelope towards him. 'I'll get a bell-boy to see you up to your room, and if there's anything I can do, just let me know.'

The name tag pinned to her uniform said *Azeb*. 'Thank you, Azeb. I think I can manage to find the room, and I'm travelling light.' He lifted the garment bag and the briefcase to show her as he turned away.

He had just reached the bank of elevators when a voice behind him softly breathed, 'James. James, there you are. I've been waiting since Monday morning. Where've you been?'

He turned and stared in confusion.

'James, what's the matter? You look as though you've seen a ghost. I got a flight straight away, the moment I received your message,' said the Principessa Sukie Tempesta.

2

Bait?

'MY MESSAGE . . .?' BOND grasped blindly for an explanation. 'I think we'd better go upstairs and talk about this in private, Sukie.'

'What a novel idea. I change all my plans, which, incidentally, happens to save my life, and you want to go upstairs and discuss it.'

He took a step towards her. 'Sukie, it's only four years since we had a clash with SPECTRE. This could well be the same people, and you know how hairy they can be. I think we should talk about this now. You could be in some danger. I sent you *no* message, and that concerns me.'

'You . . .?' she began, but Bond took her by the upper arm and propelled her into the elevator.

His room was 21st century utilitarian beehive.

'At least you have Dial-a-Movie.' Sukie gestured towards the TV, and her smile lit up his life as it had done every time they were together – which was never as often as he would have liked.

'Thank heaven you're alive.' He dumped the garment bag and briefcase. 'When and where did you get any message from me, Suke? Better still, what was the message?'

'At the Dorchester. I've still got it.' She rummaged in the

large white leather shoulder bag that matched her heavy winter coat. The clasp on the bag was a large gold-coloured letter 'T' entwined with an 'S'.

He took the envelope from her, noting that the address was typewritten: *The Principessa Tempesta, The Dorchester Hotel, To Await Arrival*. Inside was one sheet of heavy paper containing a simple typed message –

Sukie My Dear,
You could be in grave danger. Do not try to make contact, but get out of London and head to Washington DC as quickly as possible. Straight away if you can. Book yourself into a hotel and watch for me on all flights coming in from London. I should make it within twenty-four hours, but do not delay your departure. Just get out of London as quickly as you can.
As ever –

Then came his signature, which was a very good forgery, not quite right but good enough to take in Sukie.

'Not me,' he spoke curtly. 'You took it at face value?'

'Of course.' She gave a little mock curtsey. 'I know better than to disregard your advice, James; you know that.'

'And you got it when you were checking into the Dorchester.'

'I told you, yes.'

'Which was when?'

'Sunday evening. I didn't even go up to my room. I simply flew back to Heathrow and took the first flight to Dulles. To hear is to obey, O master.'

'Sure, yes. Why did you choose this hotel?'

'I didn't. I'm checked in at the Hilton up the road, but I've spent most of my time hanging around the arrivals area. It was

16

luck that latched me on to you in the end. I overheard a conversation about the arrival of a Royal Air Force plane. There were a couple of drivers talking – I guess you'd say being very insecure. One of them mentioned that some passengers from the RAF flight would be coming to this hotel. So I watched the aircraft land, then shot over here to wait and see if you were among the group, which you were.'

He detected that something was not quite right. The look in her eyes, a certain movement, a gesture. It was one of those things his intuition picked up and yet the fact of it lay just beyond the reach of his mind.

'You have a car?' he asked.

'I rented a piece of Japanese high-class stuff – a Lexus – as soon as I got here.'

'Under your own name?'

'It's the only one I've got.'

'You realize we have one hell of a serious problem?'

'It does seem pretty unusual.'

'That's like saying Perrier tastes like Krug.'

'Doesn't it?'

'Sukie, do you have any connection with Harley Bradbury?'

'The family does.'

There it was again, and this time he caught it, a slyness in the eyes: something he did not recall from the time they had spent together in the past.

'You mean your family, or the Tempestas?'

'My stepsons, their wives and the hundreds of sisters, cousins and aunts. The Tempestas, of course. They have dealings with Harley, yes.'

'So you got a special invitation to be on the inaugural flight to DC.'

'That's how it worked. I've told you before, James. The

Tempestas – my stepsons and their ladies – rarely move further than the Appian Way. Except for Venice, for the Carnival, of course, and the place they have near Pisa – and their little jaunts to the USA. We all had invitations, but I do the parties for the old family firm. Known for it.' She gave a little laugh. It was not the kind of laugh he remembered from the last time they had been together, but that could simply be a faulty recollection. Yet he had a distinct feeling about it. She seemed edgy, nervy, uncertain.

'And you came into London on Sunday straight from Rome?'

'Paris actually. I spent last Friday and Saturday in Paris. Flew to London on Sunday, and bounced straight here as soon as I got the letter you didn't send me.' The laugh again and an uncharacteristic movement of her hand, the forefinger plunging into her hair and winding some strands around it. A child's action. He had seen small children do exactly the same thing, usually accompanied by a sucking of the thumb. It was as though in the past four years Sukie Tempesta had been subjected to great stress.

'So, on Sunday night you got a message to say get out. Go to DC and wait?'

'Right.'

'And on Sunday night the only people who knew there was going to be a tragedy on Tuesday – that Harley Bradbury's Flight 299 was going to be blown to pieces – were the people providing the terror. Incidentally, you weren't the only one to miss the flight. Harley cancelled as well. And your name was still on the passenger list.'

'I didn't cancel, so I'd be a no-show.' She had slipped out of her coat revealing that she wore a neatly tailored white suit.

Bond nodded, 'They probably didn't pass that on. They'd be

anxious to get away on time, but the main question is why would anyone try to get you on a different flight by posing as me? That's what they did, Suke.'

'I understand that.' She visibly shuddered, 'Gives me goose bumps. Yuck.'

'By the same token, how would these people think they could get away with it? Did they think there was a possibility that I might actually turn up here? Incidentally, where were you when the aircraft blew up?'

Sukie had seated herself near the window, leaning back and crossing her long and exceptionally lovely legs, the finger still winding the strands of hair and her eyes flicking to and fro: again almost slyly. She also seemed to have gone a little pale. 'I was there. Over in the mid-field terminal. I saw it . . .' Her eyes were brimming now, and there was genuine distress about her body language: a particular movement deep in her eyes. 'Haven't got over it yet, James. Horrible. Absolutely horrible. That night, after the last flight had come in from the UK – and you weren't on it – I went back to the hotel. Couldn't sleep until I had written a description and drawn pictures. As for you turning up, perhaps they were banking on you *not* being here, which makes it even more sinister.'

He went over to her, bent down and enfolded her in his arms where she snuggled like a small child drawing comfort from his presence. To begin with, she was rigid, tense and he could almost feel the fear reaching out from her. Then she eventually eased herself free and led him towards the bed. 'It's been a long time, my dear James,' she whispered.

He was uncertain, not sure that this should happen so quickly, even though, in the past, he had been her lover, but she was insistent, and when it came down to it, frantic, passionately wild as though sex released some drug into her body, transforming her, so that she became a different person. Again, he wondered what had happened in the interim years. Later, after the loving, she asked what he thought was going on.

'That's what I'm here to find out. We've always been completely straight with one another. It goes without saying that I'm more than just worried about you. Someone cut you loose from flying over on Bradbury Airlines, yet sent you here using me as bait – if that isn't too arrogant.'

'Why should it be arrogant? People know we've been lovers on and off since we first met. I'm worried as well. To be honest with you, I'm terrified. Someone wanted me off that flight . . .' She stopped suddenly as though she were about to say something indiscreet, or not for his ears.

'And whoever that was must have known what was going to happen, yet could not have known I'd be here within hours of the incident – if you can call the deaths of almost five hundred people an incident. What about your stepsons? You said they knew Harley Bradbury.'

'Yes.'

'How far were they in bed with him on Bradbury Airlines?'

She cocked one eyebrow. 'I think one of their wives was in bed with him.' The sly look once more.

'Literally?'

'Is there any other way?'

'Which of the wives? Luigi's or Angelo's?'

'Luigi's. The lovely Giulliana.'

'Evidence?'

'The last time Harley came to see them in Rome, Giulliana was supposed to be staying with her mother for a couple of nights. In fact I saw her coming out of the Cardinal with him. You know the Cardinal, small but elegant. On the Via Giulia – I thought it was quite an amusing choice. They seemed rather close, and this was two days before he was due at their Palazzo.' The same laugh as before. A laugh alien to her former self.

'You've told nobody?' He was worried about her. Wondering if there was some deep problem between her and the remainder of the Tempesta family.

'James, what do you take me for? Luigi's three years older than me, and Angelo's about a year older. They've been incredibly supportive. My late husband's estate was split two ways: two thirds to me, and a third jointly to his sons, plus the companies. They accepted that, but I'm not going to get mixed up in family scandals. Please, would you come back to Italy with me? Meet them?'

'Yes, I'll come to Rome with you. Back you up. If you'll give me tips and hints when I meet the brothers Tempesta.'

'To do that we would have to go to Tuscany. They're all there at the moment. It's a kind of family tradition. March until after Easter.'

'Okay, then I'll come to Pisa with you.'

'Only if I can move in here for as long as you stay.'

'Deal. Food?'

'Just something expensive from room service.'

He called room service and ordered two chicken salads, coffee and a semi-reasonable Chardonnay – the best in a dubious wine list.

'You've become mean since I last saw you, James.' Sukie did a mock pout. 'I asked for something expensive.'

He handed her the room service menu, 'Look for yourself. You got something expensive.'

He remembered the fax handed to him on arrival, slipped the envelope out of his pocket, used his thumb to rip it open, then began to look through the pages. The first three pages consisted of the passenger manifest, and he did a mental double-take at some of the names. 'My god,' he said aloud. 'Whoever did this just got rid of half of *Who's Who*.' There were three very well-known actors on board, seven politicians, two from each party and one independent. One of the politicians was a Cabinet Minister. There were also three popular best-selling authors and two more highly regarded literary figures.

'What?' she asked as he sighed coming to the end of reading the list.

'Your name and Harley Bradbury's are still both on the manifest,' he began. It was the reason he had thought her dead. He went on to read out the other high-profile passengers, his reading punctuated by little gasps as she recognized names.

'James, I didn't know. There were half-a-dozen people I knew. Friends. Oh . . . Oh, Christ, James . . . I really didn't know . . .' She began to sob, making a dash to the bathroom when room service knocked on the door.

The waiter spoke little English, but understood the tip, which Bond slipped to him in cash.

He tapped on the bathroom door and called to Sukie.

'I'm all right. Be out in a minute.' Her voice was small, still not under control.

He laid out the lunch on the room service trolley, then turned back to the faxed documents. There was one more page which gave details of the aircraft's movements for the twenty-four hours before its final flight. He scanned it, then stopped to read it more carefully, his lips pursing in a long silent whistle.

She came into the room looking pale and shaky. If he did not know better, he would have thought she was a very frail young woman. The sight increased his concern about her.

'Sukie, are you really all right?'

'I'll get over it.' A wan smile which did not reach the eyes.

'It's just . . . well, a shock. I knew so many of those people.'
But that was not all. He could tell by the new nervous habits,
the apprehensive laugh and her almost fidgety manner.

He encouraged her to eat, and over coffee asked her if she
still wanted to join him here, at the hotel. She cheered up a little
at that, even wisecracking – 'I'd rather we joined each other.'

'That can be arranged,' glancing at his watch. 'I've got a
briefing at three-thirty. Why don't you go back to the Hilton
and move your things over here?'

'Can't I come to the briefing?'

'Your friend Harley will be there, and we might get some
flak from the NTSB people if I march in with you.'

Ten minutes later they took the elevator down to the main
lobby which was deserted except for the girl at Reception.

He took Sukie by the elbow and steered her towards the
desk.

'Azeb,' in his most suave and charming manner. 'This is the
Principessa Tempesta, from Rome. The Principessa is going to
join me here for a couple of days. She's going to collect her
luggage and move in while I am in a meeting. I'd be more than
grateful if you would see that she gets all the help and
co-operation you can muster.'

Azeb looked at Sukie as though she were a person of great
wonder. 'You're a real princess?'

'Well, a kind of dowager princess. Minor Italian royalty.
Very minor, sort of C Minor.'

'Yes, Mr Boldman, I'll see that everything is done to make
the princess comfortable.'

'Thank you, Azeb.'

They turned to move away, but she had not finished. 'What's
a dowager?' she asked.

'Like the Queen Mother.' Sukie's smile danced towards the

receptionist. For a second, she was the old Sukie, remembered with great affection. It's the Tempesta step-sons, he thought. That is where the trouble really lies.

She said she would be back in half an hour or so as he saw her into the Lexus. She lowered her window and turned her face up to be kissed, then drove smoothly away, one hand raised in temporary farewell.

The hotel looked out, through a small screen of trees, onto the huge parking lots that spread in front of the main terminal of Washington Dulles – a glass and concrete edifice which stood like some modern rendition of a sixteenth-century canopied structure erected for a king on the verge of a battlefield.

Bond thought how bleak and uninviting the environs of modern major airports had become. The romance of travel was now long gone; in its place there was only a wasteland of parking lots, fast-food joints and waiting, struggling passengers.

As he turned back into the lobby, three minibuses containing the NTSB, FAA and other teams who were coming in from the crash site pulled up in front of the hotel. As the occupants passed by, he saw the same look in their eyes: a look which was full of shock, disgust and not a little anguish.

These were the people who had seen the wreckage, close up and very personal, and it showed in the way they walked and in their faces. For a second, Bond envisaged the last moments on that aircraft as it flared and touched down bringing relief that the long journey was over. Then the noise and the fireballs exploding within the cabin, searing lungs and consuming bodies. He hoped that it had been quick for all of them.

3

Voice Mail

THE IIC – AS they called the leader of the American NTSB team
– was a broad-shouldered man with a gentle, almost fatherly,
voice. He had short-cropped grey hair and announced that his
name, for those who had yet to meet him, was Jack Hughes.
'But most people at NTSB call me Pop.' He gave a slow smile
starting at the mouth, creeping up his leathery face and settling
in the dark blue eyes which looked as though he had seen
everything there was to see in the way of disaster, pain, sorrow
and, paradoxically, happiness in the fifty or so years of his life.

Everybody had been given a chance to wash and change
before assembling in Convention Room A, part of the hotel's
Conference Suite, a series of uninviting rooms, reached by
elevator from the main lobby.

Bond had already introduced himself – as Jim Boldman
from the British Foreign Service – to Pop Hughes and the
senior member of the Farnborough trio, Bill Alexander. A nod
had sufficed for Mr and Mrs Smith who claimed to represent
the Home Office's Anti-Terrorist Department which fooled
people about as much as his own Foreign Service assertion.

He had finally put a name to 'Smith' – Peter Janson,
formerly of the Security Service's Watchers Division, cur-
rently – after several quick-and-dirty courses – he was billed

25

as an expert on terrorist operations in what was known among the more jocular members of the intelligence community as Global Terror, Inc.

Mrs 'Smith' remained a mystery, a pallid, pasty-faced young woman with a laugh which clanged rather than tinkled.

The NTSB team under Pop Hughes consisted of a serious-looking thin blonde with breasts like large peaches and a permanent scowl who answered to the unlikely nickname of Twinkle; a *wunderkind* with thick spectacles called Moan; and a second man built in the same mould as Hughes who was introduced as Greg Welles.

The two FBI Special Agents were trained in anti-terrorist counterintelligence: Special Agent Eddie Rhabb, a tough, unsmiling, no-nonsense character of few words; and Barney Newhouse, a laid back Mr Nice Guy.

Looking around the room, Bond thought the people from Boeing, and both the Airline Pilots' Association Captains, would have all made good field intelligence men for they seemed to disappear into the woodwork and would have had difficulty in catching the eye of a waiter in a restaurant.

Hughes asked Harley Bradbury and his coterie if they wanted to say anything at the start of the briefing, but Bradbury – usually an outgoing man full of charm – asked if he could wait until the end.

Everyone in the room looked, and sounded, shaken by what they had seen out on the airfield, and Hughes started a matter-of-fact general briefing.

'I want to run over the facts and where we are, at this point in time. As most of you know, we've recovered the Flight Data Recorder and the Cockpit Voice Recorder. These are being studied by our people back at Headquarters, and the results will be passed on to the Farnborough team, who will be doing some of the hard work back in the UK.

'In general terms, we've also established the position and type of what appear to be four bombs – not three as we originally thought – which led to the disaster. One was hidden in the starboard lavatory directly behind the flight deck; the second was secreted in the crew station and galley between what is normally the first and business classes. This second device, we think, was linked to a third explosive device below a floor inspection panel in the main cabin; while the last was fairly obvious to anyone who has viewed the tape – in one of the rear lavatories.

'As for type and method, I'm going to ask Special Agent Rhabb to make some remarks on this.'

Rhabb stood and looked around the room in a somewhat aggressive manner. He reminded Bond of a bull lowering its head before charging. 'The four sites of detonation were isolated during last night's examination of the wreckage,' he began. 'This was not difficult given Mr Hughes' team, who were able to map the debris very quickly. We worked under arc lights all through the night, and near the mapped areas we found the remains of at least two solenoids. We were also able to take scrapings from fragments of metal and charred wax paper in the general area of two of the sites. Our laboratories have isolated the type of explosive used. It is not the usual Semtex – international terrorism's explosive of choice. In fact the explosive used in the front and rear bombs was Comp D – Composition D.'

He paused to look around once more and let the news sink in. 'Comp D, as most of you are aware, is a product manufactured here in the United States and is not easily accessible. The Bureau, with the aid of the ATF, is doing a nationwide search at this moment, to ascertain if we can track down any missing amounts.

'The solenoids suggest that the devices were activated locally. What the Brits would call a "button job." Namely, a remote control activated from some point on the ground here at Dulles. This is borne out by news that reached me just before this briefing. It appears that before the first explosion the CVR picked up an electronic whine which alerted the aircraft's captain and second officer. You can hear the whine quite clearly and the captain's last words were, "What the hell's that . . .?" The words were immediately followed by the first explosion, and the electronic whine is consistent with a remote device being activated. The question now is how and when were the explosives placed on board and wired up?'

Rhabb again looked around, as though challenging someone to come up with the answer.

Bond slowly raised a hand and got to his feet, speaking as he did so. 'You've almost certainly got this information, or will get it pretty quickly.' He held up the last page of the fax that had been waiting for him. 'London has faxed me information regarding the aircraft's movements during the twenty-four hours prior to the tragedy. On Monday this particular aircraft – Zulu Two Four – did a package flight from the Bradbury base, which is Birmingham, to Tenerife in the Canaries. It was on the ground for approximately two hours, doing a turn round and collecting passengers from a similar package from two weeks previously, then returning to Birmingham, where it arrived at just before 17.00 hours. It was then taken over to the Bradbury maintenance hangar where it went through a complete ground check. This was completed just after 22.00, and the aircraft remained in the hangar until 08.00 when it was removed and flown to Heathrow for its 11.00 departure. It is my understanding that there was no special security watch on Zulu Two Four during a crucial ten-hour period. I presume you can collect the necessary information from Bradbury Airlines. Also, it is my understanding that the British Security Service already has investigators in Birmingham checking the status of that hangar and its accessibility during those ten hours during which the explosive devices could – and probably were – put in place . . .'

Smith/Janson cut in, obviously annoyed that Bond had provided the information before him. '. . . I have the same information, Mr Hughes,' he snapped. 'I can also confirm that the Security Service is there, on the spot – with police backup – investigating the distinct possibility that security was breached. They are convinced that the devices were placed on board during that window of opportunity.'

If anybody had doubts regarding the true nature of 'Smith's' work description, his little speech shattered them.

'Do we know if further security checks were carried out at Heathrow?' Hughes asked, a sombreness coming into his voice.

'They're looking into that . . .' began Smith.

'Unlikely . . .' Bond overlapped.

There was an uncomfortable silence followed by Pop Hughes asking if Harley Bradbury would like to comment.

'We face a problem here.' Bradbury's usual charm was there, but anyone looking carefully saw the change in his eyes: a kind of wariness underlying the concern which followed the tragedy. 'Yes, Mr . . . er . . .?'

'Boldman,' Bond lied.

'Mr Boldman's information regarding the operation and whereabouts of Zulu Two Four on the day before this cowardly act of terrorism is basically correct. However, my legal adviser,' he gestured towards a dark-suited and jowled, silver-haired man sitting to his right, 'Charles Groves feels that it would be inadvisable for me to comment on the question of security in Birmingham.'

'That indicates you could have problems in that area?' Pop Hughes seemed to be doing a relaxed good-old-boy performance, but Bradbury did not miss a beat.

'Mr Hughes, it means that I am a businessman with many companies under my general control. I have learned to share responsibility. Further, and to tell you the truth, I do not know every single thing concerning all aspects of Bradbury Airlines. It would be foolish for me to speculate at this moment. I'm awaiting a report from Birmingham. My main concern is for those who have lost their lives in this wanton act of violence, and for those whose lives have been changed by the sudden deaths of loved ones. It would be premature to speculate about the security arrangements at this moment.'

Pop shrugged. 'Okay, sir. Anything else you want to say? I should add that we all feel distress over this terrible act. Anyone who has been out there at the scene already feels the anguish, and I for one can say that, in nearly twenty years of doing this kind of work, this is the worst I have ever seen.'

There were mumbles of agreement in the room, then a moment's silence during which Bond thought he felt a slight tremor within the building. Nobody else appeared to have noticed so he put it down to an aircraft on take-off.

'What's happening now,' Hughes had started again, 'is that our good friends from the Aircraft Research Establishment at Farnborough are taking over. We have people out at the site labelling and collecting every morsel of the wreckage. We hope to have this completed by tomorrow night when a Hercules will arrive to transport the wreckage to the UK. Once there, they will do their usual thorough job of detection.' He added that at least one member of the FBI would eventually be joining the team at Farnborough, while on both sides of the Atlantic anti-terrorist and security officers would carry on with the investigation.

'We shall, of course, be eventually holding our first official Board review here. Probably in about a month,' he concluded.

The meeting broke up, but Bond hung around for ten minutes or so, talking to the people on the NTSB team and, lastly, to Smith who was still not a happy man.

'I'll carry the can for this one,' he muttered out of the corner of his mouth, which reminded Bond of a bad ventriloquist. 'They'll have me back home and I'll probably spend the rest of my days ferreting out the situation at Birmingham.'

'Nobody's claimed responsibility then?' Bond asked.

Smith thought for a minute, as though working out if he were speaking with the enemy. Eventually he decided that it was safe. 'I gather we've had a couple of crank calls and that's it. It's not the old enemy for sure. Personally, I think this is devastating for Bradbury. I wouldn't rule out big business being behind it. Those huge conglomerates would cut one other's throats. It's a dirty old world.'

'You can say that again.'

'Don't need to. You're Bond, aren't you?'

'Is that a shrewd guess or are you acting on information received, as our wonderful policemen would say?'

'They told us to expect you to be nosing around. As far as our people are concerned, you have a reputation.'

'So I've heard.'

'Remember, if you eavesdrop you never hear good of yourself.'

'You people should know.' He grinned at the Security Service man, winked, then made for the elevator.

The receptionist, Azeb, was still on duty, so he asked her if the Principessa had arrived safely.

'I haven't seen her yet, Mr Boldman. I have a key all ready for her as well. Maybe she's been held up.'

When he got to the room he saw the red message light flashing on the telephone. He scanned the telephone instructions and discovered that the hotel was equipped with a voice mail service, so he punched in the code and waited while a disembodied voice told him there was one message waiting for him, then Sukie's voice came on the tape, low and urgent.

'James, I think I have problems. I might have to go to ground. Don't worry, I'll be in touch, but things are getting a mite dangerous. If possible, I'll meet you at the Villa Tempesta, it's just outside Pisa, on the road to Viareggio. If anything does happen to me, remember the acronym COLD. I have to . . .' She was cut off with a sudden intake of breath which made the hairs on the nape of his neck tingle. The message had been logged in at three fifty-one. He grabbed the local telephone directory and riffled through the yellow pages to find the number for the nearest Hilton, punching it in as though he were trying to inflict damage on the instrument.

'I'd like to speak with one of your guests, if she hasn't checked out,' he began as soon as the operator answered. 'The Principessa Tempesta.'

There was around a minute of silence on the line, then a male voice. 'Who was it you wanted?'

'The Principessa Tempesta.'

'Who's calling.'

'Boldman. James Boldman.'

'Are you a relative, sir?'

Without even thinking, he said, 'Yes. A cousin.' Then, as the dreadful thought hit him, 'Why? And who are you?'

'Detective Pritchard. DCPD. Where are you speaking from, sir?'

Bond told him, even giving him the room number.

'Okay, sir. I would like you wait where you are. Put your telephone down and I'll call you back.'

The telephone rang again almost instantly, and it was the same voice on the line. 'Okay, sir. I'd like you to wait in the hotel. You can go down to the lobby if you like. If it helps, you'll see me arrive in a squad car within the next ten minutes.'

The line went dead and Bond thought about his safety. Was this Detective Pritchard for real? Was he something to do with what Sukie had called COLD?

In the foyer of the hotel Azeb had disappeared and there were now two uniformed doormen, not the one he had seen before.

Just over ten minutes later a police cruiser pulled up, a uniformed cop at the wheel. The passenger uncurled himself from his seat and headed into the foyer: a tall, broad-shouldered, tough and stone-faced man.

Bond thought twice about it, then decided to go along with things, walking forward to meet the approaching man who had the slightly flat-footed gait of a policeman. He wore an unbuttoned grey topcoat over a grey suit. The jacket of the suit was also unbuttoned – 'all the better to get the draw on you.'

He thrust out his hand. 'Detective Pritchard?'

'Mr Boldman?'

He nodded as the detective motioned him towards a leather settee close to the coffee shop entrance just off the foyer.

'You are James Boldman, sir?'

'Yes.'

'Have you any ID?'

He took out his Boldman passport and handed it over. The

cop had big hands, broad palms and long battered-looking
fingers.

'And your relationship to the Princess – Principessa?'

'I told you. I was her cousin, on her side of the family. The
Destry side. Why the questions?'

'I'm sorry to be the one to tell you this, Mr Boldman, but
we're pretty sure your cousin is dead.'

Bond's head came up in shock. For a second, in the evening
gloom outside, he caught a glimpse of snow starting to fall.

4

A Chill Down the Spine

WHAT HAD ONCE been the black Lexus was hauled off to the side of the road near the main entrance ramp to Dulles International. Warning cones, reflectors and yellow crime scene tapes cordoned the tangled lump of scorched and twisted metal.

Several police cruisers, a tow truck and an ambulance were parked in front and behind the remains of the vehicle, while criminalists, police photographers and a mixture of uniformed and plain-clothes officers were within the charmed circle marked by the tapes.

Two other cars were also off the road, their shaken occupants being assisted by a team from a Rescue Squad truck. Red and blue lights twinkled and portable floods bathed the obscene lump of metal, making it look like a piece of sculpture on view in a museum of modern art. Light snow whirled around the scene.

'We don't expect you to identify anything.' Detective Matt Pritchard led Bond under the tapes. 'Certainly not the body — what's left of it.'

Bond swallowed hard. Once out of the squad car he had smelled the familiar odour. The mixture of burned paint, and above it the sickly scent of singed human flesh. He wanted to gag or vomit, but kept himself in check. This was no time to

show weakness of any kind, for he knew what the big policeman was doing.

'Sorry about your loss, Mr Boldman.' Pritchard had leaned
forward and touched him briefly on the left shoulder, as they
were sitting in the hotel foyer close to the coffee shop. 'You're
the only person we can find who knew the victim . . .'

'Victim?'

'I think you'd best come and see for yourself.' The detective
stood, gave him a fleeting smile, then asked if he would please
come with him to the site.

'Site?' Bond rose, a reflex to the cop's movement.

'The murder site, Mr Boldman.'

As they walked towards the hotel door, Bond knew exactly
what was happening. He felt sick at heart about Sukie, yet at
the same time he knew the way experienced police officers'
minds worked. If Sukie were truly dead and they discovered a
family member, however distant, staying nearby then that
family member immediately became suspect. So Bond was the
prime suspect – probably the only suspect – in whatever had
happened. The cop had not asked him if he had seen her
recently, or even when he had last seen her. Those questions
would be the Sunday punches he would throw – probably with
at least one other police officer present.

In the few seconds it took to walk to the doors he debated
with himself whether to stop this now and tell the truth –
something he would eventually have to do – or wait and let
Pritchard play the thing out. The latter choice seemed to be the
obvious decision, so he kept quiet and now here he was,
standing coatless beside the tangled wreckage, freezing cold
and with the terrible stench of death in his nostrils.

Two mega-sized plain-clothes men stood downwind of the
chewed and jagged remains of what had once been the car.

'M.E. shown up yet?' Pritchard asked them.

'Just gone, Matt.'

'They're going to remove what's left of the body any minute.'

'Criminalists done everything?' from Pritchard.

'What can they do? Pictures've been taken and they've picked up a few bits and pieces.'

'Ain't gonna get no fingerprints from that. Gonna lift it onto a flatbed and take it to the vehicle lab.' He pronounced it 'vee-hickle'.

'Come take a look, Mr Boldman.' Pritchard strode through the increasingly heavy snow towards the wreck.

As they drew close, Bond could make out the general shape of the smashed metal. The rear of the car, together with the roof, had been blown away. There was, in fact, no sign of either boot or roof. The remainder of the car looked as though it had been in some kind of crusher. On the driver's side he could make out a fragment of the steering wheel. Lower, as he stood close, there was a shape: black and burned as though it were some part of a beast with a scaly body. The head had been reduced to something resembling a large charred coconut which had melted, producing three irregular holes towards the top, and a long dark gash below. As he looked, Bond also made out what had once been arms and hands, curled up in what forensic people call the typical 'boxer position' of a burned body.

He was aware of Pritchard turning and calling to the pair of big cops – 'Anything that could identify her?'

The reply was carried away on the swirling circles of snow, but the detective seemed content, and the larger of the other two cops began to trudge towards one of the cruisers.

Pritchard drew Bond back from the wreckage, saying they would not be long.

'What actually happened?'

'Well it wasn't a Fourth of July firecracker. Lucky nobody else was killed. She was just taking the bend here when the car exploded. There was one car in front and to her left, and another just pulling out to overtake. Drivers are pretty shaken but I've only had reports from over the phone. The story is that the rear exploded. The gas tank, I suspect, because a sheet of flame ripped through the car and the driver starting to overtake says he had the impression of another explosion.'

Bond sighed and shook his head, thinking poor Sukie, what had she done to deserve this?

As if reading his thoughts, the detective said that she would not have known what happened. 'There one minute, gone the next – in the twinkling of an eye, as the scriptures say. If you have to go quickly that's the way I'd like it. Boom and you're out of it.'

The big cop and his partner were tramping towards them. One carried a clear plastic evidence bag in his hand. 'This is the biggest thing they found.' He stretched the bag out towards Pritchard. 'Initials,' he said cryptically.

'Sure. You identify this, Mr Boldman?'

Within the bag, Bond could make out a blackened piece of metal. It was twisted, but the pattern was clear and visible. A letter 'T' entwined with an 'S'.

'Yes,' he nodded. 'It's the clasp from her shoulderbag.'

'Know it from the past, do you?'

'She had it with her today. Big white leather shoulderbag.'

'You seen her today?'

'This morning.'

'This morning? You saw her this morning? You didn't say nothing about that.'

'You didn't ask, and I didn't know what had happened.'

'I think we ought to go downtown and have a little talk. What you think, Stew?' turning to the larger of the two other cops.

'Kinda interesting.' Stew – a name that did not suit him – nodded sagely. 'I think we should have a long and cozy talk downtown, yeah.'

Bond stood his ground. 'No, I think we should go back to my hotel and have a short cozy talk during which I explain the facts to you. I'm with the team investigating the 747 that blew up on touch-down. I'm even working with the FBI.'

'Yeah, I heard the Fibbies were there.' A pause of a couple of beats. 'You got any proper ID, Mr Boldman?'

'If I can reach into my pocket without any of you guys getting trigger-happy?'

Pritchard nodded. 'Do it real slow then.'

Bond felt for the secret pocket in the lining of his jacket and pulled out his official ID. The one in the little leather wallet, with the laminated card inside. Slowly he handed it over to Pritchard, who bent over to look at it in the light from the floods. 'You're a spook, eh? A frigging spook with a hundred different identities!'

'Something like that.' Bond smiled at him almost ingenuously.

'A spook?' from Stew.

'A Brit spook.'

'I'm beginning to feel a shade chilly.' Bond retained the smile. 'Tell you what. Why don't we all go back and I'll buy the coffee.'

'So you're no blood relation to the Tempestas?' Matt Pritchard looked puzzled. They sat huddled together in the hotel coffee shop.

'No, I met her first in '85. She was being attacked by some

thugs behind a filling station in France – but I've told you all that.' Indeed, he had gone through all the non-classified pieces of the period when he had first met Sukie.

'That would be after Don Pasquale needed her as a live-in hot water bottle to warm his old age.' Stew sounded unconvinced and vaguely unpleasant.

'If you mean it was after the Principe Pasquale Tempesta, her husband, had died, yes.'

Matt Pritchard gave a little snicker of laughter. 'Principe, my ass.'

'Well she's certainly the Dowager Principessa . . .'

'No more a minor Italian princess than Matt's girlfriend is Princess Di. For a senior spook, Bond, you're a little naïve.'

'Look, we'd better come clean,' Pritchard sighed. 'Stew and I worked on details concerning the Tempestas for a long time. The FBI have all our notes, but we still carry a lot in our heads. You ever met the pair who are her stepsons by marriage?'

'No, but Sukie certainly told me – and I believed her – that the family ran a perfectly kosher series of businesses. And from what I recall, my people in London checked it out.'

Pritchard gave a curt little nod. 'Sure, mid-eighties we weren't doing much, or telling people much about the Tempestas. Their operations were mainly in Europe anyway. I think we were on the point of infiltrating them. If you don't believe me, there's a Fibbie coming in who knows *all* about them.'

Bond turned to see Special Agent Eddie Rhabb coming through the entrance, shoulders forward and head down in his classic charging bull stance.

Matt Pritchard waved across the room. Rhabb acknowledged the wave, and walked quickly in their direction. He gave Bond a friendly nod, but immediately looked to Pritchard. 'Is it true?' he asked, his eyes darkening.

'You mean the Tempesta woman?'

'Who else?'

'Yes, I'm afraid it's all too true and your colleague here, Mr Boldman . . .'

'Don't you mean Bond?' A friendly twinkle came into the FBI man's eye.

'Okay, there are no secrets from Fast Eddie.'

'Just call me Eddie the Rhabb.' He turned towards Bond. 'I was looking for you. Left a message on your voice mail. Don't quite understand why they're going through me, but London needs to talk with you.'

'About?'

'I suspect the Tempestas. They want you to come to Quantico with me. Tonight if possible. You'd better check with London first, but they seem very keen.' He sat and ordered coffee.

'Bond here is an old friend of the Tempesta woman.'

'I know.'

'How?' Bond asked sharply.

'I just know. There's not much about the Tempestas I don't know. We had a request from your people back in the eighties. Wanted to know all the ins and outs of *La Famiglia Tempesta*. We gave them nothing at the time. Neither did our Italian colleagues. In fact we let them think the Tempestas were on the level.'

'I'd swear Sukie thought everything was above board. She definitely believed that they were good, upstanding pillars of the community. Captains of industry.'

Rhabb chuckled. 'Sorry to disillusion you, James – I *can* call you James?'

'You can call me what you like, as long as you don't call me Jim'

'Okay. Back in – when was it you met her, '85?'

Bond nodded, then quickly told Rhabb about the meeting, and the dangers he had gone through with Sukie.

Rhabb nodded. 'Right, back then we talked to nobody about the Tempestas. And I guess Sukie had no real picture of what was going on. The family rarely strayed out of Italy. If there was anything to be done in the USA they had other people who were sent in. I doubt if she was left in the dark for long though.'

'Things didn't seem to have altered. I spent a lot of today with her, and I certainly didn't see any change. You know she was supposed to have been on that bloody aeroplane?'

'Yes, and it's possible that either the Tempesta brothers or some rivals set it up.'

'She was frightened, I can tell you that.' He explained his relationship with Sukie and how she had been about to move into the hotel with him. 'Just after the briefing broke up this afternoon I found she had left a message on my voice mail. By then she was *really* frightened. Does the acronym COLD mean anything to you?'

He saw a movement deep in the FBI man's eyes. 'I've heard the word in connection with a lot of things. The Tempesta family and COLD would make a formidable alliance.'

'Okay, just put me in the Tempesta picture.'

'You'll get a full briefing at Quantico.' Rhabb appeared to be reluctant. 'In short, the Tempestas are an organized crime family, but not strictly one of the old-time Mafia families. They *do* run a lot of companies which appear to be genuine, though I suspect the companies are there to wash dirty money. They're very powerful in Italy, don't have connections with Sicily, but control a lot of the stuff that goes down in Rome. The usual – prostitution, extortion, some nightclubs. The drug business and some clubs in the USA and UK are fairly recent: during the last few years that is. They're becoming more and more powerful, spreading their wings so to speak. Did you know they had money invested in Bradbury Airlines?'

'Sukie indicated that to me this morning.'

'Perhaps that's why she wasn't on the plane.'

'Perhaps that was why Harley Bradbury wasn't on the flight as well.'

Rhabb shifted in his chair. 'Why don't you check things out with London and we can get moving. They tell me the snow's tapering off and they're sending a chopper over to pick us up.'

Bond nodded and quickly left the table.

Back in his room he operated the security locks on his briefcase and took out the small portable scrambling device which, when plugged into the modular telephone jack, bypassed the main telephone line and allowed direct secure conversation with a number of similar units throughout the world.

He unplugged the direct line, snapped the little package of electronics into place and then plugged the telephone directly into the other end of the box. Taking an autodialler from the open briefcase, he pressed the button which gave its little sequence of beeps and tones. The distant end rang. Then—

'Duty Officer.'

'Predator.' He gave his field name. 'Someone wants me to call them.'

'Hold, Predator.'

There was a long silence and M's drowsy voice came on the line. 'You've met an old friend and now she's dead, I hear.'

'Correct.'

'Has an FBI man called Rhabb been in touch?'

'I've just spoken with him. He says you want me to go Quantico. True, sir?'

'Absolutely. You're in for a few surprises, I think. After Quantico, let me know your intentions before you do anything else.'

'Roger, sir. That it?'

'Go in peace, Predator.'

'Thank you, sir.'

'No peace for the wicked, eh?'

He heard M's short laugh as he closed the line.

The journey to the FBI Training Establishment – which shared the Marine base at Quantico, Virginia – was uncomfortable and bumpy. Though it only took them some thirty minutes to get there from Dulles, the snow had not completely left the area and twice they flew through what looked like raging blizzards which threw the craft all over the sky.

They were met at the helicopter pad by a small group of agents and driven straight into the complex of red brick buildings which made up the training quarters, plus many other facilities. It was there at Quantico that much research was done, and there that the counterintelligence people kept sensitive assets when necessary.

There were quick introductions to hard, wary-looking men – Drake, Mulett, MacRoberts, Long, and a young woman who was known only as Prime.

'She's here?' Rhabb asked.

The man called Drake answered, 'Waiting for you. Has to be out and back in circulation by the morning. It's going to be a long night.'

Behind Bond, Prime muttered something about a hard night as well.

They moved quickly through the Perspex-covered tunnels that connected various buildings and were known in the Bureau as 'The Gerbil Tubes.' Then into an elevator and up six floors.

The corridor into which they emerged was like a hotel corridor. Deep carpet under foot and doors set at some fifteen foot intervals. Bond felt he was being hustled along by the others who surrounded him.

Finally they stopped before one door and Drake knocked shave-and-a-haircut. What sounded like a familiar voice called out, 'Come in.'

Drake and Rhabb reached back and pulled Bond forward, thrusting him into the room, which was dark, suffused illumination coming from one green-shaded desk lamp in the far left corner.

5

Conjunction

SOMEBODY SWITCHED ON the overhead lights. For a few seconds, time seemed to stand still. Bond would have sworn it was Sukie Tempesta sitting in an armchair, then she seemed to dissolve and alter in what was a trick of the mind and the light.

The young woman who rose from the chair was nothing like Sukie, except perhaps for the stunning body which looked as though it had been poured into the running suit. The rest bore no resemblance to her. This girl was tall, rangy, long legs – like Sukie's – but there it ended. Black eyes to match the raven sleek short hair; wide and generous mouth; high cheekbones and a patrician nose. Very Italianate, he thought immediately as she walked towards him, a smile of apology and a gesture – arms opening, palms upwards: the body language which said she was sorry. Then, her right hand came up towards his. A firm cool grip, her hand close to her body bringing them almost face to face.

'Toni Nicolletti.' She introduced herself. He caught a faint accent, just a trace, together with the unmistakable bouquet of *Bal de Versailles* catching his nostrils.

'I'm sorry,' he said, his throat dry. 'For a moment, I thought you were someone else.' For a fraction of time a picture of Sukie again came sharp and brilliantly into his mind. It was as though the past had leaped into the present and he could feel and see her – smell her scent also – as they both stood on the deck of a hotel in Key West watching a spectacular sunset. That had been one real moment, just after they had shared great danger.

'Why am I meeting this young lady?' he asked, still inwardly shaken.

'I think we should all sit down, and I'll tell you exactly.' Rhabb motioned with his right hand, inviting them to sit.

There were not enough chairs for all of them so some sat on the floor, ranged around Bond like a group of students ready to discuss some important lesson.

Eddie began, nodding towards MacRoberts, a big ginger-haired and bearded man who looked like a wild Scottish laird beamed in from a distant century. 'Mac is our in-house Tempesta historian. He should start.'

MacRoberts' voice was as gruff as his appearance, and he spoke quickly, bursting upon his audience like a series of great rolling breakers hitting a beach.

'Right, you've heard some of this already, Mr Bond, but I'll take it all from the top. The Tempestas were around at the time of the Borgias, and they were a family rooted in sin even then. During the fifteenth and sixteenth centuries, they managed to survive the treacheries of both Cesare and his sister Lucrezia, probably because they never became involved in the more violent passions of the Borgia family. They "owned" commercial Rome by the late fifteenth century: and by that I don't mean they were leading traders – merchants, buying and selling men, owners of ships and the like. Back in those days the Tempestas were controllers, and they still are.'

MacRoberts went on for maybe half an hour, tracing the rise and rise of the Tempesta family. How, with guile and subtlety, they had gathered an army of experts around them: men who were experienced in the ways of commerce and men who were – as MacRoberts put it – 'Very good at breaking heads.'

He continued. 'Their basic plan was to grant what we would now call insurance policies, and, as we all know, the gap between insurance and extortion is very narrow. The fine print on their offers to cover losses on goods, carried by sea or land, amounted to the simple tenet, "You pay us large sums of money – up to fifty per cent of the value of your cargo – and we will see to it that your ships are safe, and your carriages and wagons go unmolested."

'If the money did not get paid on time, a ship would go down with a loss of cargo; or an overland train of wagons would be attacked and robbed. The Tempestas sat in their fashionable houses and raked in money so that the wheels of commerce could turn without hindrance.'

Without rushing the story, the FBI man showed the way in which, during the nineteenth century, the Tempestas began to run everything within the confines of Rome, from whores to places where visitors could eat, rest their weary heads, and move through the streets in safety.

'They became the only organized crime family to rule Rome and, at the same time, remained respected. The Cosa Nostra, when it came, stood no chance of taking over. By the 1920s Pasquale Tempesta was given the title of Prince, hence Principe Pasquale Tempesta. Together with his family, he was both loved and hated, while it was common knowledge that his power, and therefore the power of those close to him, was paramount.

'In many ways he was the most charming of men, yet an upcoming Mafia Don was barbecued in the garden of one of his many villas, and the man's lieutenants met various terrible ends. Even the so-called Honoured Society did not have the stomach to go after him. The police crackdown against organized crime began around 1984. Quietly in Italy, and softly over here. Pasquale's sons became over-ambitious and started to attempt a colonization of parts of the United States. By '84 we were already working on putting in our own penetration agent. Pasquale was dead by then. The estate had been well split, and the sons Luigi and Angelo appeared to be spreading their wings. That, Mr Bond, is why your people got nowhere in their search for the truth.'

There had been a period of time when both the Italian authorities and the FBI had genuinely discussed attempting to draw Sukie into their operation: especially after they discovered that she truly had no hint that the old man she had married was a man of evil power. In the end they had decided against it on two counts. First, Sukie had no training in the black arts of deception. Second, they were unsure if she would play along with them.

MacRoberts said, 'There was always the danger that she would be naïve enough to go running to her stepsons with tales out of school.' He turned towards the woman agent they called Prime, handing over the story for her to tell.

Bond estimated Prime as being in her mid-thirties. Clear skin, hardly any make-up, neat and short blonde hair and the coiled spring body of an athlete. 'I had done a lot of courses before they brought me in,' she began. 'Five years in the field at our office in Atlanta with courses sandwiched in between. Then I came here to Quantico. I was on the Training Selection Team, and to my mind that was a very big deal.

'I was brought into the picture regarding the Tempesta family, and asked to look out for someone we might possibly train as a penetration agent. Three weeks after being given the assignment, Toni Nicolletti walked into my office.

'I had a gut reaction in the first five minutes of the interview. She's a second generation Italian American with a lot of links to Rome, has a degree in computer sciences from Georgetown University, and wanted to work undercover. A very gutsy lady.' She looked across at Toni, flashing her a quick smile. 'So we put her through the normal course with a lot of other studies. We really pressurised her.' Another glance at the lovely Toni. 'She went in around the Spring of '85, and has provided gold from the first.'

'What do you do for the Tempesta brothers, then, Toni?' Bond gave her a look of admiration.

'I got to know them very well. Then they gave me a job. Tested me out for a year. Now I run all their computer operations – and practically everything they own and do is on computer. I should say it's on a huge network of computers, so I have my work cut out. I'm over here buying new hardware: Power PCs, so that we can work in both Macintosh and Windows environments. That's become essential these days.'

'So, you have access to the hard disk? You can provide almost anything?'

'She certainly does,' Prime cracked another of her rare smiles. 'What Toni is doing has become invaluable, but it's dangerous. She's running a secondary series of lines straight out of the Tempesta computers. We're getting almost every transaction, every document, spreadsheet, database as it goes onto their systems. And if we don't get it straight away, we have all the passwords. Our people go in at night and hack their way aboard so that we can check on the updates.'

'Sounds like fun.'

'I do have another job that yields extra pieces of information,' Toni Nicolletti's voice sounded wicked and bubbly, as though she were teasing a man. For a moment, Bond thought she might be teasing him, Then—

'I'm Luigi Tempesta's mistress. Oils the wheels a bit and keeps things friendly.'

He recalled Sukie's words in the hotel room near Dulles International.

'*I think one of their wives was in bed with him.*'

'*Literally?*'

'*Is there any other way?*'

'*Which of the wives? Luigi's or Angelo's.*'

'*Luigi's. The lovely Giulliana.*'

So, he wondered, was that the reason for Giulliana being unfaithful to Luigi with Harley Bradbury? Because she knew of her husband's infidelity?

'You see, James,' Eddie spoke softly and, Bond considered, probably carried a big stick – possibly a baseball bat. 'You see, Toni has provided us with a panoply of information. We now know where most of the Tempesta contacts can be located; we are aware of the names, addresses and telephone numbers of their most trusted soldiers – the hoodlums they use for strong-arm tactics. We know favourite methods, and the Attorney General's office has been supplied with information that they are collating. In brief, we are only a few steps away from a very big showdown.'

Bond nodded, but said nothing. He wanted Rhabb to come to him with the information instead of the other way around.

'Within the walls of this room only,' the FBI man looked around, clasping eyes with everyone present, ending with Bond, 'the Italian police are anxious to do the final bust. But we want them taken and brought to trial here in the United States. They are setting up one or two very worrying situations over here. Since John Gotti was put away, for instance, the

Tempesta family has moved into New York. Slowly they'll control a very large number of the old Gotti interests. Also . . .' He was cut short by the ringing of a telephone.

Looking around, Bond saw there were two instruments in the room, set side by side. One red, the other black.

Eddie reached over and quietly answered the black telephone, his eyes swivelling towards Toni Nicolletti. 'It's your boyfriend.'

The girl went quickly towards the red phone and nodded, so that Rhabb replaced the black phone as she lifted the receiver of the red one.

'*Pronto*,' Toni said in a breathless voice, using the normal form of Italian greeting on a phone. She then launched into a low and long conversation in Italian, keeping up the same quiet tone she had used when answering. She had turned her back to everyone else in the room, but there was no doubt that this was a lovers' dialogue. Of course she loved him . . . Couldn't wait to see him again tomorrow . . . Yes, both her mother and father were well, but life was not the same without him. There was a lengthy pause as she listened to obviously endearing comments being made by Luigi Tempesta. Then she was able to speak again. Yes, her flight landed at Washington National at eleven o'clock tomorrow morning . . . Of course she understood it would not be wise for him to meet her, so who was he sending? . . . Dino would be good . . . She laughed a lot at his next comment and said that was ridiculous but she could cope with it. Then another long silence followed by her giving a startled gasp . . . You're sure? . . . But I thought . . . Giulliana's not here in the States, surely . . . No . . . No . . . Was he absolutely certain? . . . Yes, of course. You did *that* . . . I'll wait to hear it all. Could the marriage be annulled? . . . Yes, she would wait to see what he had in mind.

The goodbyes and protestations of love took about another four minutes, then she replaced the receiver and gave a long sigh as she sat down.

Bond raised his eyebrows, giving Eddie Rhabb a quizzical look.

'I'd better explain to our British friend,' Rhabb began. 'James, the only way we could bring Toni in for a debrief – and we do it every time she's in the US – is to send her on a notional trip to Kansas to see her dear old Mama and Papa. We have a sweet elderly Italian lady in the Bureau who spends all her days in a room here eating, reading, sleeping, watching TV and waiting by a telephone with a Kansas number. We plug in another telephone when Toni's alone – not often – so that she can pick up. If Luigi phones, as he does regularly, Mama says she's somewhere in the house and that she'll get her. She even goes through a ritual of calling for her, and sometimes has a nice little talk with Luigi.'

'And Luigi doesn't want to go calling with Toni? Meet the old folks in Kansas?'

'Up to now, no. Luigi Tempesta's usually a very busy man when he's here.' He turned his head towards Toni, 'So what's new?'

She took a deep breath. 'He's found out about his wife, Giulliana, and Harley Bradbury.'

'How?'

'Going to tell me tomorrow.'

'Was he talking divorce there?'

'He was talking something. From what he said it was a little more terminal than divorce.'

'I don't think we're in Kansas any more,' Bond muttered. Then – 'How do you get her on a flight from Kansas to Washington National without alerting friend Luigi?'

'We provide the paperwork. One of our people does the actual flight. You have to change at Baltimore. Toni meets her, picks up the paperwork and gets on the flight. It's always worked before.'

'I hope it works this time.' Bond's eyes were on Toni. 'I'm relying on you to get me into the Villa Tempesta. Can you do that?'

'You'll have to get yourself absolutely unbreakable and untraceable ID . . .'

'We can do that,' Eddie cut in.

'Then, Mr Bond – James, may I call you James?'

'Every time.'

'We'll have to set up some long-term friendship from way back, and you'll have to find yourself in the area – the Villa's on the shore of Lake Massaciuccoli. You know where that is?'

'About half way between Pisa and Viareggio.'

'Yes,' she laughed. 'I'll give you telephone numbers and also there's a way into the computer system that goes straight to me. Only to me. It's simple and straightforward. Nobody else can get there. Nobody knows the password, except Eddie, so I'd rather give it to you in private.'

'Well, we'll leave you two together to work out the details.' The FBI man looked pleased. 'But, first, I'd like you to tell James here, the Tempesta's favourite way of silencing people. Their all-time drop-dead method.'

Toni Nicolletti raised her eyes and locked into Bond's eyes. 'They're very fond of explosives,' she said. 'Luigi likes to see people go out with a bang. He's quite casual about it. Death seems to have no lasting meaning for him. In fact, he sometimes gives the impression that it's something that happens to other people, but will never happen to him.'

They talked for a few minutes, then Rhabb said they would

meet Bond down in the restaurant.

After they had all left, Toni patted the couch on which she was sitting, inviting Bond to sit next to her. He smelled the scent again, and also her pleasant personal odour – the scent and a fresh fragrance that reminded him of a Summer day in the country: a mixture of sun-bathed trees, wild flowers and fields of wheat. Her closeness was disconcerting, and she knew it, he thought.

Carefully she went over the moves he would have to make through a computer modem to get into the Tempesta system and quickly, without being detected, to her own secret room in cyberspace. Lastly she said, 'Conjunction.'

'Conjunction?'

'That's the word that'll get you into my secret room, James. Conjunction. A good word, yes? Don't you think we should have had a love affair in the past? Luigi would find it amusing to meet someone who knew me before he staked his claim.'

'What an interesting idea.' James Bond reached over and drew her towards him. She raised her head and it was as though her black eyes swallowed him. Conjunction became more than a password as their lips met.

6

Cold Comfort

ALITALIA FLIGHT AZ 611, ex-JFK New York, landed at Rome's Leonardo da Vinci Airport at a little before seven on a cold morning, with fine drizzle blowing in waves like gunsmoke over the runways. Spring was going to be a little late this year, and seven days had passed since Bond had spent the best part of a memorable night with Toni Nicolletti in the guest room at Quantico.

He had nearly three hours to kill before his onward flight to Pisa, so he sat quietly in one of the many restaurants at da Vinci, sipping coffee and, forgoing his beloved toast, eating bread rolls with butter and jam. Around him the place bustled and the repeated announcement warning – the first five notes of *Volare* – became almost intrusive. Yet his mind drifted back to the night at Quantico and what he had learned.

There, with Toni, they had come up with what people in the world of secrets call a Legend – the outline of a past that was a deception. It would be up to people like Eddie Rhabb to make their story unbreakable: to insert false information about them into documents and databases so that, should the Tempesta brothers decide to take a look at the past, they would find everything for which they searched.

They decided that Bond would use his real name, for it was

57

possible that Sukie had told someone within the family that she had known him in the mid-eighties. It was also quite probable that the late Pasquale Tempesta's widow ('The child bride,' as Toni said she had been known within the family) had shown someone photographs of herself with him. They had taken enough at the time when they spent R&R together after the terrible dangers they had faced when extracting his house-keeper, May, and M's PA, Moneypenny, from captivity.

They decided Bond must have done a stint at Georgetown University, lecturing to the computer sciences classes over one semester. It was there that Toni had met him, and had a brief affair with him, long before she had been chosen to work for the Tempesta family.

For her part, Toni would mention that she had bumped into her former lover on the flight out to Kansas City. When she told him that she was working for the Tempestas, he had volun-teered the information that he knew Sukie, and that they had been, as he put it, 'very close'. Naturally, Toni had invited him to drop in on her should he find himself in either Rome or Tuscany.

As they lay together on the bed in Quantico, Bond started to fill in any blanks in their story.

'Sukie wanted me to join her in Italy,' he said. 'Now I find the FBI want me to do the same thing. Why?' Really he was simply thinking aloud, but Toni Nicolletti picked up on it straight away.

'Eddie, as well as all the other things he does, works mainly for the Bureau's Special Operations and Research Depart-ment,' she told him. 'He's had an agenda of his own ever since that horrible BD 299 incident: after all, he knew you were coming over to represent your organization almost before anyone else. FBI Counterintelligence has a dossier on you and

I suspect it contains details of your link with Sukie. He'll probably tell you why he wants you at the Villa, but I'm almost one hundred per cent that Eddie was put onto the case as a stalking horse, to cut you out from the rest of the experts. You must have worked out that he suspects the Tempestas of being the major force behind the bombs on 299. It's their style.'

'But you have no firm evidence of that?'

'I only know they had a big investment in Bradbury Airlines, and that Harley Bradbury was finding it difficult to keep dividends flowing back to them.'

He thought for a minute, then said that for the Tempestas to carry out such a cold blooded and ruthless act of terrorism was somewhat like cutting off their noses to spite their faces. 'If they did arrange this, then why? They would have known that any disaster of this magnitude would almost certainly reduce their chances of recouping money from their investment. Bradbury'll be hard pushed now. With something like this happening, he'll possibly go broke.'

'I didn't say they were responsible, but they have partners, and those people are more interested in paybacks of a violent kind.'

'Who're you talking about in particular?'

'I'll let Eddie tell you. In fact, I don't know if he will, particularly if he's sending you into the Tempestas' lair. He probably thinks you should go in cold, so to speak.'

'Cold,' he muttered back, and she smiled, leaned over and kissed him, then whispered, 'You've got it.'

Eddie Rhabb was patiently sitting waiting for Bond when he finally got to the canteen. 'You two must have got on very well,' sarcasm dripped from his mouth and eyes. 'Don't blame you, buddy, but we haven't got all day – or night.'

'Takes time to create a Legend.'

'Sure.' Rhabb was almost diffident. 'So, what you come up with?'

Bond told him, and the FBI man shrugged his bull-like shoulders, his head dropping. The body language was of a man on the offensive. Take no prisoners, it said. 'We can fix all that. Better take a photograph of you and do some magic on the computers. The wizards should be able to take a few years off both of you and we'll insert them somewhere. The University records are a piece of cake as well. You can be sure either Luigi or Angelo will send one of their people to check you out. Just hope they haven't already done it. From the time when you met Sukie, I mean. Those guys try to cover all the bases and they're clever as a barrel-load of monkeys.'

He ticked off all the paperwork they would need to keep up the deception, then Bond came in with the question at the forefront of his mind. 'Toni wouldn't talk to me about this, Eddie, but I have some concerns.'

'You do? What kinda concerns?'

'I simply got a feeling about you, Ed. A feeling that you were at the crash investigation for a special purpose.'

'Oh, yeah? What purpose?'

'To reel me in.'

Rhabb grunted.

'Sukie was talking about me going to Italy with her. Then she was murdered and you came along and suggested we come on a little trip here. This turns out to be a journey to meet your penetration agent. I need to know *why* you're all so keen on putting me in the same jar with the Tempesta brothers. You want to talk to me about that?'

Rhabb lifted a hand and curtly ordered more coffee. 'Sure. Sure I'll talk to you, but I'd have thought you could work that out for yourself. Why not try, James?'

'You don't like Brits, yet you've manipulated me very professionally. When it all goes down and things are set up for me to go on the grand tour to Italy, I'll be taking my instructions from my Chief in London, not you. You realize that?'

'He already knows we want you to go in.'

'Ah.'

'I talked with him for a long time yesterday. Damn it, you know I did. James, you'd better be sure here and know that I always cover my ass. I wouldn't countenance the idea of you going out among those scumbags unless the necessary authority had come from your boss. Got it?'

Bond nodded. 'Good, so were you at Dulles because you knew I was coming in? You also knew I was an old friend of Sukie Tempesta?'

'Sure I knew. At first I was concerned that perhaps the late Principessa was up to some tricks with you. When they converted her into meatloaf in that car, I even had a momentary thought that you could have been involved.'

He paused for breath and, Bond suspected, to calm down. When he spoke again it was almost a whisper. An old trick designed to make the subject strain to listen, and assure that the message was taken in loud and clear. 'We're all a mite paranoid about this,' he began. 'The Tempesta business, I mean. I wouldn't give a toss if they kept it all in their own country. Let 'em cause whatever chaos they like over there. But when they begin to raise their flags here, well, that's a different ballgame. And they *are* moving in. They're also a very sophisticated organization, and in the long run they make the old five families look like Mother Theresa, Pope John Paul, and all the saints rolled into one.'

'So why do you want me to play Daniel in the lions' den?'

'I don't know why the late Principessa wanted you. She

61

could've had altruistic reasons, though I doubt it. Me, I want to use you as bait, though I guess you already suspected that.'

'I had a feeling that Sukie was using me.'

'Not that I wanted to do the same?'

'I think that's what really worries me. You want me there for some reason. She wanted me there for another. I'm anxious that the lines don't get crossed up.'

'Yeah, so am I, because *that* is a distinct danger. Let me tell you, James, that Toni Nicolletti is not just feeding us good information, she's doing another job for us.' He raked through his short curly dark hair with splayed fingers. 'Lookit, here's the deal. The Tempestas are poised on the brink of taking over some very big concerns here in the US. We want them, and we want them bad. We could do a deal with the Italian authorities – no problem. But we've gotta fess up to it; if we did that, the thing would be split down the middle.

'I suspect that if we picked up Luigi and some of his folk here while Angelo was collared in Rome or Tuscany, it'd be years before we could put all the pieces together and get them into court in the same country. Toni's trying to get them both to come over here, and she's doing it very subtly. They have to think it's their own idea. Or at least they must believe it's the one way they can settle some of their problems – and they've got at least one huge entanglement here in the States. I hope you might be able to assist her in getting them both to come over. They're canny bastards. One time Luigi comes. The next time it's Angelo, and so on.'

'What's the big problem? What did you call it, their huge entanglement over here?'

'I don't know if you'd want to hear it.'

'Try me.'

'They've got into bed with a double-headed monster.'

'COLD?'

Rhabb almost jumped out of his seat. 'What d'you know about COLD?'

'Not a damned thing. I just heard the name. I gather it's an acronym.'

'Okay. Let me spell it out for you. COLD stands for the Children Of the Last Days.'

'Sounds like one of these nutty religious groups.'

'In a way it is. In another way it is not. In some ways it's like one of these private militias you've been hearing so much about in the papers – and they aren't funny, I can tell you. No, COLD is an organization spread across the country and made up of people who've been put out of business by our clampdown on organized crime. Some are ex-Mob, some are crazies, dangerous crazies, and some – mainly the people at the top – are highly intelligent criminals who see themselves as the answer to all the country's ills. They don't have the philosophy of the militias – that the people need to protect themselves against the federal government. These people believe that the only way to fight crime is by putting criminals into the government.'

'I thought you did that already,' Bond regretted it as soon as he had spoken. 'Sorry, Eddie, that was a bad joke.'

'Sure. These nice folks who are the leaders of COLD see the country being run almost as a police state. Deep down, I suspect some of them really think it's the only way. Let me tell you a story about them. It illustrates how COLD thinks.'

The story Eddie Rhabb told was undoubtedly true. It took place in New Jersey where COLD had a strong foothold. A local parish priest was experiencing a sharp drop in his congregation. He was a wise, sincere and holy man who at first blamed himself and his own ministry for the falling number of faithful coming to his church, but he quickly discovered the real reason. Next to the church was a parking lot where the faithful had always left their cars when they came to Mass. Over a period of two years there had been constant carjackings and muggings in the parking lot. The priest went to the local police and pleaded with them.

'Sure, Father,' the cops said. 'We'll put someone on it.'

In spite of the promise, the muggings and thefts continued, and at last a member of the congregation suggested – at a wedding reception – that the priest should speak with a friend who was there: a particularly religious man.

Reluctantly, the priest went over to this obviously powerful man and explained his problem.

'Don' worry about it, Father. It's taken care of.'

And it was. Nobody was mugged, nothing was stolen. A few young men in the area disappeared, a few ended up in hospital, but the crime rate around the church dropped like the proverbial stone.

'That,' said Eddie Rhabb, 'is rather how the old Mustache Petes of the Mob would've worked, and it's the way COLD works. Some of the top people in this organization are religious, even religious maniacs. They see this country of ours being riddled with the cancer of crime, but they're not above using old criminal methods to both deal with problems and line their own pockets.

'For instance, they are all for enforcing an anti-drug programme, but they would do it their way by killing off pushers and addicts alike; on the abortion issue they are prepared to close down every clinic or hospital that performs abortions, only they'd close them down with bombs and guns. They'd levy taxes as well, which means they would lift money from the wealthy by every kind of fraud in the book. COLD would probably give some of it back to the poor and sick, but they'd keep half for themselves. They call themselves Children Of the Last Days because they believe that we are in the Last Days, the days which will spell an end to the kind of democracy for which this country stands. Sure, they'd put paid to a lot of crime, but they'd do it by ruthless criminal means, and they would end up virtually running the country through fear. It'd be the worst possible thing to happen. It's like looking back to the old Fascist days in Italy and Germany when Hitler and Mussolini made the trains run on time and built good roads. The concept of law would be gone for ever, together with the concept of justice.'

Bond thought for a moment. 'You know all this, so what can you do about it? Why don't you get out there and arrest the ringleaders?'

'Because we don't know who they are. It's that simple. This has been brewing for a long time. We've got close to a few people, but the real brains – the people who give the orders – remain in the shadows. Now the Tempesta boys are doing deals with them. We know that, but so far they haven't led us to the heart of this organization. That's the other thing we want. The Tempestas are our pathfinders. They see COLD as a way of making easy money and they're trying to get in on the ground floor. So, James, we need you to try and get both of the brothers over here – or at least set the fuses that will eventually bring them here. We have enough evidence to charge either or both of them. We need both, and we need them to get to the heart of COLD.'

'What kind of time-scale are we talking about?'

'Like yesterday, but I guess this could linger on for years. We don't expect an overnight cure. You gotta understand that the Tempesta boys are probably not the only large dynasty built on crime that wants to get into something like this. We know the Russian Mafia are interested, though they have no damned scruples. The Chinese will probably get taken out of the picture, so they'd be edgy. As for the rest of Europe, there are a fair number of influential small groups who would buy in. James, you gotta see that the rewards would be huge.'

'And the disruption . . .'

'Would be even larger. No, we don't want the drug culture but we're hardly denting it. We want safety on the streets. We want civil and racial unrest taken out. All those things are plusses. I can even see how some Godfearing people might cheer COLD on to victory, but the price would be a ripping apart of the country's infrastructure. What's worse, if COLD, with the help of criminal factors from other countries, finally had their way, they would move on. Eventually we would be back in the Dark Ages throughout the entire world. Not in our lifetime, buddy, but eventually. So, we have to nip it all in the bud in *our* lifetime.'

In his life and dangerous time, Bond had faced many evil adversaries who appeared to be aiming for a kind of world criminal domination, but this was different. These people had a plan that appeared to be rational – at least to themselves. Crime tied to an almost Calvanistic morality which could lead to the collapse of freedom world wide.

In the days that followed, Bond had several conversations with M on a secure line to England. They also received two detailed messages from Toni Nicolletti at the Villa Tempesta, the second of which told them that she had casually dropped Bond's name into the conversation. Luigi and Angelo appeared to be very interested in him and had approved of Toni inviting him to visit should he ever find himself in Italy. So the green light came, and now he sat in Rome's premier airport.

When there was only an hour to spare before the connecting flight, he went to a public telephone and called the main number Toni had given to him for the Villa Tempesta.

He asked for Signorina Nicolletti, and was put through almost at once after giving his name.

'James,' she sounded delighted to hear him. 'Where are you? Here, in Italy?'

He told her that he had a couple of free days and that he was in Rome. She asked him to wait one moment and was quickly back on the line. 'James, Luigi Tempesta has asked if you can stay here for your couple of days. Can you fly into Pisa?'

'Only if that tower's still leaning.'

She laughed. 'As a matter of fact it is, but only just, they're preparing to put scaffolding around it because it seems to be straightening up.'

'What a coincidence.'

'James. Seriously, Luigi says he can have a car to meet you at Pisa.'

'That would be very civil. Thank you. I have checked and there's a flight that gets in around eleven-thirty.'

'Then there'll be someone there with a car. This is wonderful. Can't wait to see you.'

After hanging up, he went straight to the bank of safe-deposit boxes in the arrivals area and took out the key given to him at Quantico. His main luggage had already been booked straight through to Pisa, and he opened the assigned box which held, as promised, a neat Gucci briefcase fitted with a combination lock.

He knew what was inside: communications gear in the form of a laptop computer and various other pieces of equipment, including a miniature camera and – in a safe, shielded and hidden section – his favourite ASP 9mm automatic and three spare magazines, plus a Buck Hunter knife. The shielding would make the weapons undetectable to airport X-ray machines, while the case was so cunningly contrived that a security check of the laptop computer was unlikely to reveal the more deadly equipment.

The flight to Pisa landed at a little after eleven-thirty. It was chilly and raining in Tuscany as well as Rome, though the trees, grass and bushes showed the advanced signs of Spring.

He collected his one suitcase and walked through customs and immigration, which he had not cleared in Rome, then out to where a silver Rolls Royce stood, liveried chauffeur at the ready with a sign that said, *Mr James Bond*.

He nodded to the chauffeur and the front passenger door swung open to reveal a slim, tanned and very fit-looking young man who obviously worked at being a fighting machine. His eyes were a clear grey, and he moved with the agility associated with bodyguards. Bond considered that this one was of the élite variety as he wore an Armani suit under which the bulge of a weapon was hardly visible.

'Signor Bond,' the smile was almost frightening.

He nodded and watched the bodyguard pick up his heavy suitcase as though he were handling balsa wood, the chauffeur reaching for the briefcase.

'No, I'll keep that with me.' He had decided, back in Quantico, that he should feign practically no knowledge of the Italian language.

'Sorry, Mr Bond, but Signor Luigi prefers that we put it in the boot.' He held on to the briefcase and opened the rear door wide, allowing Bond to climb in.

As he bent his head, he caught the quick scent of an expensive male cologne, Hermès, he thought, and the man who was wearing it stretched out an immaculately manicured hand to help him in.

'James Bond,' he spoke English with little accent. 'Luigi Tempesta. I have been looking forward so much to meeting my stepmother's one-time lover, and the former lover of my mistress, I understand. Come, we have so much in common that I feel this will be a momentous day.'

7

A Judas Kiss?

HE HAD NEVER put a face, body or personality to Luigi Tempesta, and the FBI had no recent photographs. Someone had made a point of saying he was camera-shy, and the passport picture was – well, it was a passport picture and did not provide a true likeness.

Now, seeing the man for the first time, was almost a shock. For one thing he was small, just under five feet. Small and very elegant, from his thick, backswept grey hair to the impeccable dark blue suit, with a good half inch of cream silk shirt cuff protruding at his wrists, displaying large circular cufflinks fashioned from ancient Roman coins. At his neck, he wore a heavy silk tie that matched the suit and was overlaid with polka dots.

Below the sweep of his hair, Luigi Tempesta's face could have been the face of a Roman Emperor. Somehow there was a nobility about him that Bond had never suspected. He glanced forward as the Rolls pulled away from the airport and saw that the chauffeur and bodyguard sat erect, like the retainers they were. He shifted in his seat and looked back through the rear window. A sleek black Ferrari was keeping station with them some fifty yards behind.

Luigi saw the look and smiled. 'Don't worry, Mr Bond.

They're looking after us. You'll see another one ahead a couple of kilometers up the road.'

The most striking thing about the man, Bond now realized, was his eyes which were the colour of pewter. Cold and hard even when he smiled. They reminded him of the North Sea on a bitter midwinter day. Eyes that could be scary and ruthless. Certainly eyes through which you could read nothing.

'You go well-protected,' Bond said, trying to disengage from Luigi's penetrating stare.

'It's the safest way.' Luigi's smile was charm itself, yet again not reaching the eyes. 'Someone recently wrote that the wealthy should protect themselves like Renaissance princes these days.'

'The price we all pay for freedom.'

'Just so. It is particularly important in my country.' Luigi Tempesta made a tiny motion with his right hand, but the one simple movement seemed to indicate that he all but owned Italy. 'We seem to be disappearing under the weight of crime and such a lack of purpose that the young are abandoning their heritage.

'In the outlying rural areas of Italy, men and women are leaving, almost vanishing before our eyes. They vaporise to reappear in other parts of Europe, or in our overcrowded major cities, even in the United States. When this happens, when the villages die, the country begins to disappear. It causes great concern.'

He made another move with the same hand. The body language suggested concern over the smaller towns and villages. In this short period of time, Bond had discovered that Luigi possessed the extraordinary talent of using his hands to express detail behind the spoken word – like some extra sign language that was immediately apparent and accessible.

Bond simply nodded, leaning back in the leather seat. He turned to look out of the window, streaked with a fine mist of rain, glimpsing a signpost that pointed towards Viareggio. For a fractional moment he recalled the last time he had been in Tuscany: a hot, dusty, August day, with the ground parched and the red roofing tiles on buildings appearing to soak up the burning sun.

He remembered some almost forgotten poem about chanting choirboys moving through an avenue of cypresses: this last triggered by the sight of a roadside church with a stand of cypresses like a line of guards waiting to flank a bride and her groom; a child awaiting baptism, or – most likely in this part of the world – the coffin carried in that last journey of the dead.

'I'm told your villa is magnificent.' He looked towards Luigi again, not avoiding the eyes.

'Naturally, we think it's a little more than magnificent. It's been in our family's keeping for around five hundred years.' He gave a short but not unpleasant laugh. 'Mind you, Mr Bond, it's rather like the old broom that's had three new handles and four new heads but is still the old broom.'

'A lot of restoration, then?'

Luigi smiled his mirthless smile. 'That *was* what I was trying to express, yes. Externally it actually remains the same. We have a painting showing exactly how it was in 1685, and as you approach it from the lake you'd think every stone, window and tile was the same. It has been – how do you say it in English? – carefully restored?'

Bond nodded, remaining silent. He wanted to get the measure of the man and the place to which he was being taken.

'The interior has been substantially altered,' Luigi continued. 'Modernized is an unpleasant word, for my family is not what you would call modern in its outlook. The kitchens and bathrooms have been made more comfortable, as have the main rooms, but with an eye to what they were in the past. We now have good heating, and air-conditioning for the heat of summer. We also have state-of-the-art security and communications.

'My brother, Angelo, and I control many complex businesses, so it is most useful for us to be able to do so through computers which speak to other computers in faraway places. Across the world.' He made a little petulant sound. 'But, of course, you know this already. You've talked to our computer and communications sorceress, the lovely Toni. She tells me that you were a lecturer at Georgetown University when she was taking her degree in computer sciences.'

'Just for one semester. She studied under me.'

Luigi's right eyebrow went up, making a circumflex accent above the eye. 'Literally, I understand.'

'That was out of class and had nothing to do with her ability as a student.'

The little man gave another of his cheerless smiles, then shifted his body towards Bond. The disconcerting eyes appeared to alter again, this time becoming like dangerous grey lava. His voice also changed as he hissed rather than whispered. 'One small thing before we get to the Villa Tempesta, Mr James Bond. No, it's not a small thing really. I want you to remember that Toni Nicolletti now works for the Tempesta family, so she is, in her way, bound to us body and soul. She *is* one of us, and in a sense she also belongs directly to me. *Capisci*, James Bond?'

Bond gave back a smile as good – or evil – as he was receiving. 'The world has long changed since people owned other people, Luigi Tempesta. Today you must be careful to whom you express yourself in those kinds of terms.'

'It is our way still, and it would be to your advantage to remember it, Bond.'

'Oh, I *capeech* fine, Luigi.'

'Good. I'd hate us to get off on the wrong foot. Our poor young stepmother was unconscionably fond of you.'

Bond nodded. 'Yes, her death came as a terrible shock.'

'*Tragico.*'

'*Molto tragico,*' Bond had almost stared him down. 'And if I ever find the man or men that did it to her, I'll make it my responsibility to personally exact vengeance.'

'Ah.' Tempesta nodded and looked away.

After a kilometre or so Bond asked, 'Is the Villa Tempesta on this side of the lake?'

'There is a long way round which demands a drive through Viareggio itself. We find it easier to run our own vehicle-carrying barges from Torre del Lago. Pleasure boats and a transport service run from there, just a few steps from Puccini's house, where the composer's body is entombed.'

'Yes, I know it. It also sports a wonderful statue of Maestro Puccini.'

'So, you know this part of the world. Interesting.'

'I once did a little job near here.' Bond gave him his own enigmatic smile. In the back of his mind he saw the past: a velvet dark night, his quarry stumbling up a deserted beach and dying hard under Bond's hand. The man had been a traitor and needed to be silenced. It was what he had done regularly in those days, with his licence to kill and the double-O prefix.

He nodded forward, 'They your boys?' Another black car keeping them neatly boxed in. It was the first hint of the car Luigi had mentioned as they left the airport.

'Good men. They've kept out of sight well. But we're almost there.'

They had left the main road, and, in a matter of minutes, the Rolls swept into the small square adjacent to the lake. He saw the house, railed off and protected by shrubbery. There Puccini had written *La Bohème*, *Tosca* and *Madame Butterfly*. His bones now lay within the house which had known some of the composer's great moments, and the one terrible scandal – the suicide of a maid who was said to be pregnant by him. Yet, this small community contained a number of men and women who had the Puccini look. The statue still stood looking across the small square: a life-sized Puccini in overcoat and snappy trilby.

There was a ferry moored at the pier, and women like black crows shuffling up to its deck, on their way to other lakeside communities after a day's shopping. The car that had appeared just before they pulled off the main road was parked forward of the bows of the ferry, and the Rolls pulled up behind it, with the Ferrari almost on its bumper now. Just offshore, a flat, barge-like craft wallowed, ungainly, as it waited for the ferry to depart.

'If I recall it correctly,' Bond sounded offhand, 'there are a number of tributaries that run from the Lago Massaciuccoli.'

'Canals mostly. Very beautiful to traverse, and there is, of course, the canal that takes you right into the port of Viareggio. Now there's a place that's changed.' Luigi seemed to relish what he regarded as bad news. 'It was near there, on the beach, that your poet Shelley was cremated on a funeral pyre and his friend plunged his hand into the burning corpse to pull the great man's heart from his body. In those days you could do that. Now, ha! Now, you must pay for the privilege of even setting foot on the beach. In Viareggio you must pay to breathe the air.'

The ferry cast off, with a long blast on its whistle, and, as it set course for the far side of the lake, the Tempesta's vehicle barge came backing into the pier. Two men in black slacks and striped jerseys started to let down a ramp from the stern, one of them leaping ashore to make certain the heavy metal incline was secure. Within minutes, the three cars had inched their way onto the wide deck and the ramp was back in place again just before the craft backed off, turned, rocking gently in the still water, then set off, its bows pointing towards the right side of the lake.

In the distance, Bond could see the almost sensual slopes of the Tuscan hills. He had forgotten how beautiful this part of the country could be. It was not surprising it brought hordes of tourists flocking from all over the world. A man could regain his sanity and find peace just looking at the sunlight on those hills, he considered. He thought about the generations of Tempestas who had lived and rested on the shores of the lake.

As though reading his thoughts, Luigi spoke softly. 'Though we are Romans born, this is the place to which we come regularly in order to unwind, to search for the true meaning of our lives. To think on our destiny.' He moved again and his jacket fell open. Bond glimpsed the soft leather holster and the black butt of the pistol within.

His first sight of the Villa Tempesta came just as the rain started to clear and a shaft of sunlight crept through the overcast sky. It appeared to fall like a huge spotlight on the lakeside home.

There was a dock and pier down by the lake itself and above it two long solid structures running out on both sides. Boathouses, he presumed. From the pier a gravel road snaked up towards the house while a low grey stone wall ran around the property in a great square U shape, ending at the extremities of the boathouses.

The road rose up a gentle slope, and he had the impression of landscaped grounds, more cypresses, and a huge turning circle large enough to take five or six vehicles. Above this, a short flight of long grey stone steps led up to a terrace that ran the length of the house which was L-shaped, low, built from the same grey stone and topped by the familiar red terracotta tiles. The entire structure looked old and beautifully built. He wondered what tales of drama, melodrama, treachery and plotting that stone held secret.

The ramp came down and the three cars backed from the barge, each turning and moving slowly up the rise towards the steps and terrace. The arrival seemed to have been carefully choreographed, for the cars came to a halt in line: the Rolls flanked by the other two guard vehicles.

Doors started to open and slam. Luigi climbed from his side of the car, the door opened by the bodyguard, while Bond's door was held by the chauffeur.

He heard Luigi say thank you, and give the man a name, Carlo. So he turned, smiled at the chauffeur and said, '*Grazie* . . . er . . .'

'Filippo,' the chauffeur supplied, and Bond simply nodded, repeating, 'Filippo.'

He saw the bodyguard had his luggage, the suitcase and the essential briefcase. For a second, he was tempted to take the latter but thought better of it. Time enough.

The men in the other two cars were outside now: big men, mostly dressed in suits, at least two carrying short shotguns, the others certainly with concealed hand guns.

'Come, James,' Luigi lifted an arm, pointing towards the top of the short flight of long stone steps. 'See, my family has turned out to meet you.'

At the top of the steps, a foot or two back on the terrace, stood a tall slim man, whom he took to be Angelo, flanked by two equally tall women: one a spectacular slim brunette, with hair hanging around her shoulders; the other an elegant redhead who stood with her right hip thrust forward, her hand resting on the hip itself, and her breasts straining against the silk shirt she wore tucked into a very short skirt.

Which one is Giulliana, he wondered.

Angelo raised an arm in welcome, and there was a flurry of light footsteps from behind as Toni Nicolletti came running across the terrace, down the steps, arms stretched wide, then her hands resting on each of his shoulders as they came face to face.

She whispered, 'Oh, James, how good it is to see you. How wonderful.' Then she kissed him on each cheek and, over her shoulder, he saw the look of loathing on Luigi's face.

What was Toni playing at? Was this a Judas kiss, he wondered?

8

At the Villa Tempesta

BOND WHISPERED, 'CAREFUL, Toni, not so close. Luigi's going to kill us both.'

'They're going to try killing both of us anyway. Want to know what you know. Dry you out, then dump your body in the lake.'

'How touching.' Luigi's voice was cold, raw and bitter as an ice-storm. 'You should take a photograph, Maria. Call it *Ancient Lovers' Reunion*.' He spoke in English.

Bond untangled himself from Toni Nicolletti, smiled at Luigi and walked slowly up the steps.

'My brother, Angelo.' Luigi grasped Bond's shoulder, none too gently.

'Charmed. I'm glad you could visit us.' The relationship was clear from the brothers' looks. Both had similar noses, foreheads, and the same imperious manner. The arrogance of power. The same way of using their hands so that, with a gesture, they could add a subtext to conversation. This last, as he had noted from Luigi, was an uncanny talent, but there the likeness ended. Angelo was tall and slim. Together, on the terrace, the pair looked like some suave, sinister double act. Two years between them, Bond reflected, and the main difference was in stature, and the hair – Luigi's grey and distinguished; Angelo's thick, black and neatly barbered.

'Toni, I believe you have work to do,' Angelo's voice mirrored his brother's, with perfect English, hardly any trace of an accent. 'And, Mr Bond, you must meet the rest of the family.'

By this time, Bond had reached the terrace, his hand going out towards the slim brunette as Angelo introduced her – 'My wife, Maria, James Bond.' Her palm was cool and dry, the English not quite as accurate as her husband's. 'How nice to meet you, Mr Bond.'

'And my wife.' Luigi seemed to be pushing himself in; asserting his rights as the elder brother. 'My wife, Giulliana.'

The redhead, who was still standing with one hip thrust forward, as though to display her voluptuous figure, appraised him with her large brown eyes. For a moment, Bond thought he now knew what a woman felt like when eyed up by a lascivious man, for the cool brown eyes seemed to be undressing him. Giulliana was obviously a handful. Her wide and inviting mouth tilted into a smile of welcome.

Oh, what a large mouth you have. All the better to eat you with.

'I am more than happy to greet you, James. You must let me call you James, yes?'

'Giulliana, I would let you call me anything. Luigi is a very lucky man to have such a beautiful wife.'

The smile broadened. 'I wish you would tell him that.' She linked her arm through his, the outside of her thigh pressing against him. 'Let us go in to lunch.'

She led him through a pair of tall French doors into a large hallway. The floor was probably the original – planks, polished and kept to a high gloss, with three or four throw rugs which acted as stepping stones over the slippery surface.

To the far right, a wooden staircase curled its way upwards, though this was covered with a thick beige carpeting, held in place by old-fashioned brass stair-rods. The walls were painted in a dark cream colour; a huge red brick fireplace seemed to take up almost all of the wall to the right, and there were pictures everywhere; great gilt-framed oil paintings of what could only be Tempesta ancestors.

'This way.' She prodded him like a rider turning a horse, through a pair of massive double doors which led into a long low reception room, exquisitely furnished, mainly with antiques. In one corner, a beautiful angled cupboard rose from floor to ceiling, its shelves bearing rows of leather-bound books.

In the centre of the room a long refectory table was set for six. Matching high-backed chairs faced in to the place settings, which glittered with silverware and delicate china plates, each bearing a gilt coat of arms: the Tempestas again, Bond considered, looking around and seeing that these walls were also decorated with paintings – more Tempesta ancestors, mixed with the odd El Greco and, a Canaletto – inevitably a view of Venice.

The table was set out with cold meats, salads of every known description, stuffed tomatoes and eggs. Nearby, at a serving table bottlescaped with wine, Angelo expertly uncorked two bottles of champagne. His wife poured five glasses which were handed around.

'So, welcome to our home, James.' Angelo raised his glass, and the nucleus of the Tempesta family joined in this act of greeting.

They apologized for the simplicity of the meal, and, while they ate, the conversation centred mainly on the Tempesta family and its long and chequered history. Angelo told a long story about Edmondo Tempesta who, in 1446, had been the

close bodyguard of Pope Calixtus III – the first truly important
member of the Borgia family. Edmondo had saved the Pope
from an assassination attempt and was suitably rewarded with
a large sum of money. It was also said to that he inherited the
cast-off Papal mistresses, but he hoarded the money, and it was
with this capital that the Villa Tempesta was built.

Bond asked about their palazzo in Rome.

'Ah, that is another story,' Luigi said guardedly, and his wife
Giulliana said she really preferred this villa to the place in
Rome. 'My favourite is the small house in Venice.' She smiled
at Bond, as though giving him a signal. In fact, she had been
flashing her eyes in his direction all through lunch, and her
stolen glances were easily translated into elaborate invitations
– expensively printed and delivered by eye and body language.

The meal lasted barely an hour. Then Angelo pushed his
glass of chocolate mousse to one side, saying, 'I think it's time
for the ladies to withdraw so that we can discuss business.
Coffee, please, Maria.'

His wife made a little mocking bow and left, returning
quickly with coffee. Giulliana followed her sister-in-law out of
the room, giving Bond a final smouldering look. He remembered Sukie's information about her – . . . *Giulliana was supposed to be staying with her mother for a couple of nights. In
fact I saw her coming out of the Cardinal with him. You know
The Cardinal, small but elegant. On the Via Giulia – I thought
it was quite an amusing choice.*

Giulliana obviously put it about. Or was her behaviour some
other ploy? Giulliana the mantrap, sprung and waiting for
someone like himself.

The coffee was poured, and both the Tempesta brothers
leaned forward, their faces showing that there was an urgent
need to talk.

'You were, we hear, at Dulles airport when our stepmother died so horribly.'

'Yes, and it *was* horrible. You lost a very beautiful and quite incredible young stepmother, just as I lost a very good friend . . .'

'And lover,' said Luigi, his tone changing, becoming undoubtedly unpleasant.

Bond nodded, solemnly. 'Yes. I lost a lover.'

'One of many, I think, James,' from Angelo.

'Many for her, or for me?'

'I think both. But you were a favourite. She talked of you a great deal. You shared danger together and she thought you were some kind of secret agent . . .'

'I work for the government,' Bond snapped.

'She made a little joke of it,' Luigi again. 'She would speak of you with much tenderness and say that you were the spy who loved her.'

' "The spy who loved me," she used to say.' Angelo did not smile. 'So, are you in fact a British spy, James Bond?'

'More of a troubleshooter.' So that was it, he thought. Now he would have to play the cards agreed and worked out with Toni Nicolletti and Eddie Rhabb.

'It seems to be a coincidence that you met our delightful Toni on a flight to Kansas City. Were you shooting trouble there? What *do* you do in the way of troubleshooting, James? It's important that we know.'

'I work on various assignments for the British government. At the moment I'm following up on some leads concerning drug trafficking. Checking out the way one particular group of people move drugs from Colombia to the United States and then through Europe into the United Kingdom.'

'So!' abrupt, from Luigi.

This was the cover they had arranged. If the Tempestas were hand in glove with the renegade organization called COLD, they reasoned, the family would stay far away from drugs.

'And you were also assisting in examining the terror incident involving the Bradbury Airlines bombing?'

'Yes. I spent a short time at Dulles reporting back to London. In fact, there appears to be evidence that you were financially involved with Bradbury.'

Luigi nodded, and Angelo spoke. 'That is true. If Harley Bradbury goes belly-up because of this – what can I call it? – this cowardly bombing, we will be hit very hard. Not good.'

There was a short silence, then Luigi leaned forward, 'So, James. We respect you. We respect your friendship with Sukie, but I will not mince words, we also worry about you. This flight to Kansas City, when you met Toni. Can you tell us why this flight?'

'You can ask, but I can't answer fully, Luigi. I was meeting a contact who had information for me.'

'Information about what? Not about us, I hope.'

'Not unless you finance drugs going from here to there and back again.'

'You think we would be part of that business. They are the slow death of the world, the drugs. They are a destabilizer. They cost America a war. They are responsible for rising violent crime. You think we would be involved in that kind of thing? We are businessmen, James.'

'I wasn't accusing you of anything. Apart from knowing Sukie, and being nearby when she was murdered, I know of you only as businessmen. I also know you welcomed her into your family under circumstances that would make some children very angry.'

'You mean Sukie marrying our aged father?'

'Of course. I should warn you that there are some who have looked into your family history – people who knew you were investors in Bradbury Airlines – and are puzzled by Sukie's violent death. They wonder if family money played a part in *that*.'

They sat like statues, staring at him, their eyes holding back enigmatic smiles.

'Tell him, Angelo.' Luigi broke the silence.

'Sukie was the best thing that ever happened to our father, James. He was still a strong and virile man in old age. People would say, 'Oh, this is like the biblical thing. King David taking a young girl to his bed to keep him warm. I forget her name . . .'

'Abishag,' Bond supplied.

'Whatever. But it wasn't like that. There was genuine feeling between the two of them. There was physical joy as well, I assure you. Yes, sometimes we would get a little jealous for Sukie was definitely desirable, and Papa took advantage of that, and she of him as well. What do they call it in English? A spring and winter romance?'

'Something like that.'

'Tell him what really happened. Tell him the money.' Luigi's precise English slipped a little.

'Okay, I tell you something nobody knows but ourselves and the lawyers. When she accepted Papa's proposal, Sukie insisted on a pre-nuptial agreement. She wanted none of his money when he died. They sat together in this very room. Papa, Sukie, Luigi and I, and the advocates. The agreement was drawn up that she would receive nothing after his death.'

'But she inherited . . .' Bond began, and Angelo held up a hand to stop him.

'They were married in Rome. The night before the wedding, old Papa summoned us to the study where he spent a lot of his time. We arrived, together with our wives, and the advocates were also there – the lawyers. In front of us he burned the pre-nuptial agreement, and made his new will which made certain that she inherited as a Tempesta. It was fair and honest, and the Tempestas have always had a reputation for honesty. It was agreed, and we *all* agreed.'

'Even your wives?' As he said it, Bond realized that it was too flippant.

'Tempesta women always agree with the head of the family. They had to agree, and they *did* agree. Never afterwards were there any cross words. On his deathbed, Papa told Sukie what had been done and that she, as a Tempesta by marriage, should abide by it. You understand this, James Bond?'

He nodded, yes. Aloud, he said. 'It always amazes me. The honour and closeness of an old Italian family.'

'Well, you see it in action now. To be truthful, we are desolated by Sukie's death, which is one of the reasons we wanted to see you. James Bond, we doubted your integrity. I speak for both of us when I say that we still have small doubts, tiny doubts.'

'The chance meeting with Toni, for instance,' Luigi almost whispered.

'You are a troubleshooter, James. For your government. Do you ever hire yourself out to others?'

'For what purpose?'

'In this case, to find the killer or killers of our stepmother. Sukie's murderers.'

'You don't have to hire me for that,' he said evenly. 'I'm already on their trail.'

'You are?' Luigi sounded as though he had been stung.

'You have some lead? Somebody in mind?' Angelo's voice hit a high register.

'Not really. Not yet. But I am making inquiries.'

'You get a million in sterling if you find them and bring them to us.'

'No need for the money, but if you come up with any ideas . . .'

'We may already have one.' Angelo had calmed down again.

'So?'

'He's an American. A retired general who cannot stop playing soldiers. Sukie knew him. She turned down offers of marriage from him on three occasions. He is a violent man, and I would not put this thing past him.'

'He still likes playing soldiers?'

'General Brutus Clay, Retired. A genuine American hero who still wants to be active, so he has his own private army.'

'Not one of these militias we've been hearing so much about?'

Luigi made a spitting noise, and Angelo went on speaking, distaste sprinkling his words. 'No. No, not a militia. Just war games. Old soldiers who get together and play with real weapons. General Clay was a wealthy man from an even wealthier family when he first went into the United States Army. He has been retired for three years now and lives in a vast barrack-like place on high ground, in a mountainous area of Idaho.

'With him, he has some hundred men and women who served with him, are now retired but want to go on – as I said – playing soldiers. He has a fortune invested in arms and equipment. He has bought items from Russia and some of the old satellite countries. He has no aims or objectives as far as we can discover – except he has said openly that he would come to the aid of any President who might need him and his force.'

'He plays soldiers all the time?'

'Most of it. But he does take regular leaves and goes out and about – New York, LA, places like that. Cities where he drinks and whores with the best of them. He just about laid siege to Sukie.'

'And how do I get in touch with the general?'

'You go to Idaho. Spokane in Washington State has the nearest airport. I would suggest you hire a car and telephone him. Set up a meeting.'

'Give me the number.' He took a small leather pad from inside his jacket pocket and wrote down the number as Angelo read it out to him.

'You will be doing us a great favour if you investigate him, James. The man is unstable and threatened Sukie the last time she turned him down.'

'We would like to see him charged with her murder,' Luigi added. 'But death will be equally satisfactory, if you get evidence.'

'I'm not a hired killer,' he said evenly, his mind flooding suddenly with the fact that for a long time he had been just that.

They suggested that he should relax – 'Stay a few days, James. You live a busy life. Hang out here. We've an indoor pool, the works. I'll get Toni to show you to your room.' Angelo must have pressed some hidden button for a couple of minutes later there was a knock at the door and Toni came in.

He noticed that she was very deferential to the brothers, and led him to his room on the second floor, hardly looking at him.

'If you need anything just dial 88,' she said, opening the door for him.

'I . . .' he began, but she put a finger to her lips, standing just inside the room. Then he felt her fingers near his jacket pocket.

'Have a pleasant stay with us, James. See you at dinner. They usually eat around seven.'

The room was high-ceilinged, airy, with a large window looking out onto the double boathouse and the lake, which shone like a mirror under a wan sun. The rain had gone, and he stood looking across the water for a few minutes before settling down to unpack.

Dumping the briefcase on the bed, Bond did a slow and very precise search, looking for fibre optic lenses which would signify surveillance cameras. He found none so looked for signs of a bug. Nothing. Only when he was absolutely certain that the room was clean did he spin the locks on the briefcase and open it up. First he took out the automatic, making certain it contained a full magazine. Next he touched his jacket pocket and found that Toni had slipped a computer disk inside when she had touched him. Moving the laptop onto the small table which stood under the window, he slid the disk into place and opened it. Words scrolled, white on blue down the screen.

They are setting you up, I think, he read. *It is possible that they've talked to you about a retired US Army general called Clay. He would be their ideal choice. In fact I think they already have both of us tagged, and, should the opportunity arise, they will dump us within the next twelve hours or so. They want us at the bottom of the lake, so please, James, take great care. I have other vital information for you but I have to tell you myself. Scrub this disk. I will try to get to you sometime tonight. Please be ready to make a fast getaway. Love T*

Erasing the disk, he popped it among several others in a compartment in the briefcase, then set about readying himself for sudden trouble or action. When he had everything to his liking, Bond stretched out on the bed to rest.

Just before seven he changed into a dark suit before heading downstairs again. Luigi and Angelo were already waiting, though they seemed slightly strung out, as if they had some great secret they did not want either discovered or passed on.

'We're sorry,' Luigi began, 'But we're going to have to leave you in the tender hands of the ladies tonight.'

'It is necessary for us to go into Viareggio, and I don't think we'll be back until sometime in the morning,' Angelo completed. 'You'll be quite safe, though. There are four of our people here, and the ladies will take care of you, I'm sure.'

As though on cue two of the ladies – Maria and Giulliana – appeared. They seemed quite skittish at the thought of being left alone with him, though there was a great deal of hugging and kissing as they saw the two men off, waving to them as they walked across the terrace and down to the pier, where they climbed into a long motor launch, which pulled away at speed as soon as they were settled.

Toni joined them for dinner which, in spite of Bond's attempts to amuse the women with stories of life in England, and suitable jokes, dragged. At around nine-thirty Toni yawned and said she was off to bed. The two other women stayed on for half an hour and then they also made their apologies.

Bond was back in his room soon after ten.

The bed had been turned down and the curtains were drawn, so he changed yet again, this time into a pair of warm slacks and a polo shirt. He slipped his feet into his favourite moccasins, then readied the pistol and holster, putting out a short denim jacket which he could slip on very quickly when and if the time came.

It was almost eleven-thirty before he heard the quiet knock. There was no security peephole, so he unlocked the door and opened it, carefully keeping his right foot behind the corner to block any unwanted guest.

His mind told him that it had to be Toni, but when the door opened Giulliana stood there wearing a thin silk robe.

'I thought you might need company, James.' She pushed the door open, took two steps inside, kicked the door closed and, at the same time, let the robe fall from her shoulders to reveal exactly how items bought at Victoria's Secret should be worn.

He tried to back away, but she was on him like a vixen on heat, pushing him back onto the bed, rubbing her body against him, opening her legs, reaching for him, her mouth coming down hard on his and her tongue lancing into his mouth.

He struggled for a moment, then thought, 'Well, I'd better lie back and think of England.'

They had just got to the interesting part when the door crashed open and Luigi stood there, a black automatic in his hand.

'You ungrateful slut,' he began, then launched into a tirade of Italian, aimed at his wife. If this was a set-up, Bond thought, they were both good actors, for she appeared to be truly afraid, as he hauled her from the bed and back-handed her twice, leaving blood on her mouth. With one quick flick of his arm, the little Italian hurled his wife into the corner of the room.

'Bene,' he spat, raising the pistol. 'Now I have a reason to deal with you, Mr Bond.'

His arms came up in a two-handed grip on the pistol. Bond was sprawled on the bed with no way he could get to the Italian before he squeezed the trigger. From what seemed a long way off, he heard himself saying, 'Is this it? Is this really the end?'

9

If You Can't Beat 'Em

FROM BOND'S VIEWPOINT, everything seemed to move in slow motion, and his eyes became a camera with a zoom lens closing first on the wicked eye of Luigi's hand gun. He struggled to push himself off the bed upon which he was sprawled, yet all his focus was on Luigi's finger as it took up pressure on the trigger.

He finally regained his balance and rolled to his left off the bed. His first thought was that it seemed to be taking a very long time for Luigi Tempesta to squeeze the trigger. His hand moved to the pillows under which he had slid his own weapon.

Then something else happened. Luigi, who appeared to have been standing as still as a wax dummy, pitched forward, hitting his chin on the foot of the bed. He did not utter a sound as he fell.

'It's okay. Only a tranquillizer.' Toni Nicolletti stood in the doorway, a small high-powered air pistol in one hand and a more lethal Glock 9mm automatic in the other. She smiled nicely at Giulliana, whispering, 'Love the underwear, Mrs Tempesta. Goodnight.' The air pistol popped again and Giulliana seemed to freeze in place on one knee as she tried to get to her feet. Her eyes glazed over and, while Bond watched her, she slowly tipped to one side.

'Looks like I just saved you from a fate worse than death, James.' Toni raised an eyebrow as she gave him the evil-eye look.

'She was damned well raping me.'

'Yes,' Toni smiled. 'You still haven't quite recovered from the dangerous effects of Giulliana's body in all that frippery. I have a set just like that.' She did a double-take and muttered, 'Down boy. I think we should seriously try to get away from here as quickly as possible.'

Bond tried to cover his confusion and adjust his clothing. 'This a set-up? Where's Angelo?'

'A set-up, yes. I suspect to catch both Giulliana and yourself. She really cannot keep her hands off available men, so I suspect Luigi and Angelo set the trap. I know Luigi wanted to be rid of her, and that they both wanted to be rid of you – and me, come to that.'

'And Angelo?'

'Taking an enforced nap, like these two.'

'This a kinder and gentler approach to law enforcement? Or just something for the girls?'

'Watch it, James.' The little air pistol moved in her hand.

'Peace, Toni. So how do we get out of here?'

'Well, the heavies are still lurking around. There're always a couple on duty at night, so we have to avoid them. How much stuff do you want to get out with you? I mean, are clothes expendable?'

'You propositioning me, or are you serious?'

'Absolutely serious. Down in the boathouse – the one on our right going down to the pier – they have four jet-skis.'

'Water motorcycles?'

'Kind of. I know all the channels and, actually, I've already made arrangements.'

'What kind of arrangements?'

'We have a deal with the CIA Station Chief in Rome. Ever since your arrival there've been a couple of his grey-suited field officers hanging around in Viareggio. I can send a quick burst to them before we leave. I have the technology. I can also lead you out through the right canals so that we get into Viareggio Port.'

'And from there we can catch a fast cruise ship to DC, I presume.'

'Better. If we go within the next thirty minutes, the field officers will pick us up in the pine woods.'

Bond took only a moment to make a decision. 'I presume we wear wet suits. Any way I can take a jacket and this briefcase?'

She nodded. 'I have a waterproof back-pack, but I suggest you keep a weapon handy. You're carrying one, I see.'

'Always. Let's do it, Toni.'

'We haven't the time James. Come on.'

With his jacket slung over his left arm, and the ASP 9mm in his other hand, he followed Toni out of the room and down to her office, which was hidden away in the rear ground floor of the house. She moved silently, slowly and very carefully, stopping at corners, pistol ready, always alert. There was no other movement or sound from within the house, and when they were inside the office she reached back, closing and locking the door.

The curtains were drawn across a long window, and the bulk of the room was taken up by a big desk, a padded high-backed leather chair and a comfortable easy chair.

A bank of three telephones stood to the right of a computer screen and keyboard, while the computer itself stood on the floor to the left of the desk, so that she could reach down and have easy access to the disk drive and CD ROM player. One of

the telephones, he noted, was equipped with a screen and a
mass of buttons for entering and storing speed dialling numbers. He also guessed that this particular instrument was
equipped with Caller ID to check incoming calls.

By the time he had taken in the surroundings, Toni was already
behind her desk with the computer on. She typed very quickly,
then performed some keystrokes. The machine beeped twice,
and she waited, eyes anxiously watching the monitor. Another
beep and she relaxed, closed up whatever programme she had
been running, then shut down the equipment.

'They'll be waiting for us in the pine woods.' She raised her
head and smiled. 'There's even a possibility that one of them
will come through the port to meet us and guide us in. Now . . .'
she gestured towards the armchair and he saw two black wet
suits and back-packs lying across the chair.

'You really had this worked out, then?'

'I couldn't warn you.' She was already climbing into one of
the wet suits, pulling it on over her light slacks and rollneck
sweater. 'They were very much on the watch today, and they
very rarely leave the house without one of the cars, so I was
fairly certain that this was a come-on. If we leave a good trail,
they might just follow us straight to the States. On the other
hand – they presumably gave you one of their COLD contacts
in case things went wrong for them here?'

'The one you suggested on the disk. General Clay.'

'That's an old contact. The guy's as nutty as a bag of
Jamaican Mix. Crazy. I think they've used him as a hit man –
well, not him, but his extraordinary outfit. I really don't know
if he's affiliated to COLD, but I guess he's got some clout in
that direction. Go with great care, James, he's evil.'

He busied himself: packing his jacket, shoes and the briefcase into the waterproof back-pack, then followed her example

by wriggling into the wetsuit. 'What about Angelo's wife?' he asked, adjusting the legs of the suit.

'What about her?'

'Has she also gone to sleep for a while?'

'At least six hours. Great stuff these tranquillizer darts. You probably noticed that they produce severe paralysis as soon as they inject. That lasts for about a minute, then the muscles relax and they just keel over and sleep for a minimum of six hours, sometimes longer.'

'Must try some myself. Not going to get any sleep tonight. Anyway, Toni, where do we go from here?'

'There's only one way, and you'd better keep your gun within reach. That'll do nicely.' She patted a zippered pocket at the top of the thigh on the suit. 'Remember there are at least two of the Tempesta lackeys roaming around, and they're always well armed. We dodge in and out of the shadows down to the boathouse on the right at the bottom of the pier. The jet-skis are usually kept fully juiced up, so we start up a pair together as I press the button that opens up the front metal screen on the boathouse. Works like a garage door remote.'

'A lot of noise then?'

'Not really. These are pretty much high-tech and silent. But I want us both out of that place and onto the lake as quickly as possible. We'll be going diagonally across, heading towards the last of six canals that run off in the direction of the sea. No lights. You'll have to keep up by following my wake, and that could be a problem for you as it gets very dark out there.

'If you lose me then find the canal right up by Torre del Lago – where they picked up the cars. The canal curves round to your left. You'll pass an exit on your right after a while, then you come to a kind of T-junction. Go left and . . .'

'Straight on 'til morning?'

'More or less. The canal opens out into Viareggio Port. Lights when you're safely into the canal because there might be barge traffic. Not much at this time of the year, but it would be best to be on the safe side. When you get into the port, dodge through the traffic and head for the open sea; then hang a right and try to stay inland. You'll see the famous pine forests. Just pull your jet-ski over and leg it into the woods. Two men will be waiting for us.

'Yes, Ma'am.' He winked at her.

She was tightening the straps on her back-pack. Now she pulled up the hood surrounding her face, giving him a broad wink back.

Bond was already organized, and he finished off by slipping the ASP into the zippered pocket, checking that he could unzip and get his hand onto the butt with ease.

'Okay?' from Toni. 'I'll lead the way down because I've done some practice runs since I've been here. Ready?'

'Break a leg.' Bond smiled grimly and followed her along the passage and up to the hall, then through the door and onto the terrace.

There was an almost full moon, but there were also some thick clouds. Hardly any breeze around the lake, but there had to be a stiff wind up at around five or six thousand feet, for the moon was constantly being obscured by the fast moving clouds. He moved swiftly to keep up with Toni, who seemed to be sure-footed and silent, gliding in and out of the shadows. She froze when the moon peeped out from the clouds, moving on when the darkness once again covered the lake. It took almost five minutes to reach the rear of the boathouse, and the door creaked as she opened it. To both of them, the creak sounded like a warning amidst the silence.

Inside, Toni had a tiny penlight in her hand, and she had

obviously checked out the boathouse in darkness on a number of occasions. She leaned back and took Bond's hand, pulling him towards the water which he could hear lapping against the wooden decking. As his eyes adjusted, he could make out the shape of the four jet-skis bobbing, low in the water, at their mooring points.

'Let's take the ones at the end,' she whispered, leaning forward, almost overbalancing as she explained the fuel gauges with the penlight. 'They're both full.' He could see enough now to catch the smile on her face. Then he felt her lips on his. 'Okay?' she asked.

'Let's do it now.'

She moved back out of sight for a second and there was a low hum as she operated the metal door. 'You have ridden one of these before?' she asked in a slightly louder voice now.

Bond nodded. 'A couple of times. Don't worry, I'm not going to fall off.'

'Ready?'

'Okay.'

'Engines,' she all but shouted, and he lugged himself onto the wide seat of the jet-ski, made certain that it was cast off properly, and twisted the ignition a fraction of a second before Toni's machine burst into life. The machine bucked under him so that he had to throttle back before opening it smoothly. Out of the corner of his eye he saw her jet rise in the water and begin to streak out towards the open lake in a wide turn.

Advancing the throttle again, he felt the chill of wind on his face and a sense of speed, the entire machine wallowing and then rising, carrying him forward so that he could watch the white trail of her wake as she circled into the lake. Within seconds he had to ease back on the power as he took station a little behind her and to her right. If he had swung too far to the left, he would have been in line astern from her and could easily have been thrown off if he slipped into her boiling white wake.

The moon came out from behind the clouds just as he started to find the slap, bump and bucking of the machine an exhilarating challenge. It seemed to light up the whole lake, a long wide stretch of molten lead on which he rode with Toni still a little to his left and in front. There was a sudden static in the air, not quite a sound, but a tension he could almost hear, like a rush of air between the two jet-skis. It took a couple of seconds for him to realise that it was not the moon shining across the flat water, but a halogen searchlight beam, and that the other feeling was the crack caused by the air mass being punctured by high-powered bullets.

Glancing back, he saw the bows of a motor launch some fifty yards away, but bearing down upon them. In the cockpit, one of the Tempestas' men – it looked like Filippo – was firing bursts of tracer at them with a semi-automatic weapon. There was another flicker, and this time Bond threw himself forward over the steering bars of the machine as the bullets hissed into the water between them.

Looking back again, he saw that the launch was slowly making headway, catching up with them, while Toni was apparently oblivious to what was going on. Pouring on power and easing away to his right, Bond started one of the most dangerous moves a jet-skier can make. If you can't beat 'em, he thought, then you have to join them.

As he went into the hard turn, it was as though he were riding the side of a race track, curved upwards. The difference was that the surface on which he rode was insubstantial and could give way, swallowing him and toppling the jet-ski. Too much speed, or too steep an angle and the water would swing him out of control, spit him out then draw him in.

Bond was anxious to complete the manoeuvre without being unglued from the jet-ski, and this caused him to make the turn wider than he wanted. The ski bumped and juddered under him, and, as soon as he straightened up, his right hand came off the steering bars, reached for the zippered pocket, curling around the butt of the ASP automatic.

The motor launch had changed direction by around three points, beginning to angle towards him, but keeping the searchlight on Toni. He was around thirty feet from the craft when he saw another burst of tracer rip across the water, sending up a spray dangerously close to her machine.

He had the pistol out now, feeling very unsafe in the knowledge that while riding this bone-jarring little craft the chances of knocking out the man with the semi-automatic were very slim. He was steering at speed with one hand as his pistol came up, pointing in the general direction of the shooter, and he was vaguely aware that the man at the wheel was shouting a warning. He squeezed off four rounds, two quick pairs of shots, and almost lost control as Filippo's arms flew upwards, as though he were surrendering. The silhouette of the man danced a macabre jig, feet slipping, arms flailing and body starting to spin, then lifting and going over the side.

The bow of the launch turned directly towards him, and appeared to rise from the water as it increased speed. He wrenched at the steering bars of the jet-ski and roughly hauled it around. The response was sluggish as he increased the power and angle of turn, the machine juddering under him as though it would stall. Then he saw the bows miss him by a couple of feet, and he was caught in the spray of the white roil of water surging from the stern.

Again, he hauled on the steering bars: once more the jet-ski shuddered as though it would slip sideways and so let the water cover him. He felt the nose going down, and at the same moment had a spray-covered view of the motor-launch's stern. His right hand came up and he squeezed the trigger, some five or six shots in quick succession, one of which must have penetrated the side of the craft and, burning hot from the velocity, pierced the petrol tank.

Even over the engine noise and the rushing sound of water, he heard a dull thump as though from under the lake. Then the gas tank ignited in one huge explosion of fire, leaping upwards – a great plume of flame rising from the centre of what looked like a blossom: the opening of a fiery flower. The blast hit him and the jet-ski felt as though it had risen from the lake's surface – slewing, sideways on, aquaplaning away from the spray and pieces of wood and metal that seemed to be raining down around him.

The remains of the launch were foundering and burning some hundred yards away by the time he had gained control of the jet-ski. Through the flames he caught a glimpse of Toni's ski standing off around fifty yards on the far side of the wreck. He opened the throttle and headed towards her, happy to see her move a hand in a thumbs up sign. He eased back and could make out that she was instructing him to follow her. She obviously wanted him to do this as fast as possible, for her jet-ski lurched to one side and she began to accelerate across the lake. For a second he hesitated, then began to pour on power until they were both roaring forward at a very uncomfortable speed.

It took around thirty minutes before they reached the edge of the lake. By this time the moon had shaken itself free of the clouds, and he could see the bank, trees and shrubbery coming up very quickly. He thought she was heading them both straight into land, but at the last moment he glimpsed the opening that led into a wide canal. They both slowed to a more sedate pace as they passed into the canal, with its banks of overhanging foliage and grass.

He thought that by day and in summer this would be an idyllic place. For a while he steered on instinct alone, his mind slipping away to thoughts of being here, perhaps with Toni Nicolletti, in a motorized barge possibly, just drifting under warm blue skies with the scent of summer around them.

He was dragged back to the present by the sound of a deep pounding of engines from in front of them, and he caught Toni's hand signal to pull in close to the bank and cut the engine.

There were two of them, going at speed, sending out a long choppy bow wash as they travelled with the occasional blare of a klaxon and red warning lights flashing: a pair of police patrol boats heading to see what carnage had occurred on the lake. The men in charge were obviously focused only on getting out to the flaming wreckage, for they passed by without even looking towards the two jet-skis and their riders.

'Lights, I think.' Toni called back to him, so they started off again with lights spreading out from the front of the machines, still keeping up a moderately slow pace. Within another fifteen minutes they came to the junction of the canals, turning left and heading towards the Port of Viareggio. Ten minutes later the lights of the harbour became visible, together with small craft and the odd seagoing ship anchored within the port.

Nobody challenged them as they moved into the main channel and then out beyond the breakwater, turning right as they felt the sea begin to lift and drop the jet-skis. Toni led the way inshore, picked up speed and headed towards the lights that were the coastal town.

The pine woods came up first and Bond followed Toni's lead, cutting his engine as they drifted towards a narrow beach backed by the thick, sweet-smelling trees. They literally stumbled up the beach and into the trees. It had been a long time since Bond had felt this unsteady. The rolling, bumping and hard splashing of the jet-ski had set him very much off balance, and Toni clung to him trying to walk in a straight line. The blind leading the blind, he thought.

When they appeared – with a whispered 'Bill?' and their answer of 'Hilary' – the grey men were far from grey. Both were dressed in slacks, rollnecks, and sports coats: one a tall and muscular fellow with sandy hair, they eventually discovered; the other a short, slightly pugnacious African-American.

'The car's waiting,' the sandy-haired one spoke softly and with some urgency.

'C'mon,' the other one ordered. 'Ain't got all night. Move it.'

It was a long dark vehicle that Bond could not even put a name to. Not that they were given time to examine it, for the two men hustled them into the back, the sandy-haired man – who liked to be called Charley – slid in beside them, while their other bodyguard sat next to the driver whose face they did not see clearly – then or later.

'Just sit back as far as you can,' Charley told them. 'We've got nearly a two-hour drive but I got coffee here if you want some.'

'Black with no sugar,' Bond said quickly. He was beginning to feel the cold.

'Me too,' from Toni.

'Okay. Just lean back and enjoy. We don't need to talk. Save the talking for the Fibbees.'

Bond shot a quick glance towards Toni who whispered, 'Guess we're going to be sent to the Principal's office.'

He sipped his coffee and was surprised that the ride was smooth, for they were driving at a fair speed. He leaned back and thought about the last few hours. Had he accomplished anything? Doubtful. What had started as an anti-terrorist operation following Harley Bradbury's Flight BD 299 explosion at Dulles International, had turned into something quite different. First there had been Sukie's arrival back into his life, then her sudden and horrific death, which had led him to work under FBI control with his own chief's blessing.

He reflected on the sinister brothers Tempesta and their supposed link with the Children Of the Last Days, whose object in life appeared to be a complete reworking of the United States of America, with draconian changes, and the principles of organized crime to keep the citizens happy. Then the Tempestas' obvious attempt to do away with Toni and himself. No, he had definitely failed there, as had Toni. Their job had been to lure the brothers into the United States so that the authorities could prize COLD out of the woodwork and put the Tempestas away; preferably for life.

Somehow Bond did not think they had done much in the way of setting themselves up as an attractive lure.

He thought about Harley Bradbury and his part in all this, and as he thought, he became drowsy. Somewhere far away he heard music. He looked around to find that he had been transported to some magnificent masked ball. He knew instantly that he was in Venice, and recalled that during the day he had found a shop which specialized in hand-made paper. Later he had tried to find the shop again, but it seemed to have disappeared. That was the way with Venice, he considered. One square would look wonderful and clear in the morning, yet when you tried to find it again, later in the day, it had changed: a trick of the light. There was nowhere else in the whole world with light like Venice.

Out of the crowd of dancers, a lady in a beautiful eighteenth-century ball gown, her face masked, came towards him and asked him for a dance. 'It'll be a dance macabre,' she said, and he recognized Sukie's voice. As she dropped her mask for a moment so he saw the burned skull underneath. He reeled back and Toni was at his side, speaking rapidly. 'James! James! Wake up. We're here.'

She was shaking his shoulder, and he realized that he had slept almost all the way to their destination. He smiled sheepishly at her, and then shook the sleep from his head, reaching for the door handle and opening it. The car was in what seemed to be the courtyard of a farm building. They were well clear of any main road, and Charley began to shepherd them towards the door.

It was an old house, oddly Tudor in its appearance, and Charley gave the door a series of obviously coded raps. There came the sound of bolts being withdrawn, and then there was Eddie Rhabb, giving his charging bull look. 'Quickly, get inside.' He sounded brusque and Bond stepped back to let Toni go in before him.

Rhabb stood to their left as they entered a comfortable room with a fire blazing in a large brick hearth. Several leather easy chairs were placed around the hearth and he took in the fact that the wild red-headed MacRoberts was stretched out in one of them. Then he heard another voice.

'James, my boy. What in heaven's name happened? I can never let you off the leash. Death, fire, shooting and all those other charming pieces of gratuitous violence seem to follow you around like an untrained Rottweiler.' M rose from his chair, a glass of whisky in his hand and a stern expression on his face.

10

Kidnap

THEY WERE ALLOWED to go upstairs to change. Bond found that a small suitcase containing some of his own clothes – obviously lifted quietly from his flat off the King's Road – had been brought over, presumably by M. He tidied up before going downstairs again to find Toni already there, perched on the edge of one of the easy chairs, holding court. She was now dressed in a heavy blue skirt with a shirt of a lighter shade of blue, and a knotted silk scarf at the neck.

'Ah, good. You're sometimes more fussy than a woman, James. Like to take your time, eh?' M rose from his chair and gestured towards a table set for five.

They ate a simple meal of omelettes and pommes frites, with long crisp bread, all washed down with a thirst-quenching *Galestro*. When the coffee arrived, Eddie Rhabb began what was obviously to be some kind of debrief—

'So what happened out there on the lake?'

'We had to make a fast getaway, using jet-skis, and they were foolish enough to follow in a motor launch.' Long ago, Bond had learned the art of sticking to the main points and saving the detail under later.

'It happened faster than we expected,' Toni said quietly.

'Told you,' snapped the wild MacRoberts. 'When we

111

briefed you, Toni, I said it would happen very quickly once Bond turned up.'

'Could someone actually tell me what this is about?' Bond felt that something had passed him by. 'I understood that the idea was to get the Tempestas' confidence and lure them to the States so that you could lock them up and throw away the key.' He nodded towards Rhabb and MacRoberts.

'Well, that's just about what you did, isn't it?' from Rhabb. 'They were friendly, welcoming, and gave you a contact: someone who might have been involved in Sukie Tempesta's murder – Clay.'

'You been talking?' He looked, a little crossly, at Toni, who shook her head. 'They knew about that almost the moment the brothers put it to you. I'd spiked the dining room and was getting it all in my office. Essential pieces of conversation were nipping through the air to Eddie and Mac, here.'

'And from them to me,' M said quietly.

'You see, James,' Eddie leaned back, head up, out of the bull charging position, 'we figured that, as you had known Sukie so well, and simply because you were there, at Dulles, you would be immediately suspect. To the Tempestas, if *they* had no hand in the murder, you were the one possible choice. I imagine they were pretty shaken when they heard you had met Toni.'

'They seemed not to believe my story about flying to Kansas City.'

'Why should they? Toni was already a questionable member of the household. We knew that when we sent her in again. But I believe they were convinced she was material from regular organized crime. It wouldn't surprise me if she was quietly followed, and then lost, in the States. That's why they probably knew she didn't go anywhere near Kansas City. I think the general plan was to get rid of you there and then . . . the pair of you.'

'That's what it felt and looked like.'

'How did they actually set you up?' M asked, his face bland with innocence.

'You don't know, sir?'

'No, but I'd bet it was a woman. Knowing you as I do, I'd put money on it being a female of the species.' His eyes closed and he appeared to have nodded off.

'Just for your peace of mind, sir, *she* came to me, not vice versa.'

MacRoberts gave a humourless laugh. 'Giulliana. I'd put money on her.'

'Yes, Giulliana, and her husband really seemed upset about it.'

'Luigi Tempesta is always upset with her – if it's not royalty or money making a play for her.' Eddie grunted. 'If it's someone like Harley Bradbury, he couldn't care less. In fact, he probably gets all the pillow talk. Luigi is a man of rather bizarre tastes. As for his wife, if it's male and wears trousers she'll lock onto it like a missile.'

'So,' M seemed to have woken up again. 'They wine and lunch you, then what?'

'After lunch, they fed me General Clay and his merry men who roam the Idaho mountains.'

'They make any suggestions?'

'That I should get in touch with him. Even gave me his contact number. The bait was that the general had something to do with Sukie's death.'

'Then they turned you loose with the lovely Giulliana?'

'Not quite. Early in the evening, they were suddenly called away. I had a very dreary dinner – begging your pardon, Toni.'

Toni laughed. 'I could hardly get a word in. Giulliana was giving you the steamy eye, and letting you know that when her husband was away she was available.'

'But they came back, eh?' from MacRoberts.

'Just as she was trying to rape me.'

'Then the old badger game?' Eddie asked.

Bond nodded. 'In storms Luigi, ready to shoot me.'

'I wonder if he would've done that?' M mused.

Silently, MacRoberts shook his head. 'Doubt it.'

'You weren't facing his gun. I was immobilized.'

'Then Toni came riding in like a white knight and saved you,' said Eddie Rhabb.

Toni laughed. 'The new A15 tranquillizer darts work a treat. Stopped him dead. I'd already had some practice with Angelo.'

M opened one eye. 'So you – what's the expression? – hightailed it out of there?'

'On the jet-skis, yes,' Bond nodded, 'And bloody bumpy they are as well.'

'Watch your language!' snapped M, who had a thing about even the mildest of bad language.

'What I don't understand is if they intended to kill us there at the villa, why did they bother to set me up with Clay?' Bond's forehead wrinkled.

'Because the brothers Tempesta are very careful men.' Mac-Roberts took a long draft of wine. 'Clay'd be their backup. The Tempestas always have a secondary plan. They know things can go wrong, so they cover their backsides. That's excellent for them, and bad news for us.'

'The guys in the launch seemed to be playing it for keeps.' Bond described the battle on the lake.

Eddie nodded. 'That's the other problem with the Tempestas. Their men are not well-disciplined, unlike the members of

COLD who are trained to obey orders first and last.'

'Clay?' Bond asked.

'What about him?'

'They gave the impression that his was a solo outfit, strongly attached to President, country and the Declaration of Independence. Nothing to do with COLD.'

'They would,' muttered MacRoberts. 'They would never let an outsider even hear a casual mention of COLD, but I'd stake my life on the general being at least a conduit to COLD. It's well-known that he has no time for the militia movement who are geared to fighting the government. COLD wants to be the government, and I should imagine that the general wants to be Secretary of Defence.'

'So what have we really accomplished, and what do we do now?' Bond appeared to be challenging them.

'Well, James.' It was M who answered. 'If our FBI friends will allow me to put you in the picture – because my time here is limited . . .'

Rhabb glanced at his watch and said something about him having almost an hour.

'Military jet,' M explained. 'Fast devils. Got me over here faster than Concorde. Right, what have you accomplished? You've stirred up a little hornets' nest to begin with. Ms Nicolletti and yourself have become loose cannons. The brothers Tempesta probably see you as a large threat. It is even possible that they *will* both follow you into the States. You'll be going tomorrow. In plain sight. Ms Nicolletti will fly to DC, while you, James, will fly to San Francisco and then up to Spokane. They'll be expecting that, just as they'll be fairly sure you'll make a play for the general. That's another of their problems: in spite of what happened on the lake, they'll think you've fallen for their story about the general's involvement in their stepmother's death. Won't think twice about it. They are your basic psychopaths, they never learn from their mistakes. I should imagine our FBI friends will already have a watch on General Clay.' His head snapped towards Rhabb. 'Right?' he asked.

The FBI man shrugged. 'We do have someone there keeping a lookout.'

'So, you'll be reasonably protected.' M smiled, seraph-like, at Bond.

'With respect, sir, it'll be me out there and, from what everyone says, these people play for keeps.'

'Then you'll be in your element, James, won't you?' M let this last sentence hang in the air.

Bond breathed a long sigh and said he supposed he would be in his element, muttering, 'Nor rain of bullets, nor sleet of nerve gas, nor hail of fire, nor death of night, shall halt the males from SIS. I must get through.'

'You had a comment, Bond!' M said sharply.

'No, sir. No. Do the FBI have a nice little safe house like this in Idaho?'

'It's not an FBI house,' M smiled grimly. 'It's one of ours.'

Toni moved in. 'Then we're not to operate on the Clay business together?'

Eddie gave a forceful, 'No!' which settled matters for all time. 'James, your job is to sniff out Clay. Take a few soundings, see if he really has connections with COLD, then get out.'

'Before he gets me, I presume?'

M said that the job was purely routine. 'Just touch base with the man, take a look-see at him and his little gang, then return straight to London. You send in your report through me. Right?'

'Right, sir.'

Eddie Rhabb shifted in his chair. 'We will have someone looking after your interests, James. In fact, we'll have the whole area covered, and someone'll make contact using the same passwords as we did tonight.'

'And we go out under our real names? In daylight? Under no cover?'

'That would be the best way to flush them out.' MacRoberts had toned down his wild man voice to a softer, more gentle and persuasive inflection.

'What if they also decide to do it in plain sight? At the airport, for instance?'

'I do assure you, James, that we have co-operation from the Italians. Tomorrow at Pisa and Rome there will be a maximum alert. And they do know what and who they're looking for,' MacRoberts soothed.

'Well, I must be going,' M rose from his chair. 'Your fellows going to take me to that military base?' He glared at Eddie Rhabb.

The FBI man nodded. 'Then they'll come back here and wait until it's time to take James and Toni to Pisa.'

'And when's that going to be?' Toni sounded disenchanted with the way things had turned out.

'You both leave here at ten in the morning, and fly to Rome on the eleven o'clock shuttle. You, Toni, have an hour to wait for the Dulles direct; James will just make it for San Francisco.'

M nodded to each of the men and shook Toni's hand, then stood in front of Bond. 'Good luck, James. I'll see you in London. Right?'

'If I get through this particular obstacle course, yes sir.'

'You've always come back before . . . Except, well, there was one occasion when you had us worried. But you've always made it home.'

'There's a first time for everything, sir.'

M slowly nodded. 'Yes. Well, good luck,' and he was gone, with Rhabb beside him walking into the night.

'The come-back kid, eh?' Toni gave him a little crooked smile.

'Bring 'em back alive. Ride into town with their bodies slung over my saddle, that's me.'

Outside, they heard the car start up, then the meshing of the gears and the crunch of tyres on gravel.

'In good form, your boss,' Rhabb chuckled as he came back through the door followed by MacRoberts. 'He always as outspoken and unemotional as that?'

'Most of the time.' Bond forced a smile. 'Though I once saw him moved by a very good claret at his club.'

MacRoberts threw his head back and laughed. Then – 'You two had better get some rest. Tonight must've been arduous for you.'

'Yes, arduous is a good word.'

'Laborious is good as well.' Toni kept a straight face before asking what the two highly experienced officers thought would be going on at the Villa Tempesta.

'Well . . .' Eddie began.

'The Brothers Grimm'll both have nasty headaches when they wake up,' MacRoberts continued. 'I also suspect they'll be out for blood. Probably your blood. There'll be telephone calls to Idaho, I've no doubt.'

'They'll also be put out because they're two men short,' Toni added. 'Don't fancy your chances much, James.'

'Enough, if I have to face them, I'd like to do it well rested.'

His room was small but pleasant with a dormer window and a bathroom in which he could just about have swung the proverbial cat. He stripped, showered, got into bed and turned the light out.

Within a couple of minutes, as he was passing over the rim of sleep, there was a soft tapping at the door.

'Who is it?'

The door opened quietly and Toni climbed into bed next to him, rubbing herself against him like a cat. 'I came to say hello and goodbye,' she whispered, rolling on top of him and wriggling her body as she opened her legs, half kneeling. 'Wow,' she said. 'Well, hello.'

'And hello to you, Toni.'

Twenty minutes later he asked, 'Do you come here often?'

'Not as often as I'd like to.'

'Then you must visit me in London.'

She snuggled close and made him promise to come back safely from Idaho. He promised, and, holding each other, they both made a slow and comfortable descent into sleep.

This time, he dreamed of summer scents and the sun in Toni's hair as they lay together in the bottom of a punt moored among reeds, somewhere near Oxford, on a cloudless afternoon.

Then the banging began. Urgent. Persistent, and finally a hand roughly shaking his shoulder.

He opened his eyes, stretched and felt Toni's naked flank touching his thigh. The light went on and Eddie Rhabb was looking down at them, his face frowning and eyes anxious. For a moment, Bond mistook the look for one of anger – finding him in bed with one of their agents. Then he realized it was something more important and serious.

'They've got your chief. They have M!' Eddie blurted.

Bond swung his legs out of the bed and sat bolt upright. 'How? When?'

'The local cops just turned up. We had a special guard on this place. The Italians like to cover their backsides. The car was ambushed about five miles up the road and the two CIA guys're down. One of them was still alive when they got him into an ambulance. There was a road block with half-a-dozen men. They dragged M from the car and carted him away in their own vehicle.'

Bond felt his stomach turn over.

'London's sending a guy called Tanner . . .'

'Bill Tanner. He's M's Chief of Staff . . .'

'Tanner and a couple of other specialists. The local law is mobilized and the media have been cut out of the loop.'

'Give me five minutes and I'll be down.' He was in the bathroom before Eddie had left, and he could hardly recognize himself in the mirror. He took in several deep breaths as he looked at the face peering back at him. A face scoured by anguish and concern. M had always been the father James Bond could not remember.

11

Graveyard

HE GOT VERY near to fighting physically with MacRoberts and
Rhabb. 'My chief's gone adrift here while under your care, and
I'm damned well going to find him,' he shouted at one point,
fist raised to throw a punch at Eddie. All logic had disappeared,
and for almost an hour he would not listen to reason. Then
Rhabb was forced to get really tough with him.

'I understand your position, James.' He stood almost nose to
nose with Bond, literally in his face. 'I know how you must
feel. You've worked under M for a long time. It wouldn't
surprise me if you felt a little guilty about what's happened. If
you hadn't made that escape, M might not even have been here.
He insisted on seeing you. He's not a young man but he flew
over in the back seat of a jet fighter to reinforce his orders. You
were to work under my direction, and I'm bloody well going to
see that you get back to the States and meet with Clay. There's
no way you're going to go tearing around Italy causing may-
hem when what we need is some insight into this son-of-a-
bitch of a general.

'It's a lot to ask of you, I know, but when it all boils down,
you weren't asked, you were ordered. M ordered you to do this
under *my* jurisdiction and you're going to obey his orders.
Right?'

Bond turned away scowling, knowing the FBI man was right, and that he was being left-footed by the emotion he felt for his longtime superior.

'Well, make sure you get him back – and in one piece as well.' A pause, then – 'I'm sorry, Eddie. This threw me. The Old Man *has* been part of my life for years . . .'

'As long as you're not going soft and getting twitchy about being in the field.'

Once more, anger flared within him. 'You calling me a coward, Rhabb? Yes, I've been doing this job for quite a while, and I know people get burned-out from time to time, but I've never, and will never, gib at the work I do for my country. Understand?'

'Perfectly.'

Bond turned and went back upstairs to get ready for the journey. As he shaved, he heard a telephone ring once somewhere in the house, and when he carried the small case and his briefcase downstairs, he found Rhabb and MacRoberts sitting, stone-faced. Neither of them looked at him, and when he asked what was wrong, Eddie avoided his eyes.

'M's wrong, James.'

'What?'

'We think he's also being used as another lure.'

'What's happened?'

'Seven o'clock this morning, before everyone had been made aware of the seriousness of the problem, an air ambulance – a converted Lear Jet – landed at Pisa to pick up a British businessman who had been injured in a road accident. That was the story anyway. The aircraft had clearance to London but apparently deviated from its original flight plan, flew to Rome, gassed up with emergency tanks and filed a new flight plan. It was headed to Seattle, Washington State. Some story about the patient requiring special treatment that could only be given at a hospital there.'

'M's the patient?'

'Almost certainly. One of the personnel at Pisa recognized a Tempesta bodyguard as one of the nursing staff.'

'What about picking them up in Seattle? They can't even have arrived yet.'

'They've gone off the air. No radar has them. We've got military aircraft out looking and scanning every possible approach to the USA and Canada. So far, no luck.'

'They've got to be out there somewhere.'

'Yes, unless something went wrong.' He let the thought lie between them. Nobody wanted to suspect the worst possible scenario.

Toni Nicolletti came down the stairs with her case. 'More problems?' she asked.

'Serious.' Bond looked up at her, then shook his head. 'You really don't want to know.'

Eddie drove them to Pisa. 'You won't see people – unless I get one of them to make contact with you – but you'll be followed all the way. Wherever you are, my men and women will not be far behind you, James. I should imagine we'll see you in a few days. Oh, yes, you have the right to terminate the general if it becomes a necessary option.'

'I didn't even need to be told that.' Bond's eyes looked as hard as granite.

During the flight to Rome, he held Toni's hand and felt a small sadness on leaving her. But that was the way of life for him. Men and women passed like travellers on a dark night. They met, found some consolation in one another and then went on, their lives separating. On occasions – like the short time he had spent with Sukie at Dulles International – they would meet again, slake their mutual thirsts, and exchange whatever wisdom they had learned in the period spent apart. His whole life seemed to have been filled with a memory of women: sometimes a wilderness of them.

Long before the seat belt signs came on for the descent into Leonardo da Vinci, he had said his goodbyes and kissed her gently on the mouth, whispering one quick line from *The Song of Solomon*, 'Behold, thou art fair, my love; behold, thou art fair.' He saw tears start in her eyes, and wondered at his act of sentiment.

Then they were down and taxiing in to the terminal. James Bond was one of the first off the aircraft. He did not look back, or try to catch a glimpse of Toni.

During the flight to San Francisco he ate, dozed, watched a movie and gave it three thumbs down. From the airport he took a cab to The Fairmont and checked in under his own name.

On the aircraft, and on the way to the hotel, he knew there were at least two people with him. He did not look for these shadows but suspected that one of Eddie's people was ahead of him, while someone else – belonging to either the Tempestas or COLD – was lurking at a distance behind him.

He unpacked only what he needed, which included the ASP 9mm automatic and a holster which he clipped onto his belt on the right side of his back. He would have to return it to the secret section of the briefcase before going through security the next day, but on the ground he was not going to be caught without a weapon.

Next he booked himself on the first flight to Spokane in the morning; then he called the number given to him by Eddie Rhabb. They had arranged a series of fast codes to report his arrival and to pick up any news. The conversation was brief.

'I'm here,' Bond began.

'Good, and good luck.'

'News?'

'Yes, we think the man flew to Canada after all.'

'Safe?'

'No further information. You could meet up with him. Who knows?'

The distant end of the line went dead.

The flight into Spokane landed just after eight the next morning. An hour later he had started his journey, in a Ford Taurus – the only car Hertz had available – taking Interstate 90 and crossing the state line into Idaho.

In the lovely lakeside resort of Coeur d'Alene he stopped and used a public call box to dial the number given to him by the Tempestas. It rang for a long time and then clicked as though being switched automatically to another line.

'Adjutant.' The voice was clipped, businesslike.

'I need to speak with General Brutus Clay.' He held his breath as the line went silent then a low growling voice came on, 'Clay.'

'I'm a friend of the Tempesta brothers. We need to meet. Today if possible.'

'I'm conducting a tactical exercise in the field,' Clay barked.

'We still need to meet.'

'I can give you half an hour. Pencil?'

'Yes.'

'Map reference . . .' the general snapped out a series of numbers and Bond repeated them back.

'Fifteen hundred hours today.' The line clicked and went dead.

Eddie had told him to take Rand McNally maps. 'They don't do Ordnance Survey like in Europe,' he had said, 'but these'll do you fine.'

Back in the car he unfolded the map to work out the route. The map reference, it seemed, was a graveyard. Was that an omen or a warning? He sat for a moment looking across the still water of the lake and the jagged mountains beyond. It was a Swiss view, the kind of silent wonder that you did not associate with America if, like Bond, you usually only had business in the cities of that great country. He could do worse than eventually retire to a place like this. There would be climbing and skiing, fishing, boating and other water sports. But he was basically a European. Maybe it could soon pall. A year or two and the itch would catch him so he would scurry back to somewhere in the great United States of Europe, if that terror actually ever came about.

He drove on until he reached a turn-off leading to a log building on his right that sported the name of Willy's Wolf's Lair, and advertised the best steaks in the world.

Inside, girls in fringed jackets, short skirts, cowboy boots, and hats hanging behind their necks, carried trays piled with steaks that could have come from a mammoth not a cow, fries and all the trimmings.

There was a bar to his right and he slid onto a stool, ordering a Red Dog beer. He craved for a vodka martini, but common sense told him that just might be considered a girl's drink around here.

'One Red Dog? You got it.' The barman slid the bottle across to him and asked if he wanted a glass. Bond nodded and saw the eyebrows lift slightly as one was provided.

'Why, Bill?' said a voice and he looked around to see that seated next to him was a young lady in stone-washed jeans, a denim shirt and jacket, the jeans folded into tightly-laced calf-length boots. The accent was distinctly southern. He expected to hear 'Why, I do declare,' as her next line.

'Hilary?' He peered at her as though trying to recognize her from his past.

She had a round face that had seen a lot of the outdoors, the complexion was fresh, pink and white, with a wide mouth, violet eyes and a great waterfall of naturally blonde hair. 'Hilary herself. This is real strange. Ah nearly almost didn't stop off here. Just came to mind as I was driving past.' She pronounced it 'payust.' 'Man, ah ain't seen you in so long. Mah Mama'd be tickled to death about this. How are y'all?'

'Very bonny thank you,' he smiled, purposely using a favourite expression of a fictional spy. He had always wanted to say that— 'very bonny.'

'Well, you're a picture and no mistake, Bill. We gonna take a bite to eat together?'

In the event they took several bites, and she almost overwhelmed him with her constant prattle. Later, he told her that it was like being trapped in *Gone With The Wind*. This was after they had demolished steaks the size of dinner plates, mounds of fries and several cups of coffee.

'Where's your car?' he asked when they finally got outside.

'It's that old black pick-up parked over there.' Her accent had become more familiar: all trace of Scarlett O'Hara gone – presumably with the wind. 'It'll be safe enough here. Nobody's going to notice it for a few days. Place is always crowded with cars. I'll ride with you, that's what Eddie said I should do.'

'How did you know I'd drop in at Willy's Wolf's Lair?'

'I didn't. I passed you way back in Coeur d'Alene and figured you might just stop here. I was just going to leave and catch up with you when you came in. Where's the meet with Brutus Clay?'

'A graveyard just outside of a place called Murray.'

'That's an interesting place, James. I can call you James, yes?'

'Of course. Do I call you Hilary?'

She gave a little laugh. 'My real name's Felicia Heard Shifflet. Heard as in seen and not, but my friends call me Fliss.'

They drove through an eight mile stretch of mountains. 'Fourth of July Pass, they call this,' she told him. Then through tiny towns with names like Osburn, Silverton, onto Nine Mile Road, through Dobson Pass. Fliss kept up a running commentary. 'If you see small streams around here you call them cricks,' she said. 'Never say creek or they'll correct you. A crick is a crick.'

No Name Gulch. Unnamed Gulch. Pond Gulch. 'I thought they only used names like this in movies,' Bond laughed.

At a little before three in the afternoon she instructed him to turn right onto a narrow lane called Dark Road. 'We go over King's Pass and we're nearly there,' she said.

'Wouldn't have missed this for the world.' He had enjoyed the drive and her running commentary. It was all a strange mix of spectacular beauty in which small communities seemed to be hanging on by their fingernails.

It was just quarter past three when he pulled the car over and they stepped out literally into a graveyard which ran from the roadside sloping upwards to a line of trees. The grass was well kept, the graves in good condition.

'Come along, there are things you just have to see.' She held out a hand pulling him up among the gravestones. 'This is something you need to remember,' pointing at a marker which said *Capt. 'Tonk' Toncrecy. He was the model for Mark Twain's Huckleberry Finn*. There were other colourful characters – Molly b'Damn, a local whore, who had nursed sick miners through a serious epidemic of smallpox in the late 1880s.

Another lady of the night was commemorated by her nickname: Terrible Edith.

It was as he was looking at this particular marker that Bond thought he heard a distant roll of thunder. The sky was clear, and he looked around, then at Fliss. 'Thunder?' he asked, realizing as he said it that this was a different kind of thunder. The sound roared, clattered and pulsed making the ground shake underfoot.

Then he saw them: three dark grey shapes coming in over the trees. He also knew them for what they were. Relics of the Cold War: a little AH-1W Cobra, so low that you could see the TOW missiles, flanked by a pair of former Soviet Mil Mi-8s – 'Hip Fs' as they had been coded.

'I rather think the general has arrived.' Fliss pushed back her jacket, revealing a large holster which contained a small but lethal Tec-8 machine-gun.

'How does a nice girl like you get into this business?' Bond grinned as she unholstered the nasty little weapon.

'If you're carrying, I'd suggest you put a gun in your hand and make for that treeline.' She was all business now. 'General Brutus B Clay has been known to shoot first and ask questions later: and that's only if he takes a dislike to your face. Know what the B stands for?'

'Tell me.' Bond kept up with her as they approached the dense stand of trees behind which the three helicopters had disappeared.

'Brute – and I'm not joking. He was truly named Brutus Brute Clay. His mother was a Brute from somewhere in Nevada. I really think we should find cover.'

The trees were swaying and rocking as though they were being hit by a storm: which, in a way, they were. The gale came from the helicopter rotors as they set down close behind them.

The noise was still deafening. Bond grabbed Fliss by the hand, dragging her into the trees, crushing his way through the branches and bracken, not worrying about making a noise, for it was drowned out by the engines and slap of the rotor blades as the three craft settled, beginning to run down their engines. They crouched behind a thick trunk and listened to the voices. Men were passing by to their right, heading for the graveyard. Then came the gruff voice he had heard on the telephone.

'Bond? James Bond, where are you? Come on out and don't be stupid. Don't play games with me. I have an old friend of yours in my chopper.'

Silence, then the sound of footsteps. Bond edged his head around the tree and looked back through the undergrowth into the cemetery as Fliss whispered 'He's a dangerous crazy bastard.'

General Brutus Clay stood not forty yards away. He had six men with him, all dressed in battle fatigues and carrying just about everything from M-16s to Uzis.

Clay was around six feet two, his face like well-tanned leather, dark from months of wind and sun. He raised his head and shouted again.

'You're pissing me off, Bond. I talked to Luigi and Angelo. They gave me a job. They want you dead, buddy. They want you stone dead and I'm not leaving here until I've buried you with Terrible Edith. You can go in with her and your old boss will sleep with Molly b'Damn. Now, come out and face it like a man.'

12

The High Road

'BACK!' BOND WHISPERED. 'Crawl back towards the choppers.'
Behind them, the general was still shouting, raving, telling his
men to blast Bond out. As they began to crawl, on hands and
knees, through the trees, shrubs and bracken, a fusillade of
shots went down behind them. Clay's men were aiming very
low and they could hear the bullets thumping into the trees and
ground a few feet to their rear.

The reason for the low shooting became obvious as they
reached the edge of the trees. In a comparatively small space
directly behind the treeline the three helicopters were ranged in
arrow formation, their rotors slowly turning at idle. Clay was
obviously using the Cobra gunship as his personal aircraft,
painted in a flat matt black with the weapons pods on the
stubby wings fully loaded. It stood some twenty feet from
where they crouched.

The Cobra had two cockpits, one – the pilot's – mounted
above the other, which was the gunner's position. The pilot's
cockpit was empty, but looking at the forward gunner's position, a figure was visible, slumped, head down, hanging on the
straps of the safety harness. There was no doubt in Bond's
mind: from this close he did not need to see the face, but it was
unmistakably M.

He could not tell if his old chief was alive or dead, and he glanced towards Fliss, trying to calculate if she would be able to squeeze into the gunner's position and crouch down with M. Even if she could, it would be a bumpy ride.

The two Russian-made choppers behind, and to the left and right of the Cobra, looked ungainly, somewhat sinister, monsters with their twin rotors, a capacity for twenty-four passengers, and clam-shell doors at the rear which enabled light vehicles to be driven on board. Their fat, clumsy bodies packed a devastating firepower.

He dug back into his fading memory of Russian aircraft of the Cold War and recalled that the 'Hip-F' had an odd cockpit configuration. The view was excellent and covered a full 180°, but the instrumentation was laid out so that the captain of the big helicopter was seated in the right seat, not the more usual left. He lifted his head, peering to both left and right of the Cobra. A pilot sat in the right seat of each of the two 'Hip-Fs,' but because of the triangular pattern in which they had landed, Bond could see that if they ran from the treeline directly to the front of the Cobra they would not be visible to the 'Hip-F' pilots. If Fliss could get into the gunner's position, they would still be able to move the canopy. The pilot's canopy was already open so Bond would be visible only for a very short time, climbing up and getting into the cockpit.

There was, of course, an unknown factor: were the two 'Hip-Fs' still carrying troops on board? Clay had half a dozen with him in the graveyard, and the bigger helicopters had a combined capacity of forty-eight. Would the general keep these people sitting in the helicopters? He doubted it. If the general was that good, he would have had every man out and in a defensive ring around the three aircraft.

As he scanned the ground to his front, it crossed Bond's

mind that the chopper pilots had to be very skilled in order to bring the craft in to land in this tight space, for they were between the treeline and a sheer rockface. They were all trapped in the middle of mountains anyway. The eventual take-off would have to be fast and straight up in a hover; after that there would be plenty of cover, playing hide-and-seek among the jagged peaks, crevasses and valleys.

Another fusillade of bullets came down nearby. Clay and his six hotshots were moving in, so Bond quietly began to tell Fliss what they were going to do.

Her eyes opened wide. 'You can fly one of those?'

'I've flown SeaKings. Can't be much different.'

He scanned the ground in front of them, whispering again to Fliss so that she knew exactly what action to take if the general and his party came bursting through this side of trees.

'Okay. Ready?' He looked at her and saw her curt nod.

Drawing his automatic pistol, crouching low and moving very fast, Bond led her out to the Cobra.

The forward gunner's canopy exterior release slid back easily. Nobody had spotted them yet, though he kept looking back anxiously towards the line of trees. Clay and his men were obviously advancing through the dense wall of greenery, firing regularly at around 45° into the ground ahead as they drew closer to the strip of ground which harboured the helicopters.

'He's alive. Just unconscious. Normal pulse.' Fliss had leaned into the forward cockpit to monitor M.

'Can you get in?'

'It's going to be tight.' She already had one leg over the fuselage and was trying to get low, between M's legs. 'I think I'll just about fit.' The other leg went over and she squirmed her body down onto the floor. 'Okay.'

'You'll have to hang on. It's going to be one hell of a bumpy ride.'

'Just get us out of here, James. Good luck.'

He nodded and slowly made his way up to the main cockpit, keeping close in to the fuselage. His most vulnerable moment would be getting into the machine for at that point the pilot in the 'Hip' to his right and behind him, would be able to see him.

He took a deep breath and rapidly leaped up to the metal rung just below the cockpit, keeping his eyes focused on the 'Hip' which now came into view, and breathing a sigh of relief because he could clearly see the pilot in the right-hand seat, but the man was bent, with his head down looking at something low in his cockpit.

Bond hoisted himself over the side and dropped into the bucket-like seat, very aware now of the slowly moving rotors above him. He grabbed at the harness and buckled it on while scanning the instruments, switching the weapons control so that all missiles and the twin heavy M197 machine-guns which sprouted from the nose beneath the forward cockpit could be fired by the pilot. He also located the switch which turned on the missile sights in his windshield. The Cobra had gone through many alterations and changes since it had first appeared as the Bell Model 209 during the Vietnam war. Now, he thanked the designers for their foresight in allowing the pilot full control of the weapons in the event of the gunner being taken out.

His next moves had to be done in a fast and ordered sequence, for he had to get the craft off the ground in a matter of seconds, before either the group of men in the treeline, or the pilots of the 'Hips' had time to react.

He pushed forward the collective control, hearing the slight whine above him as the long two-blade rotor angled itself into a position for maximum lift. Then, in one series of movements, he grabbed the cyclic stick, eased the throttle forward and felt the machine respond, rising a shade faster than he had reckoned, as he jinked the Cobra to the left, grabbing for the canopy control so that it came down almost silently, closing off the outside air.

He kept the nose down as he rose over the trees, moving left and climbing away. There was an ominous thump, followed by two or three similar noises, and he realized that Clay's men were firing at him, running towards the two 'Hips'. He even glimpsed Clay's face as the general lifted his arms and tried to blast away with what looked like a large .45 automatic.

He jinked the chopper in the other direction, still climbing, but coming dangerously close to the top of the trees. Then he was free and away, though he guessed not for long. In every direction he saw rock, stone and mountain: a whole landscape of peaks and troughs, some of the peaks still bearing traces of snow from the previous winter.

Grabbing at the headset which he had knocked off the seat in his rush to get in, he jammed it around his ears, adjusting it as he climbed towards the nearest series of brutal, belligerent and threatening pinnacles and sheer drops. As he turned, a staccato series of beeps sounded in the earphones and he saw a square red light begin to pulse to his left, warning him that a rocket had already locked on to him. He hit the chaff and flare releases – two fist-sized knobs which would shoot a series of flares and large magnetic confetti to his rear in an attempt to confuse the incoming 57-mm rocket. At the same time he pulled up to a near-vertical climb, felt the Cobra sway and buck, then bump heavily as the rocket passed him only a few feet away.

The sky around him was cloudless and the sun was low. Another ten, maybe fifteen minutes and dusk would be on them. His only hope was to get in among the mountains and play tag with the two 'Hips' which must now be in pursuit.

They were slower and less manoeuvrable than the Cobra, but they had a long reach with their rockets. He only hoped that they were not carrying missiles. In the days of the Cold War, the 'Hips' had been the backbone of the Warsaw Pact forces, specifically redesigned to insert Spetsnaz troops. In that capacity they would almost certainly carry 'Sagger' anti-tank missiles which packed a lot of punch. If they could inflict damage on heavy armour, what would they do to a small craft like a Cobra, Bond wondered?

He opened the throttle a little more and adjusted the collective, racing towards the serrated rocks in front of him. He had confidence in being able to confuse and mislead the 'Hips' in the dangerous game of leading the larger helicopters into situations from which they would find difficulty in extracting themselves.

Another rocket lock-on warning beeped urgently. More flares and chaff, another series of jinks to left and right. This time he did not even hear or see where the rocket went, though he thought he heard a dull boom from somewhere below.

A rocky bluff was coming up fast and he had to pull up steeply to get over it, towers of stone rising to left and right. He poured on more power, saw a mountain crag about a mile distant and decided to see how close the 'Hips' had got to him. He switched one of the TOW missiles onto arm and saw the circular sight light up green on the head-up display etched and glowing in the forward windshield of the canopy.

The crag was half a mile distant now and he tipped the Cobra to one side, bringing it around in a Rate-5 turn which pressed him back against the seat. Now he was looking back above the bluff flanked by the tall sloping towers of rock. About a mile beyond, he saw one of the big helicopters bucketing along, with its partner only a distant speck behind it.

The TOW sight immediately captured the approaching target, its green diamond shape rapidly pulsing back. His thumb came down on the firing button and the Cobra seemed to stand still for a few seconds, kicking back as the missile left its rails on the port side.

He did not hang around to see if he had hit the 'Hip', but turned tail, slid over to the left and headed at full power towards the high crag lying half a mile away. His altimeter read just under ten thousand feet above sea level and the top of the upcoming peak towered above him. He thought for a second about M and Fliss crammed into the gunner's compartment and wondered if they were feeling the cold as he was. It was time, he thought, to try and work out his location so he took his eyes off the mountains and reached down, his hand searching for the maps he had pushed there, coming up eventually with a large scale map of the area and a small loose-leafed black notebook which he slipped into his pocket before trying to get a visual position.

He could see now that he was approaching a complex range of mountains which, he thought, almost certainly led to the great lake of Coeur d'Alene, and the town of the same name which had struck him so powerfully as he drove through it. As he got closer, he saw that there were three distinct and separate mountains, each rising higher than the next. This was where his end-game of tag could pay off, though it was not going to be the easiest thing to accomplish.

He reached the first peak, an updraft making the Cobra sway and bump in its turbulence. Guiding the chopper to the left, he took a complete circle around the mountain. As he completed the circle, he saw the two 'Hips' some five miles away, turned in their direction and loosed off two more of the TOW missiles, knowing that he was unlikely to score a hit. All he wanted was to signal to the approaching choppers, letting them know where he was.

They did not return fire, but just kept on coming, doggedly plodding in his direction, safe in the knowledge that they could bring him down eventually by positioning themselves far to his left and right and blasting at him with rockets.

Bond slowed and headed towards the two further peaks, then slowed again, thinking exactly what he would do in their situation. They had already seen him circle the first peak, eventually coming back to fire on them. They would, he hoped, assume that this would be his continued strategy. He slowed even more, letting the Cobra drop another thousand feet, giving the impression that he was in some kind of trouble. At the same time he allowed the machine to start an occasional see-saw movement, swinging almost fully left at one point so that he could glimpse the 'Hips'. They were undoubtedly gaining on him, and his mouth curled into a ruthless, hard smile.

Below, there were a few scattered and lonely houses, a road that clung to the side of the rockface and, in the distance, the glint of the lake which could only be Coeur d'Alene.

The two larger helicopters were getting very close now, putting some distance between each other, shaping up for the kill, he imagined, as he turned sharply behind the next huge pyramid of stone: a dangerous and terrifying mountain, full of crevices and outcrops of rock. The whole natural structure had to be almost two miles wide, and the pair of helicopters following would only be about a mile away now.

Under the natural cover of the mountain, Bond backed the Cobra off until he was hovering a mile away. If they had been following his run around the first mountain, they would, he prayed, split up, one keeping about five hundred feet above the other so that the pair could circle the mountain in different directions to catch him in a kind of pincer movement.

He armed two TOW missiles this time and waited . . . and waited. They took almost twenty minutes but, eventually, he saw one of the lumbering beasts break cover and come in from his right, turning close to the mountain. The missile locked on and, as he fired, he saw, out of the corner of his eye, the other 'Hip' lower, but coming around the left side of the rocks. As he locked on to the second helicopter so the first disintegrated in a rupture of flame with a white-hot centre.

He fired the second missile and the lone 'Hip' tried to turn in a manoeuvre that would throw it clear. From under the belly he saw the eruption of flares and chaff, but the pilot had mis-judged his turn, losing control, sliding dangerously close to the rock face then over-correcting so that the tail rotor just grazed the side of the mountain.

It was all over very quickly. The rear of the machine seemed to fold and, as it did so, the nose went down, the rotor blades flapping and buckling as they also touched the face of the sheer wall.

Its fall was ungainly, like the death of a clumsy insect. The first one had gone down fighting in one final glorious flower of flame. The second 'Hip' was like a bent, broken bug, its rotors being torn away, its body coming apart as it swung, spun and hurtled downwards, bounding off outcrops of rock. Then, far below, it made its final burst of energy, a plume of fire shooting upwards then dying quickly.

Bond turned towards the water he had seen, allowing his craft to move slowly forward, keeping the ground in sight as dusk began to turn into night and he headed in the general direction of Spokane airport, his hands testing various frequencies as he tried to make contact with air traffic control.

He wanted to tell them to provide an ambulance and get hold of Special Agent Eddie Rhabb of the FBI, who, by now, should be back in the United States.

He thought of M and Fliss up front and hoped they had come through the vicious twists and turns of his encounter with General Clay's private air force.

The Cobra was over the wide water now – the great lake which emptied into the Spokane river – and the lights were coming on in Coeur d'Alene. He had just made contact with Spokane tower when the engine coughed and started to splutter. Then it died completely.

13

Water Carnival

IN A FIXED wing aircraft the loss of power is not always disastrous. The weight of conventional aeroplanes is supported by the wings. In a light plane, loss of power at height gives you the opportunity to glide and look for some convenient flat site upon which to land while you still have control. In larger aircraft the loss of one engine is usually only dangerous at low altitudes, or if a pilot in panic confuses which engine has gone out and closes down the wrong engine leaving him with no power at all. In the latter circumstances the aircraft is inclined to plummet rather than glide.

In a helicopter, the loss of power is much more dangerous for it is the rotor blades that carry the weight and provide movement. There was little Bond could do as the Cobra began to sink rapidly, its speed increasing as it dropped out of control. The hydraulics had gone with the power, so he could not even correct the collective angle on the slow-spinning rotor above him.

Desperately he tried to restart the engine as they descended through six thousand feet. The lake lay below them and he knew the price they would pay for travelling at around eighty knots an hour when hitting the water, which would be as good as running into a brick wall. The Cobra would go from eighty to zero in one split second, breaking apart and spreading itself around like a child's toy trodden on by a large booted foot.

Again he tried to restart. There was a splutter this time, and he reckoned that the fuel lines were somehow clogged. Again. Another splutter. The altimeter showed five thousand feet . . . then four. Once more, at three thousand, and this time the splutter turned into a cough and the engine turned over, caught and began running very roughly.

The roughness made little difference; as long as the rotors could be controlled, it would be possible to make a softer landing. Gently he increased power and moved the collective control so that the angle of the rotor blades put them into a hover. The hover was not stable for the machine trembled and bucked as the engine still refused to run steadily, but it did slow them down and give him some control over the descent. He could see the lights of Coeur d'Alene just coming on off to his right. He managed to slow the descent even more and was also able to turn the craft in the direction of the town. He had already issued a Mayday to Spokane tower – noting from the board clipped to the central console that the helicopter's call sign was Romeo Alpha – and now he kept up a silent stream of conversation in his head, willing the engine to at least keep turning over as he slid the chopper towards the town's outskirts, knowing they stood more chance if he was able to put the Cobra down close to the shore.

'Romeo Alpha, Spokane Control, still losing height around two miles west of Coeur d'Alene. Can you advise hard landing? Over.' He asked into the microphone.

'Spokane Control, Romeo Alpha. We suggest ditching close inshore. Many buildings, and vehicles along the shoreline.'

'Romeo Alpha, Spokane Control. I copy. Will try ditching as

close as possible to shore. Will advise you just before we try to go in.'

It made sense. Nobody in their right mind would risk trying to make a hard landing on one of the lakeshore streets. There was traffic down there, and people moving around.

Fiddling with the cyclic and collective controls together with the throttle, he managed to get within a few yards of the lake's edge, again trying to hover with some difficulty. People were starting to gather as though waiting for disaster, but Spokane tower must have got on to the emergency services at once because a rescue squad ambulance and fire engine had appeared. He made contact again.

'Romeo Alpha, Spokane Control. We see rescue vehicles on shoreline. Am trying to ditch gently and as close to rescue team as possible. Over.'

'Spokane Control, Romeo Alpha. Listening out. Good luck.'

The trick now was to slow the Cobra so that it settled gently on the water. Even if he could manage that, he knew he would have to try and keep the helicopter just airborne with its skids touching the lake in order to let Fliss and M get out – or at least open the canopy and allow the rescue workers to get to them. Unlike the 'Hips' which he had seen blown to pieces and crash down the mountainside, the Cobra did not possess any flotation gear. For all he knew, even a soft landing might lead to a complete submergence of the chopper.

The engine was showing signs of strain. For about two minutes he listened, with rising concern, to a high-pitched whine coming from above him, and it became more and more difficult to control the machine.

He raised a hand, trying to beckon the firemen and rescue squad people to come to him as he allowed the Cobra to edge down, closer to the water.

Suddenly he had to react violently as the nose pitched back, and he realized that the forward canopy was off. He saw Fliss trying to stand up. She waved to him and gave a thumbs-up, though the shifting weight in the nose was making accurate control almost impossible. The machine yawed viciously, dipping to the left. By the time he had straightened up, Fliss was gone. Three of the rescue teams were already in the water, dragging a rope with them while others had thrown lifebuoys into the lake.

Gently, he lowered the nose a fraction to make it easier for the rescuers to get at M. With great relief he saw that his old chief was, in fact, moving as though trying to lift himself from the nose cockpit. He could see Fliss again for a second as she held onto the side of the fuselage, attempting to assist M.

Bond felt the heaviness on the nose and tried to straighten the helicopter so that he could gain a little height. Then, without warning, all hell broke loose. The engine faltered then stopped, the rotor blades slapping slowly above him. There was nothing he could do but pop his canopy just as the Cobra went completely out of control, tipped sideways and, with a terrible crunching, cracking sound, turned turtle.

Near the lake shore he had expected the water to be shallow, but now he realized that it was deep: deep, dark, cold and with a strong undertow.

He banged down on his harness release and kicked himself from the cockpit, feeling the lake pull him out as he battled the waves which dragged him down and away from the Cobra in the sluice of water that flowed out of the lake into the Spokane River.

It seemed an eternity before he surfaced, lungs bursting as he gulped for air, still being drawn away from the bank. Fighting against the current, he forced himself to swim, clothing hampering his progress as he struck out, aiming towards the point where the rescue service people seemed to be trying to anchor the ruined helicopter. As he made slow progress towards the wreckage, Bond glimpsed someone being pulled from the lake inshore, but his concentration was now totally focused on getting through the racing water and into safety. His shoulders and thighs ached, for it was like pushing against an elastic wall. His head was constantly going under, his mouth and nose taking in water.

At one point he thought that he was being ripped away from the shore; a minute later he imagined that he was working twice as hard just to stay in the same place. He was an experienced swimmer but he had never encountered such a strong cross-current. After what seemed to have been fifteen or twenty minutes – though logic told him it was less – he found himself on the verge of doing the unthinkable, giving up and just letting the water whirl him out into the lake.

By then hypothermia was setting in, for the water was freezing cold. He turned onto his back and tried to propel himself towards the shore using a rowing motion with his arms. He could only see the sky above, and felt as though a movie of his life was being screened in Technicolor in his mind. He saw wrecked bodies, women he could never forget, and some he had long forgotten: a girl covered from head to toe in gold paint; a young Japanese woman bending over him whispering endearments; his wife of hours, shattered and bleeding, bullets ripping into her as she sat next to him in a car.

He saw his flat in London; moments from the past; explosions; bodies; times of great pain and times of wonder; until they became a beautiful whirling kaleidoscope of minutes and seconds. At the centre of it all he incongruously heard a survival instructor, from long ago, shouting, 'This is not a bloody water carnival, Bond. Do it properly, man!'

It was then he knew he was dying. What a place to go, he thought with incredible clarity. After all the dangers of his life, it was all ending here in a wide, sweet yet terrible lake exit surrounded by mountains.

As he slipped into unconsciousness, he imagined that he heard voices and felt hands lifting him from the water. Angels, he wondered? Is this how it is? Angels pull you across the Styx and into the far beyond.

Darkness.

Floating.

Voices far away. Getting closer.

'He's coming back.'

'Give him a few minutes.'

'No, sir. You'll have to wait until Dr Brown allows you to speak with him. I can't allow you to stay in this room.'

Something swam into his sight, blurred, floating. A golden-haired vision. He closed his eyes, relishing the warm feeling surrounding him. Warm and comfortable. Really he had no desire to leave this cocoon. Did this happen? Was he about to be reborn?

'Mr Bond!' A woman's voice and the clapping of hands. 'James! James! Wake up James.'

He opened his eyes and heard himself groan.

A blonde woman in uniform. A nurse. Standing next to her a man in a white coat.

'You're back in the land of the living, Mr Bond. How do you feel?' from the man in the white coat.

He groaned again. 'Where am I?' His tongue clove to the roof of his mouth which felt unnaturally dry. 'Clove.' He wondered why he had thought of that word. Biblical, he presumed. If he were dead then he would naturally think in biblical terms, but whatever, his tongue clove to the roof of his mouth. 'Thirsty,' he said, realizing that it came out as a croak. A gentle hand lifted his head and he felt a glass touching his lips, then the taste of orange juice.

'Where am I?' he repeated.

'You're in hospital. Kootenai Medical Centre. My name is David Brown. I'm your doctor.'

'What am I doing here? Why do I need a doctor?' As he said it, he realized that memory was returning. Water pulling him down, freezing cold.

'You were in a helicopter that crashed in the lake,' the doctor said. 'People drown easily in that area – up near the Spokane River – and you nearly lost your life. Any of that make sense to you?'

It came back in one great rush, like a dam being opened. The Cobra and the fight with the big Russian 'Hip-Fs'. For a moment he saw the tall man with an angry, obsessed face, turning to look upwards, a large automatic pistol pumping in his hands. Then the helicopter. The chase. The loss of power. The attempt to get M out.

'Is M okay?'

'Who's M?' the doctor asked. He was a big man with a matching smile and it sounded to Bond as though he were humouring him.

'Other man in the chopper. Older man.'

'The Admiral?'

'That's the one.'

'You want the truth?'

'There'll be hell to pay if I don't get the truth.'

The nurse, who was indeed blonde but not as attractive as he had first thought, was doing things to the bed, moving his head up, propping him against pillows.

'How is he? Did he . . .?'

'The Admiral's fine.' Brown laughed. 'Too fine, in some respects. He's sitting up giving my staff merry hell. There are also some FBI people here to see you. An agent called Rhabb and one with red hair called MacRoberts. Are they okay? I mean do you know them?'

Bond nodded, 'Yes. They'll want to talk.'

'They do, but I'm not letting you see them just yet. You'll probably need some food and a little rest. That's what I'd advise.'

'What about Fliss?'

'Was Fliss the young woman who was with you?'

He nodded, his vision almost back to normal, for he saw the doctor's face go from the big smile to the big frown.

'Is she okay?'

He saw the expression on the doctor's face; in his eyes, and he knew. 'Oh, hell,' he said.

'I'm sorry. She was very brave. I don't think the Admiral would have survived if it hadn't been for her. She hauled him out of the wreck, then got stuck. The rescue squad people tried to get her up, but it was too late.'

He thought about Fliss and realized that he hardly knew her. Thought about her banter and Southern accent in the place where they had eaten. Reminded himself of her guts when the shooting began, and the fact that she did not hesitate to climb into the chopper. 'Damn,' he thought. Aloud, he muttered that women were never safe around him.

'We'll get you some food, and I have some medication I'd like you to take.'

'How long am I going to be here?'

'About five minutes if the Admiral has anything to do with it. Realistically I think you should stay in overnight. I'll see you later, then.'

The chubby nurse returned and gave him an injection, which livened him up enough to consider that she might be fun after all, but a dark-skinned orderly brought him food.

Bond had always associated hospital food with the kind of muck they had served at school but either he was ravenous, or this was better quality, for he ate the lot: a potato and leek soup, liver and bacon with the omnipresent mashed potatoes, followed by some kind of strawberry mousse which was possibly full of chemicals, he considered. Yes, a lot of stodge you would not really expect in a country obsessed by cholesterol and healthy eating.

About an hour later the nurse returned with some coffee. 'They're still waiting for you, Mr Bond. The FBI, I mean.' She wore a name badge which said *Patti*.

'What the hell, wheel 'em in,' he said.

'You're sure you're up to it, now?'

'Quite sure. I'm certain you don't want them hanging around all night.'

She gave him a cute little smile. 'The one with the red beard I don't mind. I got a thing for guys with red beards.'

Eddie Rhabb came in first, with MacRoberts trailing behind, glancing back. He wondered if Patti had signalled her compatibility. Rhabb was carrying Bond's small case and the briefcase, retrieved from the car.

'I'm so sorry about Fliss, Eddie,' he began.

Rhabb shook his head. 'She was good. Died in the line of duty, saving your boss.'

'I know. You seen him?'

'Seen him and heard him. Old M can really make you feel a heel.'

'Told you that you shouldn't have worried about him?'

'Something like that.' He paused for about three beats.

'James, I'm sorry. We let you down. We had people around but when the chips went down there was nothing we could do. By the time we managed to get the air force to send up a couple of jets it was all over.'

'So what's the score?'

MacRoberts answered. 'We'd like to hear your side of the action first, James. If you don't mind.'

Bond told them, speaking in the clipped shorthand of a good intelligence officer, dotting the Is and crossing the Ts.

'The general?' Rhabb asked. 'Was he in one of the choppers you put down?'

'I can't really tell you. An intelligent guess would say that he was. He did not like us one bit, and we took away his biggest bargaining chip.'

Rhabb nodded, saying they were sending out search parties at dawn. 'I guess we'll find out if his body's among the wreckage of those two "Hip-Fs". Certainly hope so. We've done some more digging and I don't think there's much doubt that he's tied in pretty tightly to COLD.'

'They really going to cause headaches?'

'COLD? Yes, they seem to be getting very nicely organized. Apart from people like the mad general Brutus Clay, they're all pretty sane. They really believe that the establishment might need protecting one day, and they're going to be ready to do it. They represent a clear and present danger, but I think it'll take a few years before they decide to move in and put a ring of steel around DC.'

'But the time will come?'

'Shouldn't be surprised. Unless, of course, we stamp on the Children Of the Last Days first.'

They talked a little more, and Bond asked how things were coming on regarding the destruction of Bradbury's Flight 299.

'We know where the bombs were. We think it was a button job. Apart from that, zilch. Zip. Nada. The pieces have been transported back to the UK and your boys at Farnborough are going through them. Resurrecting the aircraft. Harley Bradbury's already facing huge law suits from dependants.'

'And the Tempestas, no doubt.'

'The Tempestas seem to have disappeared. No sign of them in Rome, Tuscany or their little place in Venice. Maybe we have succeeded in getting both brothers to come over here together. Who knows.'

After some further talk Bond asked what they wanted him to do next.

'M's pulling you out,' MacRoberts sounded irritated. 'Says he has plenty for you to do without rushing around the United States being shot at by – I quote – "Trigger-happy tin soldiers who haven't had a decent military training." '

'Sounds about right for M,' Bond smiled. 'I've always suspected that he still thinks the American Revolution went the wrong way.'

'Like your crazy King George III.'

'Exactly. He often still refers to you as our Colonial Brethren.'

Finally they left and Patti came in to say goodbye – 'I'm not on duty tomorrow and I guess you'll be gone when I'm back.'

As she was leaving, she whispered a 'Good luck. You have the Wicked Witch of the Night on next.'

The Wicked Witch of the Night turned out to be a sharp and forceful black senior nurse who was not going to allow any patients to take liberties, or break the rules. She said so as soon as she made her appearance. Bond accepted her position with good humour. Years ago, a doctor had advised him that, when in hospital, you should always refer to the orderlies as 'Nurse', the nurses as 'Sister', and the Nursing Sisters as 'Matron'.

'When you actually get to matron you should spread yourself before him or her in obeisance.' He had continued, 'Because a matron is the nearest thing to god that you'll come across this side of the grave.'

That night, however, Bond had no desire to take liberties with anybody. He found himself depressed and very tired. By eleven he was sound asleep. By midnight he was dreaming peacefully.

He was just getting to the pleasant part of the dream, where a reborn Sukie Tempesta was making her presence felt, when he was dragged out of sleep by being shaken and shouted at.

'Come on, Bond. Should've been awake hours ago. We have places to go; people to see, and a plane to catch. We're heading back to London. Come on, man, shape up!'

M's gravel voice and bark drove all other things from his mind, and he wondered if he would ever hear more about COLD and the Tempesta family.

14

Interlude

THEY FLEW TO Washington DC, arriving at National around four-thirty in the afternoon, Eastern Standard Time. Because M was travelling first class, Bond managed to get upgraded, so they had more privacy. Though M was always careful about talking in any public place, he unbent his rules slightly and Bond was able to quiz him regarding the kidnap.

'As you know, it was dark, and, to be honest with you, I was a little tired,' the Old Man began. 'Actually, we all fell for the oldest trick in the book. Came around a bend in the road and there were two cars almost blocking the way. Looked as though they had been in a bit of a shunt, and there was one man hanging out of the open door. Looked as though he were injured.

'My driver and the bodyguard reacted instantly and without thought. I should have told the bodyguard to stay with me, or told the driver to go around and then call police and rescue squad people. But I was, slow, bumbling and foolish.

'They were on us like a pack of dogs. At least six of them. My driver got off one round but they took him out, then the bodyguard, without a second thought. It was obvious their orders were to kill anyone else, because they were very careful to shoot well clear of me. I'm not a fool, James, so I did not fight back. What's the point? When you reach my age you can only get yourself into trouble. If they were after secrets – and who isn't these days – they'd probably shoot me full of some damned chemical and I'd talk till the cows came home.

'Anyway, they *did* inject me and I went into a nice quiet sleep. Woke up on an aircraft. We landed somewhere – I suspect Canada – near the Washington State border, for they took me for a long drive. Most uncomfortable because I was in the boot of some car. Heard them stop at a border crossing, but I was still pretty woozy from whatever they'd shot into me. Next thing I knew they had me in some big house, under lock and key. Managed to get a shufti of what was outside. Nice view. Mountains and a lot of pine forests. Could've been in Switzerland.

'Then they started in on the question and answer game. They weren't interested in any of our deep dark secrets in Europe or the Middle East. They wanted to know how much we had on this COLD outfit, and the Tempesta brothers.'

'Who did the inquisition?' Bond asked.

'Military, or pseudo-military type, but they all had uniforms. Playing soldiers by the look of it. You know the kind of thing – "Yes, sir! No, sir! Three bags full, sir!" '

'What was he like – description, I mean – this military type?'

'American, with all those lovely white teeth colonials seem to attract to themselves. In his late fifties, though that's hard to tell. You see so many forty-year-old types over here who look sixty. Very tall. Six-two, six-three, something like that. Strikingly tall. Spent a lot of his life in the great outdoors. A bully-boy with a kind of madness in him. The sort of officer who demands obedience, but the kind you really don't want to be in charge. I got the impression that he was a terrible risk-taker. Death or glory, that ilk. See it in his eyes, eh?'

It was possibly a good description of General Brutus Clay. 'What did you tell him?' Bond asked.

'Not much *to* tell. I said the Tempestas were suspect in a lot of matters. As for these COLD people, I spun a bit of a line. Said we knew what the acronym stood for, but nobody took them seriously and we had no idea what their aims and objectives were. He got rather cross at that.'

'He would,' Bond smiled. 'How long did they keep it up?'

'Time? Doesn't have much meaning when they're trying to dry you out. I rather think they gave me a shot of soap at one point.' Soap is intelligence speak for sodium pentathol. 'Blacked out anyway and felt drunk when they brought me round. Had me wits about me, though. Didn't give 'em anything to take home.'

'How did you end up in the forward cockpit of that Cobra?' he asked.

'I recall they fed me quite well, then gave me another shot of something. Came round with that poor girl almost sitting on my lap, and the ground very unstable.'

'You know that girl died saving your life, sir.'

M nodded slowly, a brief shadow of pain passing across his eyes, like the sun going behind a cloud. 'Yes, I thanked that fellow Rhabb. Strange people these FBI types. Hearts in the right place though.'

'I'm sorry about the ride in the helicopter. Must've been a shade iffy for you.'

'No worse than being on the deck of a destroyer in a Force Ten. I remember once in the North Atlantic . . .' and he was off on some tale of escorting convoys when he was a very young sub-lieutenant. Bond knew he had had all he was likely to get out of his chief for one session.

At Washington National, M announced that he would be

staying at the Cosmos Club. ''Fraid I can't invite you, James. Give you dinner if you like, and I've got to go out to Langley tomorrow. I suppose you'd better come along with me on that one. I'd rather like us to get back on the last flight from Dulles to Heathrow tomorrow night. I can arrange the tickets through London.'

Bond used an airport courtesy telephone and called the nearest Marriott Hotel, which happened to be in an area called Crystal City where he booked a room for the night. 'I'll find it tomorrow,' M said. 'Pick you up at two in the afternoon.' He gave him a telephone number where he could be reached, then disappeared into the crowd of people heading towards the taxi rank.

Crystal City was so called because the many buildings appeared to be made out of glass. It sounded exotic but was, in fact, bizarre and ugly. Bond took a cab over and checked into a room which literally overlooked Washington National Airport. He unpacked only the things necessary for the rest of the afternoon and evening, then called FBI Headquarters in The J Edgar Hoover building to see if Eddie Rhabb had arrived back yet. The Special Agents had planned to make the journey from the Coeur d'Alene area on the previous evening but the call was a waste of time. Special Agent Rhabb was out of town on assignment, according to the secretary he managed to speak with.

'I was with him last night. He was due back in DC today.'

'Oh, he was in this morning,' the somewhat crabby girl said. 'But he was called away suddenly this afternoon.'

He thought it more prudent not to ask questions, so he called Jack Pop Hughes at NTSB.

'Hey, James. I thought all your people had gone back to Merry Old England.'

'Most of us have. I took a little side trip, Pop. Wondered if you could have dinner with me tonight? I'm a lost soul in this great city of yours and I don't want to get into trouble.'

'Well, sure that's easy enough to do here. Just take a long walk outside and trouble'll find you. Where are you?'

Bond told him.

'I'll be there about eight. Meet you in the lobby.'

Bond went downstairs, bought a packet of cigarettes, then went back to the room to sit by the window, smoking and watching the aircraft land and take off. He had given up cigarettes some time ago, but the events of the past days seemed to have got under his skin. He took a few drags on the first cigarette and stubbed it out, watched a few more aircraft then went to the jacket he had hung in one of the closets and extracted the black notebook that he had recovered from the floor of the helicopter. Still sitting in the chair by the window, he began to go through the notebook.

The first five pages were filled with telephone numbers. Next to each number there were neat initials, but the more he looked at them the less sense they made. Many, he thought, were numbers for the United States, but they were unfathomable as all the dialling codes were non-existent. Scrambled, he thought, as he started to look through the rest of the book.

There were pages of what could well have been map references, only they were also scrambled. These were followed by pages of odd hieroglyphs and numbers which made no sense. For a long time he stared at groups such as—

AM8753 ΣφΚΠΠ⊇ 14 ZOΨP 7654 ΔB*≅∃ 468H ΔΦΠΩA

The entire book was filled with similar symbols, while the odd page contained more scrambled telephone numbers, or map references. Several times he came across clear words, obviously cryptos, *Madeleine*, *Corsica*, *Backstop*, *Pepper*, *Madman*.

The book would need careful going over by someone experienced in codes and ciphers. He thought for a while, then dialled the number that M had left him for the Cosmos Club, asking for Admiral Sir Miles Messervy. M's name was never bandied about by members of the Service, though it was one of the best-kept open secrets in the trade.

M came on the line with a rather sharp, 'What do you want, Bond?'

'Just one question, sir.'

'Go ahead.'

'Are we bowing out of the COLD business?'

''Course we are, except if it ever has an effect on the United Kingdom. I trust our colonial friends will keep us informed, but as of now we'll be at least distanced from it. Why d'you want to know?'

'I'm having dinner with the IIC from the NTSB. I'm also trying to get hold of our Rhabbid friend from the FBI. This is simply a case of need-to-know, sir.'

'Well, we're still interested in the NTSB findings, of course. Anything to do with Bradbury. As for the chilly thing, just need-to-know and information only if it concerns our territories. Got it?'

'Perfectly, sir. Thank you.'

Pop Hughes, turned up just before eight, and drove them out to Jo and Mo's on Connecticut Avenue – 'Steak, seafood and fashionable,' Pop said. 'The media moguls come here a lot, and where the media come politicians cannot be far behind. But the food is terrific.'

They went for the steaks, and Bond then began a lengthy quiz regarding BD 299.

'What can I tell you, James?' Hughes threw up his hands. 'We'll eventually publish our findings, though they're already pretty well complete. You know where the bombs were planted. We're still not absolutely certain how they were detonated, though the common wisdom seems to indicate a local button. Nobody's claimed responsibility, poor old Harley Bradbury's facing massive legal action, and the remains are all being put together at Farnborough. In fact, we're looking to them to provide the true answers.'

'Reasons, though, Pop? You must have some idea about the reasons.'

Pop Hughes shrugged. 'I've got several ideas, though they all seem nutty when you think of the loss of life.'

'Nothing surprises me these days when it comes to killing innocent people. So try me.'

Hughes gave a deep sigh. 'Well, it could be purely financial. Someone might not have wanted Bradbury Airlines to continue under the same management – and indications are that some high-rollers might just take the airline off Harley's hands and foot the bill on the legal action.'

'Anyone I'd know about?'

Hughes seemed to pause. Then— 'Well, there are several conglomerates who invested. The Tempesta family from Rome . . .'

'I certainly know them.'

'They weren't in as heavily as a French consortium; or a big American investment from yet another consortium. Wall Street. An outfit called Freezeways.'

'Ah!' Bond paused. 'I'd take a good look at them if I were you, Pop.'

'Already have, and it's unlikely. They're *very* respectable. Anyway, there are other, equally mad, possibilities.'

'Go on.'

'A couple of FBI agents, Allen and Farmer, were bringing in a real sleazebag who was in the process of being extradited from London. Name of Dick "The Idiot" Kauffburger. Heavy mob ties, but had offended a lot of influential people. Believe me there are men and women in the pseudo-underworld who'd sacrifice a lot of other people to get at Kauffburger. On the whole, I think *that* was the reason, but don't quote me.'

'Any more? Fringe ideas?'

'There could be a political angle. But that would be purely British, and I don't see any of your Brit mobsters doing anything like this.'

'Don't believe it, Pop. Remember how the Iron Lady was sacrificed. The Conservative Party pulled a palace coup while she was abroad. But who knows?'

'Well, we're pretty certain about the folks who planted the bombs.'

'Oh?'

'You remember that the aircraft spent the night in the Bradbury hangars in Birmingham on the night before it was brought down to Heathrow for the first London-Washington trip.'

'Yes.'

'We're now pretty certain that's where the bombs went on board.'

'How certain?'

'One hundred and five per cent certain. Two men and one woman had access to the Bradbury aircraft on that night after the regular engineers had finished their maintenance checks. There's indisputable evidence that all three were in the hangar, on their own, for the best part of ninety minutes.'

'And?'

'And then they went missing. A guy called Daniel Paul;

another, older, man known as 'Iffy' – for Ivor – Bergman, and a girl who went by the name of Ruth Isaacs.'

'They've been picked up?'

'No, they disappeared. Didn't report in for work on the following evening. Using fake ID. The last I heard, your Security Service were checking on real ID. They think the man Paul used to be a well-known bomb-maker from the Angry Brigade, name of Mallard – naturally 'Drake' Mallard. Full name Winston Mallard: Jamaican by country. They also think the girl is formerly IRA. Nuala McBride. Ring any bells?'

'Our Nuala certainly does. So, we have a mixture of ex-terrorists doing the making and planting. I'll take a look when I get back to London, which is one of the reasons I wanted to see you, Pop. Keep in touch, will you? I'd like anything that surfaces.' He pushed a card across the table. 'Just call there and leave a number. I'll get back to you.'

'You want my number.'

Bond shook his head. 'I can get your number,' he smiled.

Back in the hotel he took another long look at the black notebook which had probably belonged to General Clay. He then went to bed and was in a deep sleep when the telephone began to ring.

His watch said five-thirty in the morning and he grunted into the telephone.

'You were trying to get hold of me last night,' Eddie Rhabb's voice sounded strong, as though he were well rested.

'Yes, I was.'

'Important?'

'Just a lot. When can we meet?'

'I'll join you at your hotel for breakfast – say eight o'clock.'

'A more reasonable time to be awake. I'll be waiting.' He catnapped until it was time to get dressed and go down to meet the FBI man who was waiting in the lobby.

'So?' Eddie asked once they had ordered breakfast.

'So, I have something for you.'

'What?'

'Only after you've told me if they found the body of Brutus Brute Clay down among the dead men in the helicopter wreckage.'

Eddie shook his head. 'The pilots were the only bodies discovered. Back at the graveyard, they found indications that a jeep, or similar transport, had been offloaded from one of the "Hip-Fs".'

'So, Brutus Clay is alive and well and living lord knows where?'

'Among his men in the mountains, we presume. So, what have you got for me?'

'Clay's little black book, all in cipher.' He handed the notebook to Rhabb.

'Shouldn't you pass that through your people?'

'I'm told we're not going to be concerned in it. Not unless it suddenly involves us directly.'

'If COLD pulls off its main agenda, it'll involve everybody.'

'I give that two more decades.'

'Wouldn't be too complacent, James. Anyway, we'll keep in touch.'

M, as he had promised, picked him up precisely at two that afternoon in a chauffeured limo in which they drove out to CIA Headquarters in Langley, Virginia, where M was closeted for several hours with his opposite number, and Bond did the rounds of his contacts.

'They're all worried stiff about this COLD thing,' M spoke quietly as they drove out to Dulles International. 'A bit panicky if you ask me.'

'I saw the FBI this morning, got the same impression.'

M grunted and made no further comment on the situation during the entire journey back to Heathrow where they both went straight into Headquarters.

During the following year the newspapers were full of Harley Bradbury's downfall and eventual bankruptcy. There were odd snippets of information from time to time – news from Eddie Rhabb that Clay had surfaced again, and that the Tempestas were still involved in a number of borderline financial dealings – including leading yet another new consortium which eventually took over the now defunct Bradbury Airlines, emerging as Triumph Airways, Inc., an organization that flourished and grew at an alarming pace.

Winston Mallard and Nuala McBride were arrested by the Metropolitan Police as they were about to board a flight to Miami. They were not charged with anything and the police – according to the Press – released them within twelve hours. Privately, however, those who worked for the Secret Intelligence Service, knew that the two former terrorists were quietly squirreled away in a big safe-house run by the Security Service in Acton. It was said that they were undergoing a spectacular hostile interrogation.

Later the same year, M called Bond in to brief him on the news received from both CIA and FBI sources. 'Paranoid,' he grumbled. 'The whole lot of them. Absolutely paranoid.' In fact 007 wondered if it was paranoia, because the latest figures collected by penetration agents showed a marked increase in the membership of COLD. Also, two agents had suddenly 'gone off the air', a euphemism for missing, believed killed. Their bodies were, in fact, discovered on Christmas Eve. They had been badly mutilated.

During an operation in Switzerland, James Bond met the lovely Fredericka von Grüsse, an officer of the Swiss Security Service. They worked together through that particular operation at the end of which Fräulein von Grüsse left the Swiss Service and was offered a permanent job by M.

Freddie von Grüsse and Bond became an item, and this seemed to please both M and a number of other people in the Service who thought that Bond should have settled down years before. Now, they all acknowledged that Freddie, or Flicka as she liked to be called, was a very good influence on him. M even turned a blind eye to the fact that they were living together in Bond's apartment off Chelsea's King's Road.

Wedding bells appeared to be in the air, and M was reported to have confided in another senior officer that 'The von Grüsse girl is a particularly good choice. Bond's mother was Swiss, you know. Though he does not seem to have inherited any Swiss sense of order from her.'

Then both Bond and Fredericka had been briefed and took over an operation which was later coded *SeaFire*. It was an intensely dangerous operation and, while the outcome was successful, Flicka von Grüsse was injured and flown back to London from Puerto Rico in a serious condition. To make matters worse, M was also just recovering from a severe illness.

The Service had changed by then. M was still at its head, but, in the aftermath of the Cold War, intelligence matters were being overseen by committee. The Service had become accountable for its actions to the politicians in power.

Then, with no warning, COLD raised its ugly head again in a dramatic and completely unexpected manner.

BOOK TWO

Cold Conspiracy

15

A Voice from the Past

BOND HAD FLOWN back from Puerto Rico in a Gulfstream ambulance aircraft, laid on from RAF Lyneham. Freddie von Grüsse, her face broken and battered, like the rest of her body, was made comfortable and tended by two nurses and one RAF doctor. Tubes ran out of her nose and mouth, the terrible scars and livid bruises which spoke of fractured bones provided the only colour in her face. The rest was a luminescent grey-white. Her eyes were closed, the only movement came from shallow breathing. Her only sustenance reached her through a drip running into her hand.

Soon after take-off he managed to get the doctor to one side. 'Is she going to make it, doc?' He was aware that his eyes showed only anxiety, and his voice sounded tired and nauseated.

'I hope so, sir.' The doctor was young, but obviously experienced. 'Hard to tell at the moment. I've examined her thoroughly, set what bones I can, and we think we've stopped the most immediate internal bleeding. When we get to Lyneham, I understand she's to be moved to another facility where they'll be able to make a more accurate prognosis.'

'What's your own prediction, doc? You can be honest with me.'

The doctor looked away and would not meet his eyes. 'I give her a forty per cent chance of recovery,' was all he could say, except for the worse part yet to come— 'If you really want the truth, sir, if she does recover, I think she'll spend the rest of her life in a wheelchair.'

Jesus, Bond thought, she would rather be dead. Freddie von Grüsse was only happy when involved in the active life. There was no way she would possibly adjust to spending her days as an invalid. It was at this moment, he later realized, that he hoped she would die.

There was an ambulance waiting at Lyneham, and he went with her to the clinic which the Secret Intelligence Service shared with the Security Service in Surrey. It was a converted old house, and even with their shrinking budget, the two services had managed to keep the place running on a proper footing. It had a dozen nurses who lived in the house, and three expert doctors also on the staff. Specialists were available at, literally, an hour's notice. The operating theatres were state-of-the-art, and if Freddie had any chance of recovering, it would be at this secret facility.

On the first evening they called in two specialists and within a couple of hours of her arrival, Freddie was on the operating table. She remained there for seven hours and it was around one o'clock in the morning that Bond got the news from the senior surgeon.

'It's touch and go.' The doctor was a bearded, grizzled man in his early sixties. 'We really can't be certain. She's in a deep coma, and there are no signs of her coming out of it in the immediate future. There's been massive bleeding in her brain – we've put that right as far as we can – but one lung was punctured and she has thirty-seven fractures in all. We've patched up the lung and drained off the fluid, but she's going to be on massive doses of antibiotics to stave off pneumonia. And, of course, we really don't know if there's been any brain damage. If she ever comes out of the coma, we'll be able to assess the situation, but I have to be honest with you, Captain Bond, I think the chances are slim. I do not think she's going to be able to live a normal life again.'

He took a cab back to London with a dark cloud of despair hanging over him. The flat seemed deserted without Freddie, and in the end he sat up for most of the night trying to decide what his future would be. That he had loved Freddie was not in dispute, but now he had to face a possible loss of her, or a life spent looking after a vegetable, and however strong his love, he could not see himself living out the years as a nurse to the once vibrant Freddie von Grüsse. She would not want it any more than he could do it.

He thought of his past, and his luck with women. Sex was one thing, but there were only four females in his life whom he had truly loved, and one he had married, only to have her killed within hours of the ceremony.

Bond had begun to wonder if his bad luck with real partners was something to do with him and his job. The following morning, tired and still in a black dog of a depression, he drove out to M's beautiful Regency manor house – Quarterdeck – on the edge of Windsor Forest.

When he had last visited M, the admiral had been a sick man, confined to his bed with a nurse in residence. This was just before the final stages of the *SeaFire* business, and Bond had been very concerned about his old chief. As it was, M had become very disillusioned about the way things were going. While he remained nominal head of the Service, everything concerning daily orders, and the running of any special operations, had to go through a powerful steering committee known

169

as MicroGlobe One. Neither M nor Bond could stomach the way in which intelligence matters were being handled in this post-Cold War era. Just as General Haig had told a special committee before World War One, 'The job of intelligence gathering has always been, and will always be, the job of the cavalry,' so both M and Bond had fought to keep a tight hand on their own autonomy, but without luck. Bond had certainly wondered if their steadfastness to the old way was as outdated as General Haig's dogmatic idiocy earlier in the century. Maybe they were wrong and the government was right in moving intelligence and security matters under its wing.

He rang the famous old ship's bell outside the stout oak door of Quarterdeck, and was overjoyed to find that it was M himself who came to the door. He looked fitter than ever, and his cold grey eyes were as damnably clear as they had been before the recent illness.

It was plain that M was very pleased to see Bond, welcoming him in with an unusual warmth; sitting him down and serving him a glass of sherry. After some idle chatter, M looked hard at his agent. 'You just here to check up on your old boss, or was there something else, James?'

Bond first told him about Freddie's condition, and M cut him off with, 'I know, my dear boy. I know all about it. You did well, and she lost out. My advice is that you get on with your life. Visit her occasionally, but whatever happens, time usually takes care of everything. Know how you feel, but you can't allow yourself to fall into the kind of depression you did after the unfortunate . . . well, after the death of your wife.'

Bond sighed. He knew all too well what M was talking about, just as he knew he had never felt quite as bad as he did now, except for those terrible months after Tracy's death.

'I've advised a lengthy leave for you. That damned committee has okayed it. So you're free for the time being, until
January 1st of next year. Relax, James. Go off to somewhere
pleasant for a while. Recharge the batteries. As I've said, time
will tell with regard to your girl, Freddie.'

At that moment, Bond had no desire to go anywhere further
than the clinic where Freddie lay like the sleeping beauty
awaiting his kiss to waken her. As he drove away and headed
his Saab towards the clinic, he cursed himself. What a damned
stupid simile, he thought.

There was absolutely no change in Freddie when he got to
the clinic. He now began what was to become months of
routine. He would rise at seven-thirty sharp, shower and do the
series of exercises which had been his practice over the years –
the twenty slow push-ups, leg lifts and toe touching. Then
breakfast, his favourite meal.

In fact he was back into his old ritual from former days, and
what would a psychiatrist have made of that? Was he searching
for some kind of inner peace? Freddie von Grüsse had pulled
him out of his normal routine during the time she shared his
flat. Was her state of suspended animation sending him back to
the safety of life as it used to be?

At around ten each morning he would visit the clinic and sit
for most of the day near Freddie, as she lay, unmoving, on the
bed facing a window which looked out on rolling fields,
scattered here and there with little copses of trees.

Sometimes he would talk to her, hoping she might suddenly
respond. Always he held her hand, occasionally pressing it,
longing for the pressure to be returned. Freddie showed no sign
of being pulled from her coma.

After he left Freddie on the following Friday afternoon, he
headed straight home, still with the black depression almost

like a visible cloud. On arrival he picked up the mail which he had not been able to go through before leaving for the clinic that morning – another break in routine which made him irritable.

He took the mail through to the room he used as a study, seated himself at his desk and began to go through the various items. There were a couple of bills to be paid, a letter forwarded from his club (he recognized the handwriting, a young woman he had been attempting to avoid for some time now). There was the latest price list from Berry Bros & Rudd, the wine merchants; a bulky envelope from The Folio Society; and a communication from American Express telling him of some splendid holiday offers that were exclusive to members only.

Last, he came to a small package with an Italian postmark. Gently, he slit the small package open with the Royal Marine Commando dagger he used as a paper knife. Inside was a cassette tape marked *James Bond Esq. Private & Confidential*.

Intrigued, he went to his bedroom, quickly returning with his Professional Walkman into which he slid the tape. Slipping the headphones over his ears, Bond pressed the *Play* button.

'Hallo, James, I do hope you remember me. If you don't, I'll use one of the code names we had to learn during that wonderful, if dangerous, time we spent together. Hellkin, James. Remember Hellkin?'

Hellkin. How could he ever forget? Her voice poured into his ears like honey and he could see her again as though she were standing in front of him, as she had first done outside the villa on the island of Ischia in the Bay of Naples.

On that day she had taken his breath away, dressed in a tank top and cut-off jeans. He recalled that at the time he had looked with such wonderment because they were cut-off very high, almost to the junction of her thighs and buttocks, giving a clear view of her long, gorgeous, slim legs and the small exquisite body.

He now saw her face again: dark, dancing eyes, snub nose, a very wide mouth which seemed to be in a perpetual smile, and the tight bubble of black curls. As he heard her voice, he could remember how she had first introduced herself – Beatrice (pronounced Beé-ah-tree-che). Beatrice Maria da Ricci, she of the Italian father and English mother. Educated at Benenden and Lady Margaret Hall, Oxford, later recruited for the SIS, and kept out of sight working in what they all referred to as Santa's Grotto, the computer rooms below the ground floor carpark at Headquarters. Finally, she was sent out into the wide world of what was then still the Cold War – or at least the autumn of the Cold War.

He remembered her kiss, her body wrapped in his, the silent vows and the horror at the moment he thought she was dead; then the fact that had lingered in his mind for years. Beatrice could easily have been the love of his life. He knew it and so did she.

He had to rewind the tape to hear what she was saying. After the introduction, her voice sounded husky. 'James, I'm truly sorry to bother you, but – as you might know – I'm still with the old firm, though some people make certain that we never see each other. I'm on an assignment now and I do not want to talk on the telephone. I think you could well be interested in what's happening here. I'm taping this in Rome and sending it to you express. By Friday I'll be in Switzerland and the target in my sights is something I am told you know about. Something called COLD.

'Friday, Saturday and Sunday nights I'll be at the Hôtel du Rhône in Geneva. Room 504. Call from downstairs first.' There was a long pause. 'James, please come if you can, for me

173

this is a matter of life or death. I want to win. I don't want to lose or die. Please.'

It would be unwise to use the telephone, so within ten minutes he was back in his car – taking his briefcase and an overnight bag – heading towards M at Quarterdeck. He could be there in just over an hour, and, if he got the okay, then Heathrow was less than an hour from M's home. With luck, he could be at Heathrow by seven at the latest. If his memory was accurate, the last flight to Geneva was a Swissair one at eight.

As he weaved through traffic, driving as fast as he dared on a busy Friday evening, he heard Beatrice's voice again and detected the sense of urgency behind it, like an undertow he could not avoid.

He wondered what he would find in room 504 at the Hôtel du Rhône, Geneva? Beatrice sounded frightened and she was a very efficient agent who did not frighten easily.

16

Need-To-Know

A LIGHT DRIZZLE began as he drove to Quarterdeck, yet even on this unpleasant English November evening, he started to feel his spirits lift, and realized what had been wrong with him. The inactivity imposed on him by the lengthy leave of absence, coupled with his concern for Freddie von Grüsse, had pushed him into a selfish despair. It had happened before. Too long away from the active life, and the dangers it provided, had brought on what he could only describe as withdrawal symptoms. He was longing to get back into the game, and here was his chance. He had to persuade M to allow him to fly to Geneva tonight and he would probably be given a chance to settle old scores.

The journey to Quarterdeck took him a little over an hour, and it was M himself who opened the door.

'James, my boy.' The Old Man's face lit up in obvious pleasure. 'Come in, come in. I'm alone tonight, the Davisons have gone into Windsor to a concert.' Mr and Mrs Davison had taken over the job of looking after M's creature comforts.

He stepped over the threshold and smelled the familiar odour of polished pine panelling, saw again the Victorian hall stand and the table on which stood the wonderfully detailed replica of *HMS Repulse*, M's last command in the Royal Navy.

It was the *Repulse*'s ship's bell that hung outside the front door.

'Can I offer you something, James? The Davisons have left me a cold collation, ham, tongue, salad, that sort of thing. There's plenty for the two of us.'

'Thank you, sir, but no. I have something of great importance to ask you and I want your authority to be out of the country in a matter of hours. First, I'd like to play you a tape which was delivered in my mail today. I listened to it and came straight out to see you.'

He looked into M's eyes and thought he saw a cloud pass over them, a sudden crease of concern appearing on his brow.

After a short pause, M said he should come and sit near the fire, so it was there in front of crackling logs and with a small glass of sherry that Bond played Beatrice Maria da Ricci's tape.

'If I get a move on, I can be in Geneva tonight, sir. I only need your instructions. You *do* know who that is on the tape?'

M stared into the fire, his face grave, as though he were trying to make a momentous decision. At last, he spoke. 'Yes, James. Yes, indeed I know who it is; just as I know you've worked with her in the past.'

'Well, sir?'

'You've put me in a quandary, James. Also, you know that, in these times, I cannot give you a briefing or permission to go into the field. The world has turned, *you* know that as well as I, and I'm troubled that Beatrice has seen fit to contact you directly: it's against all our current field rules.'

'You could still give me the nod, sir. After all, I'm on leave until the first of the year . . .'

M held up his hand as though to block the words from reaching his ears. Again, he stared into the fire for a full minute before he cleared his throat. 'This is a need-to-know business,

James. Strictly you have no need to know. If – and it would be a very large if – I took this matter in front of our masters in MicroGlobe One, it would take several days for them to make a decision to bring you in. I'll grant that I could plead a right for you to become part of an operation that has been running some time now, but my fear is that Beatrice da Ricci has been compromised. She's very good in the field, and this tape may well be some attempt to lure you back into a matter about which you have a little knowledge. For instance, I *do* know that something diabolical is coming to a head out there. Something that has to be stopped. There are people working on it who, I trust, will do the stopping. On the other hand, this cry for help, which is highly irregular, could well mean something has gone wrong.'

He went on at some length about the old Service rule of need-to-know, then, with a heavy sigh, said that he would take the risk and give Bond the full details of the situation. 'But you, in turn, must never let me down. What I'm about to tell you is in the strictest confidence. I shall deny that I ever spoke to you. Understand?'

'Absolutely, sir. Can I take it that, whatever it is you're about to share, could allow me to get to Geneva on my own time, so to speak?'

'What you do with this information is your own business. You'll have no sanction from me, and certainly there is no time to bring in the committee. However, if you do finally decide to follow up matters and head out for Geneva, I cannot stress strongly enough that you may well be putting yourself into a position of extreme danger. I should also tell you, under confidential seal, that by the time you return, I might have no pull at all – with the Foreign Office or MicroGlobe One . . .'

'What do you mean exactly?'

'I'm on the chopping block, Bond. Got too old and dodder-ing for this business, it seems. I've been told that I'm about to be retired. Could be a week, or a month, or the end of the year, but I'm basically finished, put out to graze. I even know who my replacement is to be – and, if I know you, it will not be sweet music to your ears. They're going to supplant me with a woman.'

He paused again, as if to let it sink in. But Bond would probably go on working, be it a woman, man or height-challenged monk at the head of the old firm.

'Whatever you're going to tell me, sir, I did not hear it from you. If, after listening, I decide to take a short Swiss holiday, then that's my own personal business. Are we clear?'

'You were always a joy to work with, 007. Even when bending the rules you could make it sound innocent.'

M had used the old 007 crypto, and it gladdened his heart. They were now speaking the same language.

'Cast your mind back to the terrible act of terrorism against poor old Harley Bradbury's inaugural flight to Washington Dulles International. You were sent out to represent the Secret Intelligence Service. Right?'

'Very much so, sir. We never did get our hands on the motive.'

'We didn't?'

'I gather we got two of the planters – what were their names? Winston Mallard and Nuala McBride.'

'Still have 'em, James. Bring 'em out and charge them when other bits of business have been settled.'

'There was talk of the motive being linked to a pair of FBI agents taking some mob figure back to the States. Extradition.'

'Never happened, James. Though we do know that Mallard and McBride were tied into the infamous Tempesta brothers.

In turn, we know the Tempestas are tied into that most dangerous organization, COLD.'

'The Children Of the Last Days,' Bond muttered.

'Quite. So I should also tell you that COLD and the Tempestas were behind the bombing of BD 299, and the truth about that will finally come out. I should warn you it's more than diabolical. That aircraft and all aboard were sacrificed to protect both COLD and the Tempestas from blackmail.'

'Sir?'

'We have been – to use that revolting American expression – downsizing GCHQ at the time.' GCHQ was the Government Communications Headquarters in the staid, very proper town of Cheltenham and covered everything from random telephone sweeps to the incoming data from satellites.

'One of the men we retired around that time was a fellow called Carter, Julian Carter. He worked in the anti-terrorist field. Built up names, addresses and profiles of current terrorist organizations. A very present help in trouble was our Mr Carter. He was also only a year from retirement and we gave him a golden handshake. He was on that aircraft.

'Oh, it must have been a year later that we made the connection – I should say GCHQ made the connection with our help. Somebody in Carter's old office managed to rejuvenate some deleted files. Carter used a big Cray computer, and his successor found a massive tape – several gigabytes I'm told, though I couldn't tell you what a gigabyte is. Don't hold with a lot of this modern way of securing data. The tape was marked *Carter on Freezing*.

'Now, this I didn't know until it was explained to me. It appears that when you delete files – data – from one of those hard disks or a tape, it is still there. At least until someone writes over the top of it. You know that, James?'

'As a matter of fact, yes.'

'Ah, well you would, wouldn't you? Anyway, this clever fellow brought the files back to life. Everyone went a little mad when they saw what he had got . . .'

'COLD's Order of Battle?'

'Just about, yes. Names, addresses, target cities, the whole works. They also unearthed a letter or two written on the same tape. He was offering the goods to COLD. Blackmail, as it happened.'

'Blackmailers usually keep copies . . .'

'Hold on, James. Carter was a bachelor – if you follow me. We tossed his flat. He had the information hidden away all right. Quite clever. Had a big, fat, old family Bible, only he had managed to split the thick pages and sandwich his thin database pages between them. The whole thing was a very clever fake, and what it turned up was poison. We had no idea COLD was so well organised.'

He drew attention to the dangerous part Bond had played in the operation which followed Sukie's assassination at Dulles, then asked, 'What was your impression of the aims and objectives of COLD, James?'

He covered it as succinctly as he could. COLD was almost the exact opposite of many of the part-time armies playing soldiers and occasionally bringing death and destruction in the USA. COLD was formed, not to defend people from the supposed excesses of government, but to defend the establishment against others, and, in doing so, take control. 'They seemed to be prepared to take draconian measures to wipe out crime, drugs, the Mob, you name it, sir.'

'Quite, and the Tempesta family would take control of certain aspects of the familiar old Mob. It's a chilling manifesto. Move in to protect everyone in power, pull the army and the law enforcement agencies into the net, then the coup is complete. It would be like the Puritans taking up arms to pull the country together. That was, and is, their aim, and, as far as we know, their day is nearly here, which is where our Ms Beatrice Maria da Ricci comes in.'

'How, sir?'

M sat looking into the fire again, as though searching for answers to Bond's question.

'When we were out there, and you managed to save my life, James, you'll recall Toni Nicolletti.'

'How could I . . .?'

'Forget her?'

'Quite.'

'I've sad news, then. She was found, last year, in the boot of a car. She had been shot, assassination-style, through the back of the head. About a week later your old FBI friend toddled into town. It appeared that the senior FBI people were concerned that they had been penetrated. They wanted to try a second penetration of the Tempestas. To cut a long story short, we lent them Beatrice da Ricci. She's been working in Rome, Venice and in that place they have in Tuscany for nearly a year now, and I gather down in that particular forest something connected to COLD is about to stir. So, James, you can understand why I'm a shade concerned about Beatrice's direct contact with you.'

'If she's in trouble, there should be someone there to help her.'

'Then she should follow operational procedures. Normally she would, James. You know that. My fear is she might be under someone else's control; that she's sending false signals. Heaven knows you're not exactly the most loved of men either with the Tempestas or COLD.'

'Which is probably exactly why I should go.'

M looked at him hard with his clear, piercing eyes. 'If you decide to go, I can't even send any backup. If I were you, my friend, I should make a couple of calls before you leave. Might be prudent.'

He drove back to Chelsea to find his answering machine blinking. It was the hospital. Would he call Dr Sanusi immediately. Sanusi had taken over as Freddie's regular doctor.

'I'm concerned, Mr Bond.' It was the first time he had ever heard the doctor sound anxious. He was normally bubbly and full of good humour. Upbeat was the word which usually came to mind.

'Tell me, doctor.'

'After you left today, she suddenly seemed to be coming back to us. Opened her eyes, looked around and spoke.'

'What did she say?'

'Not what you'd expect. No "where am I?" or anything like that. She said, "I can't see the *Jungfrau*. Where's the *Jungfrau* gone?" Does that mean anything to you?'

'Yes.' He was not going to fill in any details, but he had first met Freddie in the Swiss town of Interlaken. They had been thrown together while investigating the murder of a member of the British Security Service in Switzerland. The person concerned had been found dead on a beautiful green slope from which you could see the *Jungfrau*, that almost erotic mountain which looked like a woman's breast as she reclined. Was Freddie lost in a world of the past; a time when she had just met him? 'What else?' he asked.

'The episode lasted only a short time. I had hopes that she was really coming out of it, but she went into a coma again, and I fear it's deeper than before. Her pulse is very weak and she's showing fewer signs of brain activity.' Until then, one of their hopes had lain in the fact that, through sophisticated electronics, it appeared her brain was working – probably dreams invading her coma.

'Look, doctor, I'm going to be away for a few days. Do you think I should come over and see her again tonight?'

'It's up to you, Mr Bond. I really don't see that you can do anything; but there's always the chance that . . . Well, I'm fearful of how long she's going to be with us. If she reaches a point where she has to go on life support, would you want that, or would you prefer to let her go in peace?'

'It's only going to be a few days. If she has to go onto a life support system, I'll make a decision when I get back, but thank you for thinking about it.'

'It's my job. Is your job calling you away?'

'Partly, yes.'

'Going somewhere pleasant, I hope.'

'Just Switzerland. Not for long.'

At the distant end, the doctor put down the telephone. All he had told Bond was true, but he would have called him in any case. He stood up and walked to his office door and locked it. Returning to his desk, he dialled an overseas number. When the distant end answered he simply said, 'He's on his way. Seems to have swallowed it like a fish.'

Bond left his flat again half an hour later, after booking himself on an afternoon flight to Geneva the following day.

He walked up to the King's Road and found a public telephone that had escaped vandalization. Using a credit card under his Boldman alias, he dialled a number in the United States. His conversation lasted for almost thirty minutes.

The Hôtel Du Rhône in Geneva is beautifully situated close to the lake. It is said that the owner has combined the luxury of a grand hotel with modern functionality which is still visible even while Switzerland becomes, on one hand, more expensive, and, on the other, a country displaying the less pleasant aspects of the drug subculture.

This was apparent almost from the moment Bond arrived at the airport. A few years ago, graffiti would have been unthinkable. Now it was the norm, as were the ragged, unwashed teenagers who would never have been seen a decade before. In modern Switzerland the order and cleanliness were now only skin deep. It was particularly inconceivable in the cradle of Calvinism, Bond thought, though it was probably inescapable in this city where Calvin had first invented his own religious secret police and put children against parents all those years ago.

He waited in his room only long enough to unpack and arm himself from the secret compartment of his briefcase. He then rang room 504. Beatrice da Ricci sounded less positive than she had on the tape, but she did say that it was good to know he was here.

He went down one floor, tapped at her door, and there she was, smiling, obviously happy to see him, throwing her arms around his neck in a tight embrace as she moved him inside, kicking the door closed. 'You have no idea how happy I am to see you, James.' Her voice was taut as the proverbial bow string, and her eyes seemed to be pleading.

'Well, it's been a long while, Beatrice. I've been looking forward to this.'

'Not as much as I have.' This time her eyes were moving, as though indicating something was wrong.

Behind her, sitting, one on a chair, the other on a small settee, were a pair of grey-suited young men.

'Oh, you have to meet the people Eddie Rhabb assigned to

me.' She stepped back and introduced them – 'Special Agent Farmer and Special Agent Allen. They're my bodyguards while I'm here.'

He immediately remembered Pop Hughes' words concerning possible reasons for bombing Flight 299—

A couple of FBI agents, Allen and Farmer, were bringing in a real sleazebag who was in the process of being extradited from London. Name of Dick 'The Idiot' Kauffburger. Heavy mob ties, but had offended a lot of influential people the NTSB man had said. *Never happened*, M had told him only hours before.

For a second, Bond felt he was sharing Beatrice's room with snakes.

17

In Room 504

HE KEPT HIS back to the door, holding Beatrice directly in front of him while his mind worked overtime on the logic. Pop Hughes had said it was a possibility that these two FBI men had been the targets on BD 299, together with the prisoner being extradited from the UK. This meant that he was speaking only with the knowledge of going through Flight BD 299's passenger manifest before the bodies had been completely matched. Somewhere along the line Bond had heard that there were a couple of mystery bodies – or what was left of them – still unclaimed after all this time.

How had M put it? *It never happened.* Now, some four years later, it would be M who had the final body count next to the up-to-date manifest when things had been sorted out in the aftermath of the disaster.

He gazed into Beatrice's face and saw the truth combined with his logic. They had not been on the aircraft, but they were supposed to have been. This was a very frightened lady. He lifted his eyes, looking over her shoulder, and caught the smirk on Allen's face, watching it turn to a smile of victory.

Bond smiled back, giving Beatrice the same smile as he dropped his head and whispered, 'I think you've got to fly.' As he muttered, he gave her a hard push, sending her in a flurry of arms and legs to his left as he took off, head low and his right hand going for the ASP 9mm.

Allen leaped to his feet, his own right hand sliding out of sight moving towards his back, but Bond had him cold in a flying tackle which ended in a very hard head-butt to the loins. The so-called FBI man gave a little squeak of pain and clattered backwards over the sofa. Bond drew his automatic pistol, then heard the almost whispered, 'I'd drop that if you want the beautiful lady to live.'

Farmer had Beatrice in a choke-hold with his forearm across her neck and a pistol resting against her temple, but Bond banked on nobody wanting to start a shoot-out here on the hotel's fifth floor.

Allen had his handgun out but was still doubled up in pain.

'A Mexican stand-off, I believe they call this,' Bond said brightly, and at that moment, there came a hesitant knocking at the door.

'Who is it?' Farmer called out, his voice rough and constricted.

'Room Service.'

'We didn't order anything,' from Farmer, coupled with a groan from Allen.

'I think one of the gentlemen needs a little ice,' Bond called out, dropping his voice to add, 'I just might have damaged his marital prospects.'

'I have a gift, especially from the management.' The voice muffled from behind the door.

Farmer let Beatrice go, pushing her in Bond's direction. 'Don't anyone try anything stupid.' He lowered the pistol, keeping it out of sight.

'You have a wonderful way with words, Farmer. Great grammar as well.' Bond caught Beatrice and held her to one side while Allen tried to straighten up, leaning heavily on the back of the sofa.

'Just a moment,' Farmer's gravel voice rose as he walked to the door, twisted the lock and opened it a fraction.

Almost at the moment he turned the handle, the door burst inwards and the room suddenly seemed to be full of people. Bond recognized Eddie Rhabb and MacRoberts, his red hair flying. He had also seen the others somewhere. Yes, a few years ago at Quantico sitting in Toni Nicolletti's room. Their names came back unaided – Drake, Long and the female officer known only as Prime. Each one of them was armed and it became quickly apparent that, whatever their other faults, Allen and Farmer had the good sense not to attempt a pitched battle.

'The Swiss police are downstairs,' Eddie said loudly. 'They want words with you two specimens. I suspect sooner rather than later, though we're also going to be allowed some time with you.' He stood, feet apart, shoulders hunched and his head down in the charging bull position. His face was scarlet with a mixture of the rage he had obviously built up and the relief he now felt.

He turned to Bond. 'I'm sorry we had to use a little duplicity to get you here, James, but we need you and we're aware of the situation in your Service. An application through channels – as they say – would have resulted in a blunt "No" from that committee which seems to run you all these days.'

Bond shrugged, really not comprehending what was going on, but spotting half a dozen Swiss policemen just outside the door.

Rhabb turned to the newcomers and motioned them in, telling Allen and Farmer that they would be taken out of the hotel through the rear entrance. 'There'll be no unfortunate publicity, gentlemen. Your names aren't going to get on any official documents and I assure you there'll be no problem about extradition because nobody's going to hear about extradition. You have no rights, so I'm not going to read them to you. I've never heard of you, in fact, and none of these other officers have ever seen you. In fact, none of us are here.'

The Swiss policemen had patted down the two prisoners, snapped handcuffs onto them, and were leading them out towards the service elevator.

'I'd get a doctor to the one who's having problems walking,' Bond said as they left. 'I would never want to be called a spoilsport.'

Prime, the female agent, grinned, 'I would,' she gloated. 'I'd botch a circumcision on both of them.'

MacRoberts as wild-haired as ever, was dealing with any damage they had caused to the door. 'Good for you, Prime.' He looked towards Bond. 'I don't think our Prime likes men very much.'

'Try me sometime,' Prime flirted back.

'If it's not too much of a problem, could somebody tell me what's going on?' Bond stood with an arm around Beatrice's shoulders, his remark addressed to nobody in particular.

Eddie Rhabb turned to Long and told him to call room service to get them some coffee, 'Oh, yeah and some of that gateau cake they have. That would be good.'

'Yes,' Bond smiled, 'Gateau cake would be delicious, but I should order one or the other.'

'Gateau means cake, sir.' Prime raised her eyebrows.

'Whatever.'

Long crouched over the telephone muttering. '. . . and toot suite as well,' he finished.

They arranged themselves around the room, with Eddie Rhabb standing in front of the fireplace, lifting himself up and down on the balls of his feet, waiting for them to settle and the coffee and cake to arrive.

'You look as delicious as ever,' Bond told Beatrice quietly.

'So do you, James. You don't know how many times I've tried to see you since our little adventure.'

'What kept you away?'

'M and his Chief of Staff mainly. Moneypenny on one occasion. Then I heard you had got yourself heavily involved with a Swiss lady. True?'

He nodded. 'True, but we don't know what's going to happen. She's been in a coma for some time. The doctors aren't very hopeful.'

'Oh, James, I'm sorry.'

'I seem to bring bad luck to women.' He looked grim and the sparkle had gone from his eyes.

'You could only bring good luck to me,' she whispered.

Again he thought about his feelings after the operation they had shared. *The woman who could become the woman of my life.* He looked at her, memories flooding back, and wondered why he had not fought to keep her then.

The coffee and cakes eventually arrived, looking and smelling wonderful, though the waiters seemed a little taken back by the sheer muscle gathered in the room. Once they were all quiet, Rhabb said he would have to start at the beginning if Bond was to be brought up to date.

It appeared that, about seven months earlier, they had successfully managed to insert Beatrice into the Tempesta menage – 'Though those two fake FBI heavies will tell you that she's far from trusted,' he added.

'They *are* fakes then?'

'More than you'll ever know. They even sprung a particularly nasty killer in London, then managed to disappear by setting up three other people on the Bradbury Airlines flight to Dulles. We knew they weren't kosher but, for a very short time, we were under the impression they were dead.'

'Yes, Pop Hughes, the IIC of the NTSB team told me about them, and how they could have been the target of the bombing.'

'Sure,' Rhabb threw back his head. 'Sure, nice people the old folks in COLD and the Tempesta family. You know the real reason all those people were killed, James?'

'As a matter of fact, yes. M told me last night.'

Rhabb expelled a lungful of air. 'Allen and Farmer have been on the Tempesta payroll for a long time. They're also card-carrying members of COLD. As soon as the Tempestas accepted Beatrice as one of the household, that precious pair were assigned to keep an eye on her. Wherever she went, they were never far behind, but we did manage to get around that. You see, James, something big is about to go down with COLD and the Tempestas. We thought you might like to be in on it. Also, you're probably the best person in the world to act as a sort of decoy.'

'So you set about luring me, using the charming Ms da Ricci.'

'Something like that. As I said, it would have taken an age to get you officially, so as soon as we heard from Beatrice that things had started to pop, we performed a little duplicity of our own: to draw you, and also to left-foot Messrs Allen and Farmer.'

'How did you go about that, Eddie? I'm always interested in duplicity.'

Rhabb took a mouthful of cream cake and chewed enthusiastically while Prime made some comment about tough members of the Bureau gorging themselves on expenses. 'What we did,' he paused to wash down the cake with an enormous drink of coffee. 'What we did was have Beatrice send a daily report. We have this cute little gizmo, see. This electronic sending device. Fits in her bra, doesn't it, B?'

'The name's Beatrice,' she accented the Italian pronunciation. 'Yes, Eddie, it fits in my bra, but I usually just get good hiding places for it. Your friends and mine, the Tempestas, have WHS.'

'Whatsat?'

'Wandering Hand Syndrome. So I keep it hidden elsewhere.'

'Okay,' Rhabb shrugged. 'She's good. Very good. Transposes her report to a small tape – one of those very little ones – connected to her computer. She inserts the tape into the gizmo and sends it in one quick high-speed burst every night at 10pm usually.'

'Sometimes later,' Beatrice confided.

'Couple of weeks ago she tells us that she's being sent out from the Tuscan place. Gave us the dates. Everything. Had to pick up documents for Angelo in Rome, then come on down here to do things with banks. Well, this is the place for it, right? Doing things with banks.'

'Has been known,' Bond, full of sarcasm. 'The Swiss do a good line in banks.'

'We knew where she would be and what dates. We also knew exactly how the two shadows operated. Best of all, she told us about this upcoming gathering. Next weekend it appears the main leaders – area commanders – of COLD are to be at the Villa Tempesta for a special briefing. Whoever is the real mover and shaker of COLD is going to be there. A plot and some kind of party to celebrate. Our general feeling about it is that they're going to make their move and that couldn't be better as far as we're concerned. The move has to be on American soil, so we felt it would be good to deal with them here, on Italian soil. Means we don't have to get our own hands dirty; don't have legal battles; don't use up too much of the tax dollars fixing these guys. The Italians do it so much better, they just keep people in jail for a hundred and one years then they have the trial.'

'We'd be part of it, naturally, but it's the best way to go.'

'Saves a lot of paperwork as well,' Bond said, with his tongue firmly in his cheek.

'That also. Anyway, we came to the conclusion that, if we could separate her from her twin shadows, we could kind of get you interested: in a purely unofficial way.'

They had picked her up in Rome, cutting Allan and Farmer off, done a debrief in an old CIA safe-house, where she made the tape giving details of her movements and when she would be in Geneva. Hotel. Room number. The whole works.

'She had requested this room presumably?' from Bond.

'Luigi and Angelo requested it. They like to know where and when she moves, which was our only small error.'

'It went wrong?' Bond arched an eyebrow.

'The shadows got worried. They lost her for over two hours in Rome. To them this is a complete disaster because Angelo and Luigi like to get nightly reports back giving all her movements. They want everything, even when she . . . No, forget it. Just trust me, James. The terrible twins lose her for two hours and it's two hours of unaccountable time. We presume they call in and get their whatsits chewed off. She arrives in Geneva and they are waiting for her. They point out that the Tempesta brothers are a little piqued. From now, they say, we must have a *mélange à three*, as the French put it.'

'*Ménage à trois*, Eddie,' Prime corrected with a wince.

'Whatever. Anyhow, we're there, listening to all this, and the tape's already gone to you . . .'

'In the mail?'

'No, actually it was popped through your letter box by one of our people in London, but now we have to bring in the Swiss, and thank heaven the Swiss cops are fans of the Bureau. They'll do everything in their power to assist – just like the Italians who are really looking forward to next weekend. You saw how we managed things today, and I think you'd agree it was nicely done. The moment we heard last night that you were coming . . .' He stopped suddenly as though he had said the wrong thing.

'Last night? You have a line in to M?'

'No, we have a line in to that nice doctor at your private clinic. He telephoned us last night. Had everything except your flight number.'

'Okay.' Bond nodded slowly as though he could not believe what tricks the FBI were getting up to. 'But as I understand it, Beatrice goes home on Monday . . .'

'Yes, first thing on Monday morning I return to the Tempesta salt mines,' she acknowledged.

'Won't they be expecting her little friends to come in just behind her?'

'Yes, well, they'll be out of luck. That's one of the things I have to do before Monday evening. Either Allen or Farmer – maybe even both of them – will have to talk to the brothers on the telephone.'

'How are they going to explain their absence?' He already suspected just what Eddie Rhabb had in mind.

'They're going to have run into you, I think, James, and maybe you'll even have to do away with them. Even people

195

like Allen and Farmer sometimes lose – sometimes they lose big time.'

'And you are also thinking about me being present somewhere in or around the Villa Tempesta next weekend, while they're putting together their plan to turn the United States into a State of United Zombies?'

'That is the idea, if you'll go along with it. But, James, you will, won't you? I mean how could you resist . . .'

'Working with me again?' Beatrice gave him her most beautiful smile.

'You have a plan to infiltrate and exfiltrate me?'

'We have a skeleton plan. We thought Beatrice could explain it to you over dinner tonight. Geneva can be quite a romantic place. Dinner for two. Candlelight. That guy who plays soft piano music in the bar downstairs.'

'I don't suppose I've any option.'

Beatrice passed on yet another of her smiles. 'It's either dinner with me or a few weeks in a Swiss jail. We've all come too far to pull back now, James dear. Also the food isn't so good in the Swiss jails.'

'You're on. After all, I've got nothing better to do. Might as well save the future of the United States. Better than wasting away in a Swiss jail.' As he said it, Bond wondered what he was letting himself in for.

18

The Unravelling

'DON'T YOU GET a little fed up with all this, James?' She looked across the table, and Bond thought, not for the first time, that he might have made a terrible mistake walking away from her after the one operation they had worked on together – a momentous occasion when they had, literally, saved three world leaders from possible extinction. The fact that all three were now out of power was neither here nor there. Beatrice Maria da Ricci was here and now, causing his mind and body to enter a state of confusion. He focused on her question.

'What is there to get fed up with?'

'Well, I was officially sent in by the Service. You were basically conned into coming out here only to find that you're a sort of errand boy for the FBI. It's not even a job for your own country.'

'Beatrice, that's what I've always been – a kind of lethal errand boy. I follow orders, then use my own initiative to get the job done. Officially I'm on leave, but while this is an operation concerned primarily with the United States, it does have a knock-on effect as far as England is concerned. If these COLD people manage to pull off their stunt, it could plunge the whole world into misery. In a year or so, with COLD in control of the USA, the world itself would be taken back into the Stone

Age. I suppose it's the world's unspoken greatest fear – an American isolationist policy which would take them off the board altogether; make them self-supporting; allow them to get on with taming their own country by brute force, and probably a lot of ignorance as well. So, the answer is no. No, I don't feel like an errand boy; I'm glad I'm here. When it's all over, there'll be hell to pay back home, but the times are out of joint. Things aren't what they were. For me life's much more dangerous now than it was in the middle of the Cold War. Also, I'd like to see America still playing a part in world affairs, even if they do it badly.'

They sat in the restaurant of the Hôtel du Rhône, among the white napery, glittering silverware, lights glinting off the crystal glasses and the bar pianist playing old romantic standards.

Beatrice had put on a plain cocktail dress, dark blue with a plunging neckline, bare back and a simple strand of what looked like diamonds at her throat. Around them, money and rank occupied the other tables: mostly retired money. The couples looked socially very acceptable, and Bond thought of M's old comment in Switzerland— 'Berne is about politics,' he would say. 'Zurich concerns itself with money; but Geneva has its faded social circle. If you want to hobnob with Swiss residents who keep their money in Zurich, and their pretensions intact, then join the dying breed in Geneva.'

He looked across at Beatrice. 'Remember the last dinner we had together?'

She gave a little nod and a wan smile. 'The Rock Hotel, Gibraltar. After that bit of business inside the old rock itself.'

'I still owe you a life for that, remember?'

'You'll pay, James.'

'I always pay my debts – eventually. We could be approaching settlement day. I just hope that Eddie Rhabb manages to get those two thugs to say the right thing on the telephone to Angelo and Luigi.'

'I'm sure he will. Old Eddie has a surprising knack of getting what he wants. He got you, James.'

He smiled, genuinely amused, wondering who had actually asked for him: Rhabb or da Ricci? Aloud he said, 'Eddie's changed his tune a little, Beatrice. My first job working with him was to try and draw both Tempestas to the United States because he didn't trust the Italians to do the right job. Now, he says he'd rather leave it to the Italians and work matters from a distance.'

She thought for a moment. Then— 'It's probably circumstances. The COLD threat is very close. I'm sure of that, and I've given them a rundown on it. I believe Eddie's genuinely scared. When they first briefed me, he mentioned that until recently he really didn't take COLD seriously. It appears he takes them *very* seriously now. Sees them as a true threat to his country. What they've been planning could happen, and for the first time he's come to see that.'

The food arrived and they had agreed not to talk about the minutiae of the operation until later. They had tonight and tomorrow to get everything settled and in order. So now they ate *Raclette*, that very special appetizer of hot Gomser cheese spread over small cooked potatoes, served with baby gherkins and small white pickled onions; followed by *Geschnetzeltes*, delicious veal fillets on a bed of the inevitable *Rösti* which Bond said he always thought of as 'the nursery of food of Switzerland' – the golden savoury potato cakes which were a great complement to any meat dish.

They drank a very good Beaune with the *Raclette*, deciding it was so pleasant that they would stay with it through the veal dish. Then, in spite of Beatrice's good natured attempts at refusal, the waiter insisted that they try at least a small slice of *Zuger Kirschtorte* with its distinctive alcoholic cherry flavour that burst delightfully on the tongue, infusing the taste buds and making a gastronomic fireworks display to end an exceptional meal.

As they ate, Bond scanned the room. He knew that Eddie Rhabb would not allow them the luxury of being alone in the restaurant, but the surveillance team was invisible. Only later did they discover that an elderly couple – equipped with a communications package which gave them a direct line to a van parked up the street – had been loaned to the FBI by the local police. The pair were both former police officers who delighted in doing any work of this kind.

They ordered coffee to be sent up to Room 504 and, while they waited for it, Beatrice went first to the ornamental bedhead, then to one of the large lamps which looked as though it had been fashioned from a stone jar.

Bond watched, amused, as she prised a listening device from the bedhead, and removed another from the lamp. She took them into the bathroom, crushed them under her foot, then flushed them down the toilet. Going to the main closet, she removed her briefcase, opened it and took out a small handheld communicator which she looked at carefully, setting a small dial to the right frequency. 'I checked out the wavelength they had those two bugs on.' She smiled a catlike smile, pressed the *Send* button and spoke quietly, but clearly, into the business end of the device. 'Eddie, or whoever's wearing headphones and listening in, I'll give you a shout through my own personal bug if we need help. See you all tomorrow.'

Bond leaned back and applauded. Beatrice simply repeated her smile. 'We're going to do all the final bits and pieces tomorrow with Eddie,' she said in her normal voice. 'Before anything else, I have to tell you what I know, and lead you through what I think's going to happen.'

After the room service waiter brought the tray, she took a clipboard from the briefcase, allowing Bond to pour the coffee. 'You remembered.' She sounded pleased and looked happy. 'You remembered that I like it black with sugar.'

'You're not easily forgettable, Beatrice. Now, let me in on all the secrets.'

'First, I know you've been in the villa, but I don't know how much of it you've seen. Tell me.'

He described the entrance from the lake side, with its two boathouses and the gravel drive up to the hall entrance. Then the dining room, the room he had been given for that one disturbed night, and the main secretary's office.

'Right.' She patted the sofa, indicating that he should come and sit beside her. On the clipboard she had several sheets of plans which he recognized immediately as the villa on Lake Massaciuccoli. 'Then you don't know about the extensive gardens at the back of the house, nor have you seen the truly enormous ballroom.'

He shook his head. 'Show me.'

She turned to a plan view depicting a very large garden at the back of the property, augmenting the plan with photographs – cypress trees, shaded stone walks, statuary, fountains, a large rose garden, and – judging by some of the photographs – water tricks: secret fountains that sprayed out or upwards if you stepped on a particular flagstone.

The garden stretched right back to the rise that signalled the beginning of the Tuscan foothills, the extent of the property marked by a long irregular line of fir and cypresses. Beyond these was a stretch of open ground, and to the far right of the garden stood a long and large greenhouse with what appeared to be a gardener's cottage detached from the house.

'This,' she showed him the cottage on both plan and photograph, 'is where you'll stay for most of the time. 'While I haven't yet earned their trust, it's my cottage: my quarters. I've no doubt that they have it wired for *son et lumière* but, with luck, I'll have all that stuff disconnected by the time you arrive. I'll arrange things so that the system goes on the blink. I don't think they'll have time to work on it, because there's going to be far too much for the staff to do.

'Now, the ballroom – and this is equally important as you'll see.' She pointed to the plans. Under almost the entire length of the house, in place of cellars, ran a massive room. In separate photographs she showed him the huge underground ballroom, beautifully appointed with moulded cornices, four great chandeliers and wall lighting which was mainly used to show off the paintings. He recognized a couple of large Picassos, a Matisse, and at least one Schamberg that, if he remembered correctly, had been missing from the New York Museum of Modern Art for the past thirty years.

'Quite a place,' he muttered.

'Yes, and it's going to be used twice over next weekend. Something's happening there on Saturday afternoon, and it will be in use all day on Sunday. It's on Sunday that the area commanders of COLD are going to be there. Not enough spare rooms in the villa to put them up for the whole weekend so the visit has been arranged as some kind of special tour. They're all coming by bus – mainly staying in Viareggio and Pisa over the Saturday night and being brought out to the villa by the boatload on Sunday.'

She told him that she was reading between the lines, but it appeared the event was to be a full briefing of COLD's area commanders. 'Whatever the scheme, it's going to take place very soon. I'd say within a month. That's why we have to stop things now, while they're all together.'

'What about the Saturday? What's going to happen then? You talked about a party.'

'I truly don't know. All I can gather is that they'll be using the ballroom, there's going to be some kind of celebration, and the really big shots of COLD are going to be there. I overheard a conversation between the brothers and they seemed to be very excited about what was to take place. One of them – one of the people coming – has not been at the villa for a long time, I know that. But these are the controlling elements of COLD, so I presume they're going to have a knees-up and a general bit of planning before the arrival of the area commanders. With regard to that, I did hear somebody say it would be the last opportunity before *Blizzard*, which I can only presume is their rather obvious code name for COLD's main op.'

'Do I get to see any of this?'

'You'll have a ringside seat, my dear. That's the beauty of having you in the cottage. Someone really planned ahead when they refurbished the villa . . . look . . .' She drew out the plans again. 'I found this by accident, then checked it out.' Her finger traced a line from what was obviously a large fireplace in the cottage to a tunnel which ran below the ground, ending, it seemed, behind one wall of the ballroom.

'There's a set of stairs which run down from the fireplace – beautifully camouflaged and cut from stone. These lead to the passage – and it's a proper passage, high roof, plenty of room to move about. It comes to a stop just on the far side of the panelling in the ballroom, and there's a concealed squint – well, more than a squint really, it's a fairly large one-way mirror. You get a grandstand view of practically the entire room. Magnificent.'

Bond gave a long, contemplative, 'Mmmmmm?'

'What's the matter?'

'People build places like that for a purpose. You *are* certain that they're not going to throw you out of the cottage while this is going on?'

'Nobody's suggested it.'

'Beatrice, they don't have to suggest it. They simply do it. Maybe they want to shoot a video of whatever's happening. Perhaps they'll only let you know at the last minute.'

'Well, I'll be in touch regularly once I'm back there. I can alert you to anything else that's going on.'

'I'm not happy about that, but Eddie's obviously got things well covered, so I guess we'll just have to play things on the fly.'

'That's your forte, isn't it, James? That's what turns you from lethal errand boy to the man you really are.'

'What're you talking about?'

'Using your initiative.'

'Beatrice, my darling girl, I always use my initiative. Now, how are they going to get me in, how are they going to get me out, and what kind of backup am I going to get?'

'You're going in by parachute. The rest is up to Eddie. He's the one to tell you. Okay?'

'If you say so. When?'

'When what?'

'When's he going to tell me?'

'Tomorrow. He'll give you the whole thing, even tell you the bit about how I'm going to distract the Tempesta hoodlums and meet you in the garden; take you to my little cottage.'

'Oh, grandma, what big eyes you have.'

'No, you don't have to dress up. We're not going to play Little Red Riding Hood.'

'That's odd.'

'What?'

He told her about Freddie and his sudden thought of her as the Sleeping Beauty. 'I'm not the kind of man who goes around thinking of fairy tales. I just don't know where that came from.'

She went very solemn. 'Your friend, Freddie. Is she really very bad?'

'The worst. They don't give her much chance of recovery.'

'You going to be able to cope with that?'

'I'm already coping with it, Beatrice my dear. I know that we're not going to be together for the rest of our lives.'

'You been unfaithful to her, James?'

'I haven't been running around – how would Eddie put it . . .? "Boffing the bimbos prolly." ' He wickedly imitated Eddie's pronunciation of the word 'probably'.

They both laughed, then, 'I'm not a bimbo, James,' she said in a small voice.

'I know, dear Beatrice. Oh, I do know.'

They reached for each other at the same moment, and his ·mouth searched for hers. When their lips met and their mouths opened, it was as though two people had been parched with thirst for an age – years maybe. They drank from each other's mouths, slaking the terrible craving, then feeling the hungry need one for the other.

It was a slow and beautiful unravelling of the love they had once felt for each other, and when it was over they remained hungry for more. Eventually, they fell asleep wrapped together, dropping deeply and contentedly into a safety that neither had experienced in a long time.

The clamour of the telephone wakened them, and Bond glanced at his watch. It was just after four in the morning.

'I'd better,' she slurred with sleep and leaned over him to

pick up the receiver, listening for a moment. Then, 'James,' she said, 'it's for you.'

He knew before Eddie Rhabb even said it—

'James, I'm sorry, it's very bad news for you. I'm coming over to see how we should handle it. Your lady friend, Fredericka von Grüsse, died about an hour ago. The doctor, Sanusi, just called me.'

19

Lazarus

IT WAS BEATRICE who wept. After he had put down the telephone, Bond sat on the bed and told her. No frills, just 'Freddie's dead. About an hour ago.' She began weeping, rocking backwards and forwards, a keening requiem for a woman she had never met.

Between the tears she blurted, 'Oh, God. We should have waited.' Then she ran into the bathroom and locked the door, her sobs sounding, in the bedroom, like the stutter of a dying engine.

He felt nothing. Later, he presumed that he had already done his grieving all those months ago when he had held her wrecked body in Puerto Rico, thinking she had died there and then. Even when he saw she was alive, he had been certain that she was dying, and now it was a sombre and sobering moment as he realized that whenever he had visited her in the clinic it was always to say goodbye.

Eventually, Beatrice came out from the bathroom, her face clear, the tears washed away. He held her close, telling her of the conclusions to which he had come. When she spoke, there was no sign of emotion in her voice. 'I'm sorry, James. It's been so wonderful to be with you again, then I thought this, Freddie's death, might change everything between us. It's so horrible. She's been lying there for so long, I guess it suddenly hit me that she had died instead of me.'

For a moment he did not understand, then their earlier time came back to him and he remembered there was a period in 1989 when, for several days, he had thought she was dead also.

A few minutes later, Eddie Rhabb arrived, blurting out, 'James, I don't know what we do. I can't really have you flying back for a funeral. If you return now, they'll almost certainly latch on to you – your own people, I mean, and maybe the Tempestas.' He paused, as though breathless. 'On the other hand, I have no real claim on you. I've asked you to go in, and we both know how dangerous it's going to be . . .'

'Eddie, it's okay. Freddie wanted to be cremated. If you can get back to Sanusi, tell him to go ahead with the funeral. When this business is over, I'll take her ashes and sprinkle them in the place she wanted just outside Interlaken. It sounds cold and ruthless, but it's the only way.'

'You're a prince, James.' Eddie was gone almost before he had finished talking.

'Fast Eddie,' Beatrice said, coming back to her normal self.

They went back to bed, dozed some more, then woke and ordered breakfast which was brought by a waiter who looked at them disapprovingly.

They had just finished eating when Eddie returned. 'I didn't bring any of the others,' he grinned. 'None of their business what you two do in your own time.'

'Decent of you, Eddie.' Bond was pretty certain that Rhabb had passed on the word.

'I've talked to Sanusi again.' Rhabb helped himself to some coffee. 'It appears that your old boss has told them you're somewhere abroad on vacation. So people are looking for you.

You'll have to keep your head down.'

'How are your couple of bad guys?'

'Being very co-operative. We've offered them some sort of immunity and I think they get the message. They're being kept very secure and we've let them hear a couple of conversations. They're starting to believe that the days of both COLD and their immediate bosses are numbered. They're like all the other rats. The policy seems to be that they leave the sinking ship. Beatrice's told you what she knows?'

'About some ceremony for the bigwigs on Saturday, and a gathering of the clans on Sunday.'

'That's when we want to hit them. Sunday. But should anything go wrong, you're going to have to call us in earlier.'

'Who exactly is "us"?'

'I thought you realized, or had at least worked it out. We've got full co-operation from the Leatherheads.'

The Leatherheads is the nick-name for the Italian counter-terrorist unit: the NOCS – Nucleo Operativo Centrale di Sicurezza. This is the special force that deals with anything from terrorist operations to hostage rescue. Made up from an élite group of highly trained members of the Carabinieri, this force comes under Italy's COMSUBIN who are charged with military operations first, and counterterrorist action only if it is thought to be a danger to the country. The NOCS arm is expert, disciplined, and a definite force to be reckoned with. Rhabb had obviously presented the Italian administration with enough information to convince them that COLD was as much a danger to Italy as it was to America.

'You think they'll eventually extradite the General to the States, Eddie? Strikes me that's what is bound to happen in the long run.'

'We'll face that when and if it *does* happen. The main object of what we're going to call *Antifreeze* is to secure and cut off the main leaders of COLD which, we're pretty certain, include Luigi and Angelo Tempesta. Once they're out of it, we'll almost certainly have the foot soldiers of COLD neutralized.' He inclined his head towards Beatrice, 'She's shown you the plans and photographs?' Bond nodded.

'Okay, we'll go over the main points – your infiltration, communications and our main link to the Italian Special Forces – later. When Beatrice has gone back into the bosom of the Tempesta family, we'll have five days to get you up to full speed, James. You go in during the early hours of Saturday morning.'

'How?'

'By parachute, of course. The DZ is that open ground behind the Tempestas' garden. We're going to be dead accurate.'

'The accent being on accurate, not dead, I presume.'

'There'll be people ahead of you, James. The Italians are putting a troop of their people into that space about three hours before you arrive, and they're not going to have the luxury of parachutes. They're walking in – your Royal Marine Commandos call it "yomping" – then they'll be digging in. None of those nice folks in the Tempesta household are going to have a clue.'

'Talking about that, how much muscle's in the villa?'

It was Beatrice who answered. 'You killed two of them on the lake. At least that's what I understood . . .'

'Yes. Got in our way. Was it a guy called Filippo, and another . . .?'

'Filippo and Carlo, yes. They were old muscle, old retainers.'

'So who's there now?'

'Head of security is a guy called Alessandro. Under him there are five – no, six thugs.' She began counting them off on

Lazarus

her fingers— 'Roberto, Tomaso, Edmundo, Giorgio, Enrico and Saul. They're all young, big men. Muscles on their muscles. Tomaso is a body builder. All of them have been trained in most of the black arts: silent killing; knives; all weapons and plenty of the other stuff: feet, hands and the rougher forms of karate. They're an intimidating bunch. Oh, and Saul has a thing about me. I have to be very careful with him.'

'You've forgotten one,' Eddie nudged her.

'Who?'

'The guy our two little friends sprung from London.'

'Oh, my god, yes. Kauffburger. He's the main bodyguard for the brothers. He'd kill you with two fingers; the guy's a psycho. Give him a funny look and he'd kill you. Very big, exceptionally nasty, but he seems to respect the brothers and does as he's told. He's the kind of monster who strangles cats just for the hell of it.'

'Chews nails and spits fire for the encore. Know the type well.' Already, in his mind, Bond was going through the arsenal he wanted to take with him. Now he only hoped that Eddie would be able to get his hands on everything.

He asked Beatrice if he was going to be safe, holed up in her cottage, and she said he would be. 'Anyway, it'll only be for the rest of Saturday, and over the Saturday night. I'm taking in a little package Eddie's fixing for me. At around the time of your jump, it's going to make a big bang in the boathouse, okay, Eddie?'

'Sure, it's your basic flash-bang. Lots of sound and fury but no damage. It should draw the duty hoodlums away from the DZ.'

'How many guard the house at night?' Bond looked at Beatrice.

'Two are on constant patrol of the grounds, though they

don't usually come right to the back of the garden. They always seem to suspect a frontal attack. But two outside and there's usually one other guy patrolling the inside of the house.'

'Communications, Eddie?' His mind was really working now. Later, he thought, he would make a list.

Eddie went quiet, becoming focused on the communications. 'You're both going in with homers implanted. We did Beatrice's in Rome, a week ago . . .'

'In my rear end,' she pouted.

'That's what that lump is,' Bond smiled.

'There's a lump? You have a lump there?' Eddie sounded worried.

'Joke, Eddie.'

'In rather poor taste, I thought.' She stuck her nose in the air.

'It's a tiny thing. You have a little sore patch for a couple of days. We're doing you tomorrow, James.'

'Hurts like hell.' Beatrice massaged her right buttock. 'Just kidding,' she added when she saw Eddie's look of concern.

'So, we get implanted homing devices, what else?'

'You're both going to carry small communication packs with you. Beatrice already has hers. It's disguised as a lipstick holder. That's the first one and she knows exactly how to work it. There's an anti-clockwise movement at the base. This releases a small plunger which she presses. Immediately it is set, the thing broadcasts a constant Mayday signal. Once that goes off, we capture it. There'll be someone listening from the moment she goes back tomorrow, just in case something comes up before the weekend.'

On the Mayday call, he told them, the troop of special forces behind the house would go in— 'Straight away, no messing around. They'll all know who Beatrice is, so she won't get hit.

But, if necessary, they'll take anyone and everyone out.'

At the same moment two transport aircraft would take off from Pisa, parachuting in another batch of élite forces, while a pair of high speed police motor launches would come in from the lake.

'So she gets the lipstick. What's for me, some of that lip salve?' Bond asked.

Eddie held up his hand. 'She has a secondary emergency pack built into a belt. We have a similar one for you, James. That's a twist and bang thing as well. Somewhat like a scaled-down parachute or pilot's safety release. So, you both have belts that do the same job. You, James, also have a nice ball-point pen. Not one of those silver or gold, expensive-looking things you see in the movies. This is just a cheap plastic pen, but it contains everything.'

'All the gubbins.'

'Gubbins? What's with gubbins?'

'The doobries.'

'James, come on. You Brits slay me with your funny words. Gubbins and doobries.'

'The works, Eddie.'

After a little more gentle pulling of Eddie's leg, they worked out the rest of the day. Beatrice would get her final briefing that afternoon. 'Give the two of you a chance to have dinner tonight. Just you two alone.'

'You're all heart, Eddie.'

'Sure, that's what they all say. Then we pick up Beatrice at nine o'clock sharp in the morning.'

'You're taking her to the airport?'

'No, I meant *we* kinda figuratively. One of our guys comes around with a cab. His face is unknown here, so there's no sweat. He'll be here at nine in the morning, and I want you back in your room by then, James. Back here with the door locked.' He paused by the door of Beatrice's suite. 'And with all your doobries.'

Beatrice went out just after two that afternoon and Bond settled back to read a book he had brought from London: a treatise on the tricks of a gambler. He had a tendency to read everything he could about gambling, card sharping and the like as it had paid off many times in the past.

Beatrice did not get back until nearly six that evening. 'Gave me just about everything but the cyanide pill.' She smiled. 'I'll say this for Eddie Rhabb, he really covers everything. Oh, and I met the Italian captain who'll be in charge of the special forces at the back of the villa. Big, good-looking man. Quite fanciable in an Italian kind of way.'

They sent down for dinner from room service and spent what she said was 'A cozy evening by the fire.' Certainly, Bond admitted, fires were lit that night.

To make certain that they were both ready for the meeting in the early hours of the following Saturday morning, they decided on somewhat flippant code names to be whispered in the dark. She was to be *Red Fox* while Bond would be *Grey Fox*. 'That should fox them,' he quipped.

'Tell it to Eddie,' Beatrice laughed. 'Once I'm gone, they're moving you out of here tomorrow. Thought you'd like to know.'

'The man is always the last to know.'

'In your case, James, you're the first to know.' She wrapped herself around him and pulled him very close. 'You're the first to know that I love you very much.'

The room seemed empty and dismal after she left the following morning. There was no awkwardness, no tears, no fuss. 'See you early Saturday morning,' was all she said.

He returned to his own room, realizing he had hardly used it since checking in. Then, at three in the afternoon, Eddie appeared, this time with MacRoberts in tow.

'She get off all right?' he said, feeling stupid at asking such a silly question.

Eddie nodded. 'We're doing the business with those two greaseballs at around six tonight. We'll know the exact time; we've got a couple of guys down near the lakeside, they're going to phone in as soon as she's been picked up, then we work the phones with the greaseballs, let them lay the news on the Tempestas.'

'Where are they, by Puccini's old house?'

Eddie nodded, then added, 'Oh, James, just one other thing. They sent through a picture this morning. Some dame arrived and was greeted by Luigi. Mucho respecto. Take a look, will you? See if you can place her.'

With a bemused but worried look, Eddie handed over a computer-enhanced copy of a faxed colour print and Bond glanced down at it, not suspecting anything. Then his heart pounded and he could hardly believe his eyes. He had to take a second, longer look.

'Holy Lazarus,' he breathed. 'It can't be.'

They had got a very good shot of her head and shoulders. She was looking back over one shoulder, her hair blowing in the slight breeze as one of Luigi's men stretched out a hand to help her into a launch.

He swallowed, his throat suddenly very dry. He was looking down at a clear and beautiful picture of the Principessa Sukie Tempesta, whose remains he had seen in the dreadful car bombing at Dulles International. Risen from the grave. Impossible. He felt very sick.

20

A Close Call

'WE BOTH KNOW this lady, here in the picture, is dead.' Eddie looked at Bond as though he were crazy. 'But she was there, by the lakeside, this morning. She was going out to the villa.'

'Washington Dulles International. Same day as the London flight got bombed. Bradbury Airlines.' He stopped and glared angrily at Rhabb. 'You were there too! I *knew* this woman, Eddie. She was a dear friend. I saw the car and I saw her charred and burned body – what was left of it. Eddie, get the hell out of here and check it out.' He stopped, catching his breath, realizing he had been shouting.

'Hey, James, calm down.' MacRoberts put a hand on his shoulder.

'It's all very well telling me to calm down!' He shook the hand from his shoulder. 'If this lady is still alive, I've been conned and she's not what I've always thought. There's some connection they probably wanted to keep hidden all these years.'

'Okay, James, okay,' muttered Eddie. 'We'll get back to the safe house where Prime, Drake and Long are looking after the greaseballs. I'll make the call from there. If you'll get yourself ready to check out of here, we'll get one of our drivers over to pick you up.'

Bond nodded, still angry. 'How many people have you actually got here, Eddie?'

'Only the guys you've seen, plus two drivers. Prime and Drake have both been working on our two fake junior G-men, preparing a script for the call to the villa. Drake's a doctor, by the way. We weren't taking any chances. The car'll be here in about ten minutes.'

The two FBI men left, Eddie walking very purposefully, head down in his charging bull mode.

As he got his two bags together, Bond hesitated, wondering if he should keep his automatic on him or pack it back into the briefcase's secure compartment. He felt edgy, his nerves strung out as though stretched to their limit. He went out onto the balcony and took several deep breaths, trying to think through the various possible reasons for Sukie to have died a counterfeit death.

The answers to every equation came up skewed and unpleasant. People change, he reasoned. When he had worked with Sukie all those years ago, her elderly husband had already died, but she insisted that her stepsons were just plain and ordinary businessmen.

She had been in danger then, but that was because of him, and the maze of the operation in which he was embroiled. She had not become part of that deadly time on purpose, but had been an innocent bystander sucked in to the peril in which he had found himself. Now, he reasoned, she could have been part of the Tempesta family's duplicity, and connected with COLD even back then in the mid-eighties.

He recalled the small pang of suspicion he felt when he ran into her at the hotel after having arrived following the atrocious bombing of DB 299. Were his first feelings at that moment justified? He still could not work out how she managed to falsify her death in the car.

The telephone rang in the room behind him: the bell-boy informing him that his car was waiting for him.

He carried his bags down to the foyer and settled his account with his Boldman American Express card, then went outside where a clear-eyed young man, built like a boxer, was waiting with a shining and sleek old Rover.

'Mr Boldman, sir? Mr Rhabb says he's waiting for you and asked me to tell you that you were correct about the lady.'

He settled into the rear of the Rover and soon understood the young man was a professional driver with a great deal of expertise. They took a long and involved route which entailed a lot of doubling back, slowing down at junctions, with the driver's eyes flicking quickly up to the rear view mirrors, and sudden unsignalled turns.

Eventually, once the driver was certain they were not being followed, he headed out of town, travelling along the lakeside for a couple of kilometres, finally turning into a concealed driveway and pulling up in front of a small house, set high so that its windows afforded a good view of the entrance and road below.

'Of course I was bloody right!' Bond was still aggressive towards Eddie. He rarely liked having his word questioned, and Eddie himself had been offhand about the truth.

'You were right about the lady. Killed with a car bomb. It's a puzzle. According to all records, she's been right off the board since then.'

'So how do you figure it, James?' MacRoberts asked.

'I don't. Except that it stinks. That lady knows quite a lot about me. She knows how I operate, and I was with her a couple of hours before she was killed – or seemed to be killed. In fact, she was coming back to my hotel to stay with me.'

'Give us your worse-case scenario, then, James.'

'Sukie Tempesta's been around, Ed. She's no fool, and it's obvious now that her ties to her stepsons – that's a laugh – are much stronger than I ever imagined. If that's the case, she went missing on purpose. It's too late to pull Beatrice back, and I've a horrible feeling that, if Sukie's been in the shadows out there, she's probably not the only one. Worst case? Our *Operation Antifreeze* could be utterly compromised. We've got thcsc two ex-FBI agents who got one psycho out of jail and brought him back to Italy, but we had no idea Sukie was alive.

'If she's been wandering around, untraceable because she's officially dead, lord knows how many other people are also out and about in the real world – even here.'

'Nobody's been on our tails since we've been in Geneva. I'd stake my life on that.' Eddie had his head down and shoulders hunched, a sure sign that he was on the offensive.

'I'm not so concerned with here – Geneva – my worry is that you've got Italian Special Forces implicated. Do we know if they're leaky? What's the record?'

Rhabb thought for a full minute. 'They're airtight and leak-proof. I'd put my pension on that. Nothing's been done over open telephone lines. All of them were brought, by night, into a closed facility where they often do training just outside Pisa. No calls in or out. No extra bodies in or out. They're self-sufficient, and only their senior officers know what's going on.'

'Then I'd have those senior officers checked by a good plumber,' Bond snapped.

'Well, they're all there, in Pisa, more or less under lock and key.'

'Then for the safety of this little war game, I suggest someone has a go at them and tests the envelope of their security.'

Eddie did not argue, or hesitate. He opened his mouth, but before he could say anything, MacRoberts slammed his hand down. 'I'll go and do the job myself. I'd like Dr Drake with me in case we have to do any deep analysis, or even a chemical, but I suppose you want him here until after Beatrice is on her way to the villa. You'll want him to be on hand when whichever of the two bozos does the telephone call.'

'It's going to be the one who calls himself Allen – real name Stanley Kzolowitz, and yes, I'd like Drake here. After we've done the call, and the minders turn up to take those two back to the States, we'll all be in Pisa. Go and check if the jet's here – in Geneva. If it is, you can take it to Pisa and send it back.'

'They'll need your authorization, Eddie.' MacRoberts gave him a blank look.

'Okay. If you want something done, you do it yourself.' He walked rapidly and noisily out of the room towards the rear of the house.

'Eddie sometimes forgets he's in charge, and the Bureau gets picky about instructions and signatures, that kind of thing.'

'It's the same in all well-regulated families.' Bond gave him a quizzical look. 'You're certain nothing's going to go wrong with this telephone call to the villa? That Allen, or Kzolowitz, or whatever his name is, will play it straight?'

MacRoberts gave a huge shrug. 'If he doesn't, then he gets a bullet through the noggin and we send in the Italian Fifth Cavalry to salvage what they can. The local cops will then have to cut out all the American guys who've started turning up in hotels in Pisa and Viareggio. Means we'll get them all, but I don't know how we're going to hold them.'

They were in a long wide room which took up most of the front of the house. Big picture windows claimed the bulk of the front wall, and Bond had noticed that the door through which Eddie had gone led to some kind of lobby. He had glimpsed stairs going to the next floor. 'Where're you keeping the prisoners?' he asked.

'We have a secure room upstairs. It's been like a doctor's operating theatre most of the time. Those guys are slippery as young kids covered with soap . . .'

'So you gave them Soap?'

'We have something better than Soap. Soap's a bit of an anachronism these days. You guys still use it?'

'No, but Soap's what we still call the drugs we *do* use.'

Eddie came charging back into the room, an official-looking piece of paper in his hand. 'There you go, Mac. The Gulfstream's sitting there waiting for you. Pete's going to drive you and bring back the pair of minders; and for heaven's sake, make sure that plane comes straight back to Geneva for us.'

'Consider it done, Eddie. See you later.' He raised a hand to James as he left the room at speed. A moment later they watched from the picture window as he climbed into the car which swept away down the drive and onto the road back towards town.

'James, Drake says he'd like to do your implant now, if you don't mind.'

'Implant?'

'Your homing device. Won't take a minute, but the sooner it's done the easier it'll be. Take twenty-four to forty-eight hours for the marks to go away.'

Bond nodded, murmuring, 'And on her behind, for the sake of the blind, was the same information in Braille.'

'You what?'

'Last line of a vulgar limerick, Eddie, don't worry about it.'

Drake appeared in the doorway carrying what looked like a

staple gun. 'Down with them, James. I know it looks lethal, but it's very fast. Just a little prick.'

'I know,' he sighed, presenting his rear end to the doctor who swabbed a portion of his right buttock and then put the nose of the gun close to the skin.

In fact, it was just a slight sting, and Drake had a plaster over the insertion point in a second. He said that the plaster should stay on for twenty-four hours, after which the implanted homer would remain in place for around a couple of weeks. 'You'll feel it work its way to the surface of the skin and finally it'll just drop out,' he said.

Prime came in, looking very neat in jeans and a T-shirt, which proclaimed that **Men Should Come With Instructions**.

'Hi, James,' she greeted him as though they were old friends, then passed a single sheet of paper over to Eddie. 'That's it. He's read the thing and promises to stick to it.'

As Eddie scanned the paper, Prime mouthed to Bond that this was the script Kzolowitz was going to read over the telephone to the villa.

'Looks okay to me,' Eddie nodded, glancing at his watch. 'It's almost time for the call.' He frowned. 'Prime, I'd like a wire into his ear so I can feed him lines just in case. You want to come up and see all this in action?'

The two men who had passed themselves off as FBI agents did not look happy. They were shackled to metal chairs which, in turn, were bolted to the floor.

'Okay.' Eddie put the script in front of Kzolowitz. 'This is another fine mess you've gotten us into, Stanley.' It didn't even bring a smile. Stanley looked as miserable as any man can get.

'I'm going to tell you this once and once only. My friend here,' indicating Long who had been baby-sitting the two

223

men, 'he's going to have a rather large .45 Colt automatic in one of your ears when you make this call. There will be a little microphone stuck in your other ear just in case you have to make responses that aren't in the script. I shall be feeding you the right responses. If you deviate by a syllable, Mr Long is going to pull the trigger and the little earpiece will be ruined, together with most of your head. Stanley, we're not kidding about this. We really will kill you.' He turned to look at the other man. 'And you will follow within a second, right? Good. I really don't want any mock heroics because they would be useless. Whatever's going on at the villa's already started. We have a report that the gathering has begun in Pisa and Viareggio for Sunday's big meeting. As that takes place, there will be a nasty accident, I can promise you that. *If* you blow the lid off and they cancel the proceedings, we'll still see that every likely candidate in the area will be arrested. We will also blow the villa and its occupants to pieces. So don't take chances. It's not worth it. You understand me?'

'I want to ask one thing.' His face was the colour of parchment.

'Can't promise to answer, but ask away.'

'You *will* keep to the bargain.'

'What bargain was that?'

'Oh, Christ. The bargain we made. We go back to the States and straight into the witness protection programme. It's gotta be that way. You don't know what these guys're like. They'll get to you in prison, or out.'

'You'll be safe, Stanley. I promise you'll be safe.'

From another room, Prime called out that they had just got the message. 'Beatrice is boarding the launch now. They're telling me there's a bit of an argument about our two friends being missing. They apparently had orders to wait for them.'

By the time she had finished speaking, Long was on the move, bringing in a telephone which he placed in front of the unfortunate Kzolowitz. There was a separate instrument attached to the phone and a line ran out into the hallway. Eddie plugged the earpiece into Kzolowitz's ear, slipped the earphones with a microphone attachment over his head, as Long showed the Colt for the first time.

'I shall be in the hall, out of the line of fire, in case you make a mistake.' Eddie gave Kzolowitz a hard look which spoke of ruthlessness and brutality as yet undreamed of. 'Okay, dial the villa and do your stuff now.'

Bond moved behind Long, and Kzolowitz dialled, his hand shaking badly.

At the distant end, the telephone began to burp out its high-pitched tone. After three rings it was picked up.

'*Pronto*,' Luigi said at the distant end.

'Luigi, it's Stan.'

'Where the hell you been, Stan? The guys just reported you haven't turned up with the da Ricci broad.'

'We had to let her go on, Luigi—'

'Mr Tempesta to you.'

'Okay . . . Okay, Mr Tempesta, but we got problems. That guy you put us all on alert about. The one who took out two of your best people a few years ago . . .'

'You mean that bastard Bond?'

'That's the guy.'

'What about him?'

'We spotted him in Geneva. He didn't get near da Ricci, but we saw him twice. Seemed to be on vacation.'

'At this time of the year? Don't be more stupid than you are already, Stanley. You know where he is now?'

'He's staying at a small hotel. He's there now. What you

want us to do, Lui— Mr Tempesta?'

'Get hold of him. Get hold of him and bring him back here. The Ice Queen has a job for him.' There was a low, and distinctly evil chuckle from Luigi.

'Okay, boss, okay, we'll haul him out now. Any problems we'll call back.'

'Just do it, Stanley. Don't even bother to call back if you don't get him, but keep looking over your shoulder because if you fail on this one you'll be a walking corpse.' He closed the line.

Kzolowitz leaned over and threw up, retching violently.

'Bit of a close call,' Bond said dryly.

21

Antifreeze

THEY WAITED FOR almost two hours before the car, with Pete at the wheel, turned into the driveway. Pete, Bond recognized, was the driver who had brought him from the hotel.

While they waited, Prime and Long busied themselves cleaning up the house, and Eddie sat staring into space.

'Penny for them, Ed?'

'Hey, James. I'm just a tiny bit worried about any leaks. They're tracking Beatrice's homer and she seems to be moving around kinda normally; but I hope to heaven I'm not sending the pair of you in to some kinda ambush.'

Bond nodded. 'Know what you mean, Eddie, but it's a chance we have to take. As you people say, I believe, it goes with the territory. If anything gets crazy early on, I presume Beatrice will hit the Mayday button.'

'She will, and, incidentally, I've decided to move things forward a day as far as the first troop is concerned. The guys will now be in position late on Friday night. That's why I'm anxious to get to Pisa as soon as possible. At least once we're there I can get that fixed up and also make certain one team is standing at the ready as from tonight. Just in case.'

A second car turned into the driveway. 'Good,' from Eddie. 'That's Joe, our other driver.' He raised his voice, 'Okay guys, get the two phonies down here, in shackles. They've got a long flight ahead of them.'

They brought Kzolowitz, and his sidekick – whose real name turned out to be a rather prosaic John Betts – down from the secure room and put them in the lead car with Long who still had his Colt .45 in view.

It took the best part of forty-five minutes to drive out to the airport, where they went through a security checkpoint: the drivers showing authorization passes as they went. For the first time, Bond realized that both cars had tinted windows and the airport security people did not attempt to lean in to see who was inside.

They drew up close to the gangway of an anonymous-looking C-20 Gulfstream III. A young man in grey flannels and smart blazer – obviously FBI acting as a steward – came bounding down the steps to assist Long with the two prisoners, while Eddie remained seated until they were all aboard.

'I want all of us up there and in the aircraft in double-quick time,' Eddie commanded. 'Doc Drake first, then you, James, and you'll find me right behind you. We're pretty well hidden from any possible cameras but I'm not taking no chances.'

Not for the first time, Bond noticed that, in moments of stress, Eddie's grammar seemed to go a shade awry.

Almost before they got into the aircraft, the pilots started the engines, and one of them came on the PA system telling them they would be underway in a matter of minutes as they had immediate clearance. He also gave the flying time to Pisa and added, 'Those of you who will be making the onward flight to Washington DC with us will be pleased to hear that our steward, Michael, will be serving you with a full meal tonight. The rest of you only get coffee for the Pisa leg of the trip.'

It was around nine forty-five when they landed at Pisa.

Long and Prime were going on with the two prisoners, while Doc Drake and Eddie were staying with Bond through the entire operation. Prime even gave Bond a chaste kiss on the cheek as he left. Long shook his hand and they both wished him good luck. Eddie raised his eyebrows when Prime was out of earshot, and remarked that the kiss was a first in his experience.

MacRoberts was waiting for them in the back of a limo, with the partition closed off so that the military driver could not listen in to the conversation.

'They've assured me nobody's got any information out. The senior officers seem to be very conscious of the stealth required,' he began. Then he pointed out the facts. First, nobody except the three troop leaders and the overall commander had known any details concerning *Antifreeze* before they were brought into the special facility which lay at the far side of the airport. 'There are no public telephones, and the troops aren't allowed to use any of the very few official phones. All calls are automatically logged, and must have an explanation of the call noted. It's all computerized, and there can't be any slip-ups.'

'Yeah,' Eddie drawled, 'Nothing can go wrong, go wrong, go wrong.'

However, once they were inside the large barracks building, he seemed to relax, and by the time he had spent an hour with the Commanding Officer – a General Bolletti – he had become even more positive, announcing to the members of his team that one troop was being briefed now and would be on permanent standby within the hour. 'The general tells me they can be airborne in a matter of five minutes. If you look outside, you'll see the two converted RC-12M aircraft just a spit away. These guys're on the ball.'

Bond was given a room to himself, up on the second floor, and, while the place was run on a strict military basis, he was kept apart from the troops, except for one viewing when he was paraded in front of the entire force so they would be able to recognize him in the field.

This was done on the following morning, after which Eddie and one of the troop commanders had a long discussion regarding Bond's infiltration. They decided that a HALO (High Altitude Low Opening) jump was too risky. The DZ was limited, and they would be flying relatively close to high ground which swept up from the back of the Villa Tempesta, climbing rapidly once past the more or less flat open land behind the villa into which the first troop would now be moving, on foot, in the early hours of Friday morning.

Beatrice had been told when to expect him to parachute in – mainly so that she could set the misdirection whizz-bang in the boathouse – and the young pilot assigned to the task was the one who made the ultimate suggestion. He was convinced that he could reach the end of the lake, above the area close to Puccini's house, at around ten thousand feet. Then, he told them, he could cut the engine of the little Cessna he was going to fly, and so glide noiselessly over the lake, arriving silently over the DZ at around eight hundred feet. This would make for an accurate jump which would put Bond right on target.

During the rest of the week a lot of time was spent discussing what he should take in with him – apart from the electronic Mayday flashers. They wanted him to wear a wet suit in case he was forced into the water, but he vetoed this in favour of a normal jump suit. He also demanded comfortable canvas shoes, not military style boots. As for arms he was concerned only with taking his own automatic pistol and four extra magazines – one lightly taped to the butt for speed loading. He also chose the old style Sykes-Fairburn commando dagger because it was the one with which he was most familiar and expert. Against Eddie's advice, he refused grenades, flash-bangs, smoke or any other explosives. 'I think the Italian lads will have enough to go around – if we get that far.'

Once this had been settled, he spent the remaining days alternating between resting and taking violent exercise in the gymnasium, which was cleared for him at certain times of day. He worried a little, not so much about the upcoming operation, but for Beatrice, even though each morning and evening the FBI people told him that she appeared to be moving about the villa and estate perfectly normally.

Late on the Thursday morning, the troop that would be in the field behind the house, left by helicopter to be taken to the vantage point from which they could reach the DZ by the early hours of Friday. Once there, and safely hidden they would send back regular reports. The first of these came on the Friday morning, with the news that a team of caterers had been brought into the villa by the lake.

Looking at the report, Eddie said, 'Seems they're getting themselves ready for one heckuva big party. Plenty of booze and lots of stuff to eat – from the soup to the nuts.'

'Ask them if it looks as though the caterers are staying on, or leaving waiters behind.'

When the afternoon report came in, it appeared that the caterers had left and everything was being kept in refrigerators. Bond recalled that the kitchen and cooking area seemed to be at the back of the house, so he presumed that the troops were getting in very close with binoculars.

The Cessna took off at just a little before one in the morning, and at one forty-five his pilot gave him the thumbs-up, cutting his engine at just over ten thousand feet and starting to glide down in a long spiral towards the area of the villa.

Bond watched the altimeter unwinding and at two thousand feet he slid back the door on the right hand side, the pilot using a lot of rudder to maintain control with the wind buffeting inside the cockpit.

They had maintained radio silence so now the pilot yelled a good luck at him, telling him to watch for the Morse Code flash from the DZ. Bond nodded and climbed halfway out onto the wing strut.

Just as he saw the light glimmer up ahead, he was also aware of a larger flash and thud from the direction of the boathouse. Beatrice was doing her work. He peered into the darkness until he saw the pinpoint of light almost directly beneath him. Then he pushed off and felt that old, wonderful tingle as he fell, arms and legs outstretched, into the darkness below. He pulled the cord almost straight away, still enjoying what he usually thought of as one of the ultimate highs, dropping unfettered towards an earth he could not see. The jerk on his harness seemed only a light pull, and when he peered upwards, he could not even see his canopy which was matt black for this night jump.

A whole series of memories flickered across his mind: night jumps when the ground had come up sooner than estimated; night jumps when he had hit turbulence and started to oscillate almost out of control. Tonight it was picture-perfect: he was able to judge his angle of descent; spill air from the canopy; he felt the ground effect as soon as it was close, and broke his speed, landing lightly on his feet, running as the canopy came down around him, unclipping his harness and letting it fall away. He almost missed the shadow of the man who ran in from his hiding place to bundle up the parachute and drag it off out of sight.

He stood for a moment, quite still, smelling the air, feeling a cool breeze off the lake. The misdirection appeared to have worked, for there were shouts coming from the far side of the house, down by the water.

He was almost able to see now, so he set off, quietly and not too fast, towards the left hand side of the line of trees, which he had yet to find, but knew were there. Five minutes later he was directly in front of them and making his way, as silently as possible, through the branches and undergrowth.

He came out on the other side, and felt, rather than saw, someone else close by. He whispered low, 'Red Fox?' and felt his heart leap as he heard the soft reply, 'Grey Fox?'

She was nearer than he thought, and he reached her in less than two full strides, feeling her hand close on his as she led him quickly past what he knew must be the greenhouse, and on to a door which she opened, not switching on the light until it was closed behind them.

After the embrace which went on for a considerable time, she took him through the pin-neat little room into a small kitchen. Bond stopped for a moment. 'No bedroom?' he asked.

'The couch converts into a bed,' she whispered. 'But we've got a problem. They've moved me back into the house.'

'Ah. Right. Is everything else okay?'

'They've been very active tonight,' she was still whispering. 'I don't know what's going on.'

'Well, there's the briefing on Sunday and some kind of party later today.'

'Yes, but there *is* definitely something else going on. A woman arrived . . .'

'I know. A dead woman arrived.'

'What . . .?'

He told her about Sukie; that he had virtually seen her killed

233

yet here she was, as though raised from the dead, and welcomed back to her stepsons' villa with a lot of excitement.

She looked bewildered, dumbstruck, and as she stood there looking at him, there was a sudden thundering at the door: a banging and a rattling as someone tried to open up.

'Stay here.' She put a hand to her lips and called out that she was coming.

He heard the door being opened, felt the ASP in his hand, with the safety off, nose down, two-handed grip. James Bond, ready for anything, he thought.

'I am Kauffburger. They send me from the house. I have to look around. They got some maniac on the loose, I think.'

There was a little cry from Beatrice. It was enough, Bond threw open the kitchen door and stepped out, to find his pistol pointing at a huge barrel-chested man with a mop of thick blond hair, a mouth full of gold teeth, hands the size of pitchforks, and eyes which almost looked red.

'Stay just where you are!' he said, the pistol pointing directly at this monster's chest. Then—

'Well, if it isn't my dear old friend Bond, James Bond,' Sukie Tempesta said, stepping out from behind Kauffburger. 'Down, boy.' She patted the huge man almost playfully. 'James, I'm so glad you dropped in. You're just the man I wanted. I've a job for you. You see, I'm getting married tomorrow and I can't think of anyone nicer to give me away.'

22

Die Like a Gentleman

'OH, PUT THE gun away, James. Don't be foolish,' Sukie continued, as the huge man who was Kauffburger took a pace forward. He had the face of an idiot child, the kind of inbred relic you used to find in rural areas, places where incest still thrived among small, lonely communities.

He felt his finger take up the pressure on the trigger, then, with alarming speed, Kauffburger was on him, one hand crushing like a vice around his right wrist, twisting and causing a sharp burst of unbearable pain as the gun fell from his fingers.

'Guns is dangerous,' Kauffburger's voice was a deep monotone, slow and searching as though he genuinely had to call up the words from his brain before they would form a sentence. 'Shouldn't play with guns. They can hurt people. I know that 'cause when I was little kid I played with my Daddy's gun and it went off. Killed my baby brother. We had to put him in the ground 'cause he was deader 'n a doornail.' The man's big foot made a small movement and the gun skittered across the floor.

Bond, massaging his wrist, looked at Beatrice who glanced back, her eyes asking if she should hit the Mayday button? He simply moved his own eyes from left to right, signalling 'No' without turning his head.

'You're dead,' he said, looking straight at Sukie.

'I know. It's wonderful being dead. You can move across frontiers and go all over the place with a new name. But now I'm about to come into my true inheritance.'

Bond recalled meeting her in the hotel at Dulles International, and the strange way she had acted at times. There had been something very odd about her then. Out of the corner of his eye, he saw Kauffburger leering at Beatrice, and Sukie spoke sharply to him, telling him to back off.

'How did you manage that trick? Getting yourself blown up with a car bomb?' He forced his voice to come out in a relaxed slow drawl, drawing attention to the fact that he was not in any way concerned about his situation.

Sukie Tempesta laughed. She had altered terribly, her hair dyed almost frost-white, her eyes narrow and speaking of a kind of madness. 'You almost spoiled all that, James Bond. I had two reasons for being at Dulles. The first you can probably guess . . .'

He suddenly knew what she meant. 'Flight DB 299.' He said it aloud, not really thinking about it, yet once more seeing the horror as he had done first in M's office: the big jet touching down, then the flowering death, spurting flame and smoke leaping from inside the Boeing 747-400, scattering burning remains of both aircraft and passengers along the runway.

Sukie was speaking again, and it came out like a voice-over on the screen of his mind which reran the vivid images that had been the start of all this. 'Yes,' she said. 'Yes, I had the remote. You know the security at Dulles is rather poor. I stood there inside the building and watched as the plane came in. I had the remote in my pocket and they told me that it had a range of almost three miles. I could have sat in a coffee shop and done it, but I wanted to make certain. There was this man, you see . . .'

Once more he saw the slyness in her eyes, more prominent now than it had been in the Dulles hotel. 'I know all about Julian Carter,' he said.

'Clever you. He was a blackmailer, James. He deserved to die.'

'With all those innocent people?'

She gave a vulpine grin. 'Well, there was that, of course, but you see, we wanted to bankrupt Bradbury, and we did. What happened to him by the way? You never hear anything about Harley Bradbury these days.'

'He's making a come-back, actually. Some people are like that, they drop to rock bottom and then claw their way back.'

'Good for old Harley. I suppose we should have killed him off like the others, but Luigi organized things so that he wasn't even on that plane.'

Keep her talking, he thought. While she was talking, Sukie seemed to be in a dream world, reliving old triumphs. 'So you were the button lady for DB 299. You said you came to Dulles for two reasons.' He took half a step towards her, but Kauffburger moved over and gave him a slight push in the chest. A slight push from Kauffburger had him reeling back to the wall behind. 'That man doesn't know his own strength.'

Sukie was taking no notice, still off on a monologue of her own. 'Yes, and you nearly messed up the whole thing, James. I actually had a room at that hotel. One there and one at the other place – the Hilton. I got the fright of my life when you came waltzing in. Though I'd never ruled you out. Carried that nice little forged note from you for a long time. Good, wasn't it? You had to be turned to my advantage though. I quickly realized that. You would be a first-class witness of my terrible death. Clever of me, I think.'

'Very clever, Sukie. You came up to my room and played games.'

'Nice games, James – as long as a girl doesn't take you too seriously.' She shifted her eyes to look at Beatrice. 'I do hope you don't take this man too seriously, my dear. He's your basic sexist: gathers himself cherries while he may, then when he's had his fill, he just leaves the ladies feeling lonely and used.' He heard her in the past, at their last meeting, bounding nervously from subject to subject, her mind out of control.

Beatrice stiffened and gave Sukie a look of contempt. 'I've known James for a long time, and I've always found him to be a complete gentleman. What he does with girls is always fair play. I reckon every female who's been with him has done that of her own choosing – even you, Principessa. I bet you didn't say no to him. I didn't, and I had enough good sense to work it out. I knew the score. But, then, I'm lucky because he came back to me, and I think he's probably here to stay.'

'Oh, he's here to stay all right. You're here to stay as well, Beatrice. You've both earned the death sentence, I should imagine, and it'll be carried out: quite soon if you don't co-operate. Tomorrow night if you decide to go along with what I shall propose.'

'Sukie, how did you do it?' Bond asked again.

'Do what? Oh, my death and incineration. Yes, well . . . Yes, I came to do the airliner first. Then I was going to get myself killed. Your sudden appearance, James, *was* turned to my advantage as you now know.' The sly child stirring deep in her eyes.

She went on talking until the whole story was out. She had stayed in the hotels near Washington Dulles International for ten days prior to being the trigger for the Bradbury Airlines disaster. During that time she shuttled between the two places, alternating nights at each and looking for the perfect victim. 'It had to be somebody roughly my build and age,' she told them, and she had found the perfect young woman at the Hilton. 'She was Mexican, just a smidgen younger than me, but who was counting?'

Sukie had become friendly with the girl, who worked as a chambermaid on the floor where Sukie's room was situated. 'I could see that she'd be easy. She had that look. You know, the look that says "Why should she have it all? Why has she got money? Why can't I get a better job and make more than they pay me here?" I played her like a fish, James. You would've been proud of me.'

'I wonder.'

Eventually, Sukie had offered her a job in Italy as her personal maid, at a ludicrous salary. Nothing would be difficult. She would love it in Italy – especially with all that money. She could get the visa and work permit in no time. 'And of course she fell for it. Yes, she said. When can I leave, she said.

'I told her there was no time like the present, and she handed in her notice. The management were not pleased, especially when she came to work for me the next day, all tarted up in good clothes – clothes that I had bought her.

'Luigi sent someone in to do the car. There was a little switch, under the dash. All I had to do was flick it on and fifteen minutes later the whole thing would go up. It would take one telephone call to Luigi's man and he'd be round at the back of the hotel to pick me up. It went like clockwork. She had a driving licence and I'd already checked her out in the car.

'When I left you, James, I went straight back to the hotel and told her to meet me at the back entrance. I got the bell boys to put my luggage in the car. I'd changed my handbag and threw the one you'd already seen into the front passenger seat.

'The rest was simple. I tipped magnificently, drove around the block and then shot up to the back of the hotel. Carlotta was waiting – that was her name, Carlotta. I told her to take the car over to the other hotel where you were waiting for me – no doubt expectantly, James.'

'Go on.'

'I activated the bomb as I got out and she drove off to her destiny. Luigi's man was waiting for me and he drove me to National where I took a flight to New York under another name – with all the right papers and things, of course. But you know about stuff like that, don't you, James? I spent time in Paris, in the South of France, all over the place. Having occasional meetings, of course, because the plans were well advanced by then.' She gave a very nasty high-pitched laugh. 'And now we're on the verge of doing everything we planned. I think it would be a good idea if you took me up on my offer. Give me away tomorrow, James – I mean today, of course. Today's my wedding day, can you believe it? Give me away and I'll see to it that you both live until tomorrow night, after you've heard all that's going to happen next month.

'We're going to change the world, my dear. We're going to do away with crime and the violence of the streets. We will own the United States and we'll really see the American Dream. It's all going to happen. Tough on crime – oh, very tough on crime, summary execution if you're caught with dope on you; your thing cut off for rape; hands severed for theft and slow lingering deaths for murder. It'll take a few months, but it's what the people really want, isn't it? Safety. The country working again, self-sufficient, making everything we need. Utterly isolationist. Eventually the world will come to heel because they won't have a market in the good old US of A, will they?'

'Who are you marrying, Sukie? Who's going to be your husband?'

She did a little capering dance, giggling, her mind out of touch with reality. 'I am going to be the joint leader of COLD – you know about COLD, James?'

'Just about everything.'

'Well, they call me the Ice Queen – one of my code names – and he will be the Ice King. I'll have to argue for you to be spared, but I think he'll see the irony. After all, James, you were responsible for the fact that he now walks on prosthetic legs; and for the disfigurement. His poor face. They say the plastic surgery will eventually bring him back to near normal, but it's taking a long time. It was you, wasn't it, James? It was you who shot my lovely General Brutus Clay out of the skies?' Her face seemed to alter, becoming pinched, any beauty washed away: the eyes hard like granite chips, iced over with her particular brand of lunacy.

'You're marrying . . .' He was about to say, 'that killer!' but he just stopped himself in time. 'Congratulations, Sukie. You're marrying a legend.'

'I know, isn't it wonderful?'

'Marvellous. Yes, of course, I'll give you away.'

She began capering around again. Bond wondered what had collapsed her mind – turned her from being a poised, intelligent and beautiful young woman into this caricature. The signs had all been there at their last meeting, yet he had not taken them into account.

'Come,' she said finally. 'I think we should all go over to the house. Something was going on tonight. There was some kind of explosion, and my dear stepsons were alarmed. They're so proud of the marriage.'

'Really?'

'Of course, really. They're ecstatic. Come.'

She led the way, opening the door for Kauffburger who held Bond and Beatrice by the scruff of their necks, almost lifting them off the ground as he hurried them along. Sukie kicked the door closed after them. Bond watched carefully. His automatic pistol was still lying on the cottage floor, with the spare magazine attached to it.

The house was now a blaze of light and Sukie pushed past Kauffburger and his two prisoners, heading to a door which took them into the kitchen area towards the entrance hallway that Bond remembered from his last violent visit to this place.

'Hey! Hey! Anybody! Look what I've found!' Sukie was moving ahead, shouting as she went. The first people they saw were Luigi and Angelo, flanked by bodyguards as they came down the stairs.

'So, the ubiquitous Mr Bond,' Luigi positively purred.

'And here without an invitation.' Angelo joined his brother. 'Drop them, Kauffburger.'

Kauffburger was nothing if not literal. He simply let go of Beatrice and Bond, sending them sprawling onto the floor.

'Being here without an invitation means that you are trespassing, and you know what happens to trespassers, Mr Bond? Trespassers will be shot.'

'Not until I've had some time with him.' The gravel gruff voice came from the top of the stairs.

Sukie shrieked. 'Brutie! Oh Brutie, don't come down yet. It's Saturday. You mustn't see your bride before the ceremony. Please, please stay out of sight. I need to talk to you.'

General Brutus Brute Clay chuckled, low in the register: a sinister, repellent series of little laughs. 'I'll stay out of sight, my darling girl, until you've made yourself scarce. Tell me when I can come down, for I'm very anxious to see this Mr Bond.'

'I'm not going until I've asked you an important question. I've made a decision about the wedding service. A slight change in arrangements and I want you to give it your blessing.'

'My blessing is certainly better than my cursing. Come on, then. What is it you want?'

'Well . . .' she stood on one leg, the other foot lifted from the floor and turned back against her calf: a stance that reminded Bond of a stork, or a small child. It was her near-vicious childishness that brought out a feeling of pity in him.

'Well . . .' she began again.

'Come on, woman! Out with it!' Clay spoke quietly, though the words sounded commanding.

'I just thought of a beautiful irony, Brutie. I would like Mr Bond to give me away at the ceremony.'

'I'm giving you away,' Luigi yelled.

'Stop!' This time, Clay did shout, a military bark from upstairs. 'It is Sukie's day. Today, her wedding day. Her idea is good. As she says, it has a nice touch of irony. Certainly he shall give you away, my dear. Then, when the guests have gone . . .' His voice dropped, dripping honey, '. . . Before we partake of the joys of our nuptial night . . . Well, let's wait and see what's for the best.'

'No! No! One minute, Brutie. I thought of a greater irony. How would it be if we kept him, like a pet? I think he should know of what is about to happen to the world. First he should give me away; then he should remain here and listen to your briefing on Sunday, which will be masterful. After that, well, you must do what you like with him, and his trollop Beatrice. Say yes, Brutie.'

'It has an even more ironic twist. Mind you, I would really prefer to shoot him now: slowly, first his feet, then the knees, hands, elbows and so on, taking my time about it.' There was a pause during which they heard a long, noisy intake of breath. 'But perhaps we'll find some other purpose for them. Who knows, they could make a good pair of hostages.'

'You can do whatever you like with them, Brutie.'

The whole thing made Bond feel physically sick when he remembered how this lovely young woman used to be. Seeing her, and hearing her, reduced to a wild crazed woman made him feel a great anguish on her behalf. Had she, in fact, always been mad, bad, dangerous to know? It was quite possible that her symptoms were only brought to the fore when she was close to the Tempesta family, or assisting them. In their short time together in the past she could easily have hidden the psychological fissures.

'Anything? Yes, let it be like this. He'll give you away; he'll stay for the briefing on Sunday; then we'll make up our minds about him – and his trollop, as you call her. Now, I'm coming down, Sukie, so get away unless you want our marriage to be built on bad luck.'

She gave a little squeak and ran with tiny little steps, to the door leading to the back of the house. As she reached it, she turned and called directly to Bond. 'It's all very easy. I died like a lady, James. I only hope, when the time comes, you can die like a gentleman.'

There was movement from the top of the stairs.

23

Wedding Bells

THE TALL FIGURE came thudding slowly down the stairs, stiff-legged, rolling at each tread, grunting occasionally. It was like watching a robot as the man he had last seen in the strange graveyard in Idaho negotiated his way down to the hall.

Worse was to come as he turned, standing feet apart to keep his balance, to look at Beatrice and Bond. The effect was so horrific that Beatrice gave a little cry.

General Brutus Clay's face seemed to be made up of partly-hanging flaps of skin. The top of his head was a crinkle of skin, the flaps coming down from his forehead and joined to his jaw. There were four misshapen holes where there had once been eyes, nose and mouth, though parts of these features were discernible: the glint of eyes moving behind the layers of skin, a nostril rebuilt with part of the nose, and a gaping oval which moved, like the mouth of a ventriloquist's dummy, as he spoke. Where the ears had been there were now two little knobs, like small shells.

'Take a good look, Mr James von Richthofen Bond. Take a very good look, because this is what you did to me when you played ring-a-roses around that damned mountainside. One day I'll have a reasonable face, but it will take years of surgery and eons of pain for me. However, I have a woman who loves me, and a great future, as you will hear tomorrow. For now, I just want you to look and ponder on what can happen to anyone. Mr Bond, I can promise you nothing but an eventual very slow death. When, how and where is another matter. Because my bride is – how can I put it – a little simple: not the woman she once was, I will be kind to your woman. She might even live – a pleasant asset as a relaxing aid for those who work under me. She could work well under them.'

His head turned, in a jerky movement, towards Luigi and Angelo with their little knot of bodyguards. 'I would be obliged if you would search these two now, and take care. Remove everything from them that could be classified as a weapon. I've known and respected men like Bond before, and one thing I know about them: they have a way of disguising even the most normal of objects.'

The men descended on them and began frisking them – in Beatrice's case it was more a matter of groping rather than patting down. They had Bond's commando dagger, the spare magazines for the ASP, and everything else from him quickly enough. They even took the pen; the man who found it tossed the little plastic item to Kauffburger who grasped it as though he had just been handed the most expensive Mont Blanc fountain pen. He all but grovelled in front of the thug.

'Now,' Luigi sounded utterly deflated, and was obviously very angry at the General stealing his thunder and allowing Bond to play at being father of the bride. 'Now, take them up to Beatrice's room. Remove anything there with which they can arm themselves, and lock the door.' He turned to look straight at Beatrice, 'You've probably already realized, Ms da Ricci, that your new room is escape-proof. You cannot have failed to notice the bars on the windows, and the fact that your door is made of steel. Just behave yourself, and please, the pair of you, don't try anything stupid. I would love to have the opportunity of overriding the General's orders.'

They were hustled up the stairs, along a wide passage until they reached the back of the house and a door set into a steel framework. As the three men were opening the door to push their captives inside, Angelo called after them. 'Because I wish for my stepmother's wedding to be good and a proper ceremony, I'll see if we can find a morning suit to fit Bond.'

'Fly me back to London and I'll pick up my own,' he shouted back.

They were pushed together on the bed, and one of the men covered them with a pistol while the other two went through the cupboards, drawers and dressing table. They piled things they thought of as possible weapons into a trash bag and, after half an hour of searching, seeming satisfied, leaving, turning the key in the lock behind them.

Beatrice, threw her arms around him and wept quietly on his shoulder. 'James . . .?' she began with a sob.

'Don't. You should already know the room is almost certainly bugged.' He got off the bed and did a long search, looking mainly for any sign of fibre optic cables from which pictures could be captured. After a long inspection he decided that they were only pulling in sound. He went over to the dressing table, seeing, to his surprise, that they had left the telephone pad and pencil in place. He looked for the lipstick with the electronics for sending the Mayday signal, but could not see it so he mimed to her, asking if she had the thing.

She shook her head and he scowled grimly. Carrying the pad and pencil over to her, he sat down and began to write:

We haven't got the lipstick or the pen, but we still have the belts. I think we should wait it out and signal tomorrow. If you really cannot bear that, I shall send the signal now. I love you.

She smiled and took the pad and pencil from him:

But will you love me tomorrow, James? Yes, with you I can get through everything, and, of course, we must wait. What do you make of the mad stepmother? Incidentally, I've always loved you.

He took the pad and wrote:

Good, we'll do something about that when we get back to London. In the meantime, try and rest. If anything goes terribly wrong, just activate the Mayday. I shall do the same. As for the stepmother, she's obviously cracked – a sociopath, possibly a paranoid schizophrenic as well. My guess is that her stepsons and the General became aware of her weaknesses and then played on them. Motive? Money, the family and whatever this crazy plan happens to be.

She responded with:

Are we going to get back to London?

He only just stopped himself from writing 'Cross my heart and hope to die.' Instead he simply scribbled:

Of course.

They were both tired and soon dropped off to sleep, wakened only by the rattle of the key in the door and the entrance of Luigi and two of his men. They carried a morning suit, shirt, cufflinks, tie, socks and shoes.

Rarely was he shy in front of Beatrice, but on this occasion, with other men present, he felt decidedly embarrassed as he stripped to his underpants and tried on the clothing they had brought.

Beatrice did not make it any easier by commenting that his blue boxers went well with his eyes, but even Bond, fastidious about matters of dress, had to admit that the morning suit was a perfect fit and could have been made for him.

'How did you do so well with the fit?' he asked Luigi.

'Not me. Saul here. He used to work for an undertaker. He can work out anyone's measurements at a glance.'

'Ask a stupid question.' He grimaced at Beatrice.

'You gotta 'nour,' Saul told them in his best English.

Bond turned with a smile to Beatrice. 'Well, my darling, what are you going to wear?'

'I'm changing in the bathroom, dear.' She gave him a sly little grin.

'Leave the door open.' Pause. 'Please.'

A little less than an hour later they were both ready with Beatrice asking again and again if he thought the hat was okay with the suit. The suit, as it happened, looked as if it were a genuine Chanel – and probably was.

'You are certain about the hat?' she asked again as the heavy mob turned up at the door.

This time it was Roberto in charge, and his English was three shades better than Saul's. 'You godda stay wid us,' he began.

'Did you live in New York for long?' Bond asked, then, turning to Beatrice said yes, the hat was perfect.

'I lived out in Joisey. I was lookin' after dis guy who needed looking after.'

'How did you find that out?'

'He got whacked. Some junky whacked him wid a nine mil piece, just as he was getting outa da car. His own fault. I always tell him, wait for me before ya ged outa the car.'

'Must look pretty bad on your résumé.'

'Excuse me?'

'Your CV, your record.'

'I ain't got no record.'

'I mean your employment record.'

'No, looks pretty good ashly. I whacked the guy right dere on de spot. Took his head clean off. Had a permit as well. De cops couldn't hang a thing on me.'

'You were saying we had to stay with you?'

'Sure. Beatrice here, she stays wid Enrico. You stay wid me. No stoopid tricks else I take *your* head off, okay?'

'I'll be very well behaved.'

'Good. Now da boss says you can stay on for a while at the reception, only ya gotta be handcuffed ta me, right?'

'As rain.'

'That means "yes" in Brit talk?'

'Affirmative.'

They arrived at the top of the stairs and Roberto whispered. 'I like you, Mr Bond. Look, ya gotta unnerstand this is nothin' personal. It's all business.'

'Isn't it always?'

'Tell me about it.'

People were arriving in motor launches and passing through the main hallway, heading for the stairs which descended into the ballroom.

'We godda go in here.' Roberto tapped at a door. There was a flurry of noise and little female shrieks from inside. Then the door was opened by Giulliana, Luigi's wife. 'Mr Bond,' she smiled at him and spoke with a throatiness. 'You bastard. I heard you were here. Too bad you can't stay. Come in.'

Angelo's wife, Maria, did not even look at him, but Sukie's face broke into a big smile. She was in white with a lot of lace and frills.

'You look wonderful, Sukie.'

'It's nice, isn't it?' She smiled at him. The smile seemed to engulf him and he felt desolate about what had happened to her. 'Giulliana and Maria are my matrons of honour.'

'I suspected as much.'

Then Angelo appeared in the doorway. 'Right on time, Sukie, your bridegroom awaits.'

'Ready?' Bond asked and she gave him a little smile, bit her lower lip and put the veil down over her face.

'On with the motley, then.' Bond offered his arm and they set off towards the ballroom which had miraculously become a church. The windows were fake, of course, because there were no real windows, but these were good fakes. The wedding guests filled the huge room, row upon row of them. An altar with flickering candles stood at the end of what passed as the aisle, a priest stood in readiness, dressed in cassock, surplice and stole, holding a breviary and signing for the General and his best man to rise as the bride was about to enter.

The Tempestas were doing the whole thing in style, for an organ began to pipe up the wedding march. They began the stately walk towards the priest, doing it the American way with a pause at each step, the matrons of honour throwing rose petals out of little baskets in front of the bride. 'So she can slip on one and break her neck,' Bond thought, looked up and saw the terrible face of General Brutus Clay, the oval that was his mouth skewed in what was meant to be a smile.

The service was slow and long, with four hymns and a short sermon – in Italian – by the priest, who had obviously been brought in specially for the day as he looked slightly confused.

As soon as it was over and the happy couple were headed up the aisle, Roberto materialized beside Bond, swiftly slipping a handcuff on his right wrist, then onto Bond's left wrist. He grinned and said, 'We godda keep yer right arm free for da embibin', okay? Good word, em-bibe.'

'I think it's a very good word, but I also think it's pronounced imbibing.'

'Really?'

The whole of the main floor of the house had been turned into one giant cocktail party, and the newlyweds greeted everyone at the door.

'Sorry I haven't brought you a present, my dear Sukie, but this was a shade unexpected,' he greeted her.

'You gave me the best present of all, James. You gave me away. That's what you do very well.'

'Yes, I suppose so.'

'Hey, Mr B, let's get wid de champagne, huh?'

'Yes, let's do that.' He was looking forward to Roberto doing his 'embibin'. In fact, as he toured the house, shackled to Roberto like the Count of Monte Cristo chained to his dungeon wall, Bond positively pressed champagne onto Roberto. Not only champagne, but champagne cocktails – with a large amount of brandy.

He caught sight of Beatrice, looking as though she were being dragged reluctantly around the party, and winked at her. By this time the drinks were beginning to take their toll, and Roberto was the best friend he ever had. 'Hot in here, isn't it?' Roberto slurred at him.

'Why don't we take a stroll in the garden, Roberto? I think you need some air.' He needed more than air for he threw up in the rose garden, and staggered very unsteadily in the direction of the greenhouse. At one point they narrowly missed getting sprayed by one of the water tricks. Eventually Robert ended up in a heap, with the help of a sharp chopping blow to the back of his neck.

The keys were in the man's waistcoat pocket and Bond had the cuff off his wrist very quickly. In all it was off for around twenty seconds, allowing him just enough time to get into Beatrice's cottage, scoop his ASP automatic and the spare magazine from the floor, slip it into the back of his trousers and return to the cuffed position.

So far so good, he thought. He pulled a dead-weight Roberto back to the rose garden and then called for help, which arrived in the shape of two of the other staff, guns drawn.

Angelo was sent for. 'Nearly threw up over my shoes,' Bond remarked, and Angelo was within an ace of apologizing. 'I think we should get you back to your room,' was his only comment. At the door he said he would have Beatrice brought up, and would see that they got some of the left-over sandwiches and cakes. 'We need the suit back as well,' he leered.

Aloud, Bond said, 'As if I were going to take it anywhere.'

Beatrice was back within the half hour, by which time, Bond had changed into his own shirt, the jump suit and trainers. He greeted her happily from his prone position on the bed.

'My feet are killing me.' Beatrice hobbled over, sat down, and pried her feet from the offending shoes.

He smiled at her. 'I suggest we have a nice evening in. Quiet, you know? Look what I found.' He lifted a pillow to give her a quick flash of the pistol.

'How . . .?'

'My guide, comforter and friend got very drunk and passed out. Shouldn't be surprised if drink is his undoing.'

24

A Day of Days

TWO OF THE toughs brought trays piled with sandwiches and cakes, plus a bottle of wine. They also removed the morning suit. They even wished them goodnight – in Italian.

The prisoners ate, drank and talked about the wedding, mainly for the benefit of anyone listening in from the bugs, making catty remarks about some of the guests. Then, for a long time, they made love. 'That black doesn't really go with your eyes,' he said as he undressed her, getting his own back for her remarks about his underwear when he had changed into the morning suit.

They made love again later, then dropped down the long tunnel towards sleep.

'How wonderful a day for you.' Brutus Clay stood at the foot of the bed, and, for a second, they both thought they had plunged into a nightmare as they looked up at this weird thing, with its flaps of healing flesh and half nose, the eyes sunken into the head behind two ragged holes in the skin; the fish mouth moving unnaturally.

'I'd give anything for a day like this. Your day of days. A day when you know, with absolute certainty, that you are going to hear the massive extent of our plans for a new world which you may or may not be around to enjoy or appreciate. The briefing

255

starts in an hour. My people are arriving at this very moment. So, until later.' He gave a mock bow and stumped slowly to the door, stiff-legged.

'This is it, then.' Bond gave her a long and loving hug. 'I'd wear simple clothes, jeans and things. Just use your common sense and don't precipitate matters too quickly. Keep calm.'

'And if we're separated?'

'Play it by ear.'

They showered together and dressed. Bond retrieved his automatic pistol and pushed it down hard into his waistband, behind his right hip.

Two of the Tempesta bodyguards – Tomaso and Enrico – arrived slightly less than an hour later.

'You don' needa da handcuffs this time,' one of them said. 'The peoples down there, they gotta plenty guns.'

They were preparing to leave the room when Tomaso spoke sharply, telling Bond and Beatrice to spread their arms and legs, place their hands wide upon the wall and assume the classic position for a search.

'What's dis?' Tomaso's hand reached the butt of the pistol wedged into Bond's waistband. 'Hey, Mr Bond, we're not allowed da weapons. Dis is-a very naughty. Not allowed.' He tucked the gun into his own belt, leaving Bond with a feeling of nakedness.

They were led from the room, down the stairs, to the lowest level – to the ballroom. The church had disappeared. Instead, the chairs had been rearranged into a large semi-circle set in front of a raised dais. The room was alive with the buzz of conversation from the fifty or so men present. They were mainly built in the same mould: mostly tall and rangy, with complexions that spoke of long days spent outside in the open air. If you saw any of these men in public places, next to you in a restaurant, or standing in line in a supermarket, you would tag them as former soldiers – veterans of recent past wars. Some of them, Bond noted, wore sidearms.

The bodyguards led them to the back row, seated them together, flanking them. One or two of the men turned around and looked at them, their eyes wary and suspicious.

Beatrice flicked her eyes towards a high mirror running along the wall to their right. She moved, raising her lips to his ear. 'Push it from this end and it'll slide back, okay?' It was the mirror through which they had originally intended to view what was going on in the ballroom.

Enrico snapped, 'Silencio.'

'Oh, shut up.' Bond was in no mood to be badgered by these creeps. By now he was filled with a dreadful anxiety. The people around them all looked like hard fighters, and in his mind he could see that a pitched battle with the Leatherheads could easily go either way. The assault on the Villa Tempesta could end up with many of these people getting away, and their plan – whatever it was – going into operation. This was not how he imagined it: a pushover for those whom he regarded as being on the side of the angels.

They had been in the ballroom for less than five minutes when there was a stir and Brutus Clay entered, walking the length of the room, decked out in battledress showing a chest full of medal ribbons, and the three stars on his shoulder tabs which marked him out as a general.

Everyone shuffled to their feet and began to applaud as Clay walked to the dais. He made motions with his hands for them to sit down. The noise finally stopped as the General waited for silence which came very quickly.

'Welcome,' Clay began. 'We thought long and hard about where to hold this final briefing and came to the conclusion that we should call you – my most important officers – to this place, which is far from the prying eyes and ears of those who might prove difficult. I think it is safe to say that here, in this beautiful villa, is the last place they would expect to find us.

'Speaking of the villa, I have to thank our good friends, Luigi and Angelo Tempesta, who have not only allowed us to meet here, but also have provided us with the bulk of our weapons for the forthcoming operation. They also suggested the way you should make this trip – coming under the guise of three coach tours. I trust you have enjoyed the visits you have made en route. Just as I hope your wives have a pleasant day today, seeing the local sights under the guidance of Luigi's and Angelo's wives.' He paused, looking around the room before continuing.

'You're all aware that I'm not yet back to being my handsome self,' Clay began, setting off a ripple of laughter. 'I think it is only fair to tell you that the man who did this to me is here in this room, the man who caused my helicopter to crash. I'm lucky to be alive, and some of you already know that my pilot got me out, minus my legs and with my face almost destroyed. The killer's name is Bond and he's sitting at the back. James, why don't you show yourself? Stand up.'

Slowly, he got to his feet to a horrific barrage of boos and hisses. 'Sit down again, man,' Clay commanded. 'It will not surprise you when I say this man, and his accomplice, are my hostages and, as such, may well come in very useful.'

Applause, and Bond whispered, 'Author! Author!' Beatrice smiled, but looked very pale and uncertain. The point now, he thought, was to time the Mayday call. He wanted to be in possession of the main facts of COLD's plans before sending

258

out the signal. He also considered the length of time it would take for the counterterrorist force to get on the scene. He presumed the troop up in the field behind the house would hold off until the aircraft appeared, and had started their run-in to drop the remaining two troops. It would have to be a matter of instinct, and he would be the sole judge.

'*Operation Blizzard*,' Clay began, '*Operation Blizzard* is the first step in our overall dedicated strategy to turn our great country around, and put the people back on a course that will lead them to the true American Dream.

'Within days of the first tactical and strategic moves, the people will be behind us, and you all know the indications are that the major law enforcement agencies throughout the country, together with the military – the Army, Navy and Air Force – are considered by our analysts as allies not enemies. So, we must strike quickly and make our aims and claims known to all.

'For this reason *Operation Blizzard* will start on the morning of Christmas Day. The first strikes, which will be massive, are not aimed at killing innocent civilians, most of whom will be gathered around their trees, or watching their children opening their presents.

'Now, I need each of the area commanders to stand and state their targets. We'll go first with New York.'

A big man, with a shaved head and a rough commanding presence got to his feet. 'We've spent a lot of time deciding on targets, sir. The more obvious ones are out as we will need to use them as soon as you take control of the day-to-day running of the country, with the assistance of the President. We have finally decided that our bombs will be set first in the theatre district, around Times Square. As you have pointed out many times, the country has been undermined by radicals and pornographers. We won't be needing the buildings around Times Square for a while.'

'How many bombs?' Clay asked, nodding his pleasure at the choice of targets.

'Three in all, sir, but they'll be big enough to cause considerable damage. We also feel that we should detonate another two large bombs close to the United Nations building, but not near enough to cause any structural damage.'

'Good. Good.' Clay made the odd bobbing motion with his head. 'While I think of it, is everybody clear about the fact that we do not – repeat not – use any commercial explosives? We use only the home-made variety. Anybody not clear on this point? Let me see a show of hands from those who already have enough home-made explosives to carry out our first objectives.'

Every hand in the room was raised.

'The American people must be made aware that these explosions, covering the length and breadth of the land, have been detonated by terrorists – possibly home-grown, though more probably of foreign origin. Only if this ruse is punched home can we expect total co-operation.'

There were murmurs of approval as he went on talking. 'This is why I've made it plain that targets must be chosen with an eye to no significant loss of life. This is also the reason why I have designated Christmas morning for the first strike, and I should say here and now that we want all bombs to explode at the same moment. That is 09.00 in the morning EST, which will be 06.00 Pacific Time. You must be accurate. The detonations must be to the second. Understood?'

A murmur of consent, after which Brutus Clay began checking all the targets that had been chosen. In the major cities they were almost all Government buildings, but with consideration given to the fact that some large structures had to remain standing, as they would be needed for use by the planning elements of COLD.

To his rising horror and concern, Bond heard of the plans in large cities throughout the United States. The orders were already clean-cut and clear – the seizing of TV and radio stations; the securing of all National Guard armouries, the neutralizing of law enforcement agencies and military bases. It was all standard *coup d'état* procedure, played by the book, and he knew that, if there were enough people with allegiance to General Clay, the entire operation stood a definite chance of success. Even if it failed, the country would be split in two and the ensuing problems would result in what amounted to a second civil war, with chaos as the outcome.

As he continued to listen, he saw in sharp focus that this was not simply a harebrained scheme, but one built on sound military strategy, with carefully laid tactical operations that could be carried through with devastating results.

In Washington DC the targets chosen were almost pedestrian – small government offices mainly, plus Union Station. They were anxious that things like the Washington Monument and the Lincoln Memorial, plus the various museums, should not be damaged. 'Our heritage and links to the past have to remain,' Clay said, applauding the choices.

For almost two hours the litany of targets went on, covering every major city in the country. Seattle, Atlantic City, Jersey City, Phoenix, Chicago, Atlanta, Richmond and so on, and so on *ad infinitum*. The extent of the bombings was huge and very carefully considered, but as the plan emerged, Bond could see that this man, and these people who were all part of COLD were on a path which could well alter the course of world history for ever.

This was particularly clear as Clay got to the main strategy of what was to happen immediately after the bombings had taken place. He appeared to have six thousand trained and armed men who would first descend on Washington DC. They would move in, take over communications centres, ring the White House and the Capitol, claiming to be a defensive force there to control any plunge into panic following the nationwide explosions. 'We will be there to take charge and defend,' Clay stated, and – even with his ravished and damaged face – you could sense the way in which he instilled his force with the idea that his agenda would and could work. The only sign of madness lay in the fact of the General obviously believing, to his very core, that the American people would all rise up and back him, something that was not necessarily true.

He would be with the contingent surrounding the White House. 'Unless there is a sudden change, the President plans to be at the White House for Christmas,' he told them. 'As soon as we have secured the area, I shall enter the White House with a small group of officers. There, I shall offer my services to the President and suggest that he makes an immediate television and radio broadcast to the nation. I shall even have the text with me. In fact, I intend to read this to you during our afternoon session.'

Bond had reached breaking point. The aims of COLD and the way in which they planned to carry them out were all too possible. They would not have the luxury of waiting to deal with matters on Christmas morning. This had to be stopped now, and here on the shores of this Italian lake. He leaned over and whispered, 'Now,' to Beatrice whose hand moved towards her belt. For good measure, Bond twisted the buckle on his belt and pushed down, adding his own Mayday signal.

Now, all they could do was sit back and wait, so he shifted his position. Enrico was on his left and he could see the man's pistol only an arm's length away. When things started to happen, he could at least make a grab for the weapon.

They waited, expecting the assault to begin at any moment.

25

Clay Pigeon

UP ON THE dais, Clay was answering questions from various area commanders regarding the individual actions to be taken in major cities and towns: all the usual minutiae of *coups d'état* – the securing of radio and television stations; the guarding of major civic buildings, the amount of violence that was authorized against anyone who did not comply with instructions. Then he began speaking again:

'We must immediately show people how we are going to deal with the most pressing problems.' He had reached his barking stage now. Snapping the words out and becoming the dictator – the leader he really wanted to be. At last they were seeing the true reason for the entire plan: the greater glorification, and total power of General Brutus Brute Clay.

'The American people have pleaded again and again for strong leadership; for something to be done about the blot that lies over our country. A serious and sensible solution to our method of government where a President from one party can be held to ransom by a Senate ruled by a different faction. This is an idiotic situation, and we must stop it, change it. We must also be ruthless,' the voice rising. 'We must do the unpalatable things that have required doing for decades. The problem of drugs and serious crime – in particular street crime – is to be dealt with from the word go. Anyone in possession of drugs will be shot out of hand, whether it be a small amount of marijuana, or a larger amount of cocaine. There will be no appeal. Shoot them and string them up from lampposts.

'Rape will be punished by the most obvious method, an immediate removal of the offender's private parts – no matter if he bleeds to death. Looting and stealing will be similarly treated. The cutting off of a thief's hand is an old and well-tried method. So you do it. I cannot urge too strongly . . .' He paused as there was a noise from the doors at the back, behind where Bond and Beatrice were sitting.

A man ran down the aisle to their right, and Bond immediately recognized him as his drunken guard from the previous night, Roberto, who was now talking rapidly into the General's ear. Clay was suddenly alert, his face flushed with anger. He spoke briefly to Roberto, who came back down the aisle as Clay began to speak:

'Gentlemen, it appears that we have a small problem. This villa is about to come under attack . . .' As he said it, so came the sound of two or three random shots from far away above them. 'There is a contingent of troops moving in from the rear of the house, and two aircraft are dropping airborne troops, ringing the entire villa and its grounds.' He paused, looking around these, his trusted lieutenants. 'I see no real danger to *Operation Blizzard*. There are enough of you – trained soldiers all – to deal with this matter. Go, fight with all the tenacity and skill you possess, then make your way home. I will be in touch by the usual method.'

As he started to move off the dais, so Bond reacted, his arm snaking out towards Enrico's pistol which was still in the man's waistband.

'James!' Beatrice shrieked, and a second later he froze,

feeling the cold metal against his neck.

'I hate to do dis to ya, Mr Bond, but just stand up.' Roberto had made a circle and come up close behind him.

Both Enrico and Tomaso were now on their feet, weapons drawn, waiting as Clay came towards them, his clumping rolling gait more pronounced as he tried to walk quickly. The remainder of the men in the room were moving out very fast indeed, and with the kind of military precision that made Bond's stomach turn over.

Clay reached the long mirror and his hand went out to grasp its surround, pushing so that the long oblong moved with a rumble to one side. 'Through here!' he ordered, looking at Bond and Beatrice. 'Watch them, lads. Now we *need* these hostages. Understand?'

The three men grunted their assent and began to herd their captives in the direction of the opening in the wall. Once through, Clay turned left and, Beatrice reflexed— 'That's the wrong way,' she shouted.

Clay gave a loud one-note laugh. 'You know far too much about the villa.' His hand came back and caught her a heavy blow across the cheek, sending her almost sprawling against the wall. 'We're not going to the little cottage,' Clay rasped. 'There's a much better way of making our escape.' Then, almost as an aside, he commanded 'Cuff them.'

Bond felt the clamp of metal on his left wrist and saw that Roberto had one cuff around his own right wrist, once more handcuffing them together. Glancing across, he saw that Tomaso was doing the same to Beatrice.

The high tunnel was lit by lights recessed in the tiled curved roof, and the General strode ahead, as best he could, grunting with every step and goading them on, a Colt .45 automatic in his right hand.

Finally they came to what looked like a solid stone wall, and Clay slammed the palm of his left hand against a crack in the stone. He laughed again and shouted 'Open Sesame.'

With hardly any noise the stone wall slid to one side revealing a lift cage which Clay entered, motioning the others to get in quickly. Above them the sounds of fighting became more distinct, machine gun fire mingling with single shots and explosions.

Roberto hauled Bond in and Clay touched a button. They began to move upwards, eventually stopping in what looked like a broom cupboard.

'When the Tempestas made changes to this place, they were wise enough to provide several cunning escape routes.' Clay sounded offhand, as though he were a tour guide. 'Good. Now everybody out and turn right.'

They were in one of the upstairs passages, leading to the bedrooms. 'Head for my quarters,' the General shouted above what was now a cacophony of shots and explosions. At the end of the passage he threw open a door which took them into a sumptuously furnished bedroom. As Bond stepped inside, he froze in shock.

The centrepiece of the room was a huge circular bed: above it a canopy of glass. Sukie Tempesta lay naked and sprawled across the bed, her head twisted oddly to one side and streaks of blood drying rapidly from long slices and cuts criss-crossing her body. 'You bastard,' he yelled at Brutus Clay. 'You sadistic bastard.'

The General turned and looked him straight in the eye. 'She was no good to me, Bond. Only good for one thing, and that ended last night. You *do* realize that she was a diagnosed psychopath? Did you know that she actually killed her husband – Luigi's and Angelo's father? She killed him as she made love to him, poor old man. Throttled him. Gave much pleasure doing that to old Pasquale. Then, one night it went too far. Like it went too far last night. Come.' He clumped across the room, Tomaso pulling Beatrice behind him with Enrico pushing her.

Roberto gave Bond's hand a gentle pull and whispered, 'Dis guy's crazy, Mr B. He'll see us all in hell.' Bond simply nodded, but the nod contained a wealth of meaning. 'Then do something about it,' he was saying.

Clay led them into a dressing room, opened a cupboard door and pressed a button. A panel slid back to reveal another lift cage. 'Hurry! Hurry! Get in!' he barked at them, sounding as though his throat was bone-dry. As Roberto and Bond got into the cage behind the others, Clay shut the grille and they began to descend rapidly. 'If Luigi and Angelo haven't made it, I'm not waiting for them,' Clay muttered. Above them an explosion rocked the house. Then another as the cage stopped and the gates opened.

Now they were in another tunnel. 'Not far to go.' He was off again in his rolling strange stumping walk, leading them forward. Bond felt Roberto's hand on his wrist and saw the man unlock the cuff. 'Pretend we'se still stuck together,' the hoodlum whispered. In front of them they could glimpse light, while the sounds of battle still raged above and behind them.

Quite suddenly they emerged into the boathouse which stood to the left of the house, looking from the main door. Rocking gently on its moorings was a large motor launch, high with a pilot's cockpit rising from the centre. For'ard of the cockpit two fixed forward-firing MG3 7.62mm machine-guns rested menacingly, while a third MG3 was swivel-mounted in the stern.

'Cast off those lines,' Clay was commanding. 'The Tempesta boys haven't got here, so we'll go without them.' The ground shook to yet another, heavier, explosion, and Clay clambered clumsily on board, hauling himself up the steps to the cockpit, readying the launch. Tomaso and Enrico pulled Beatrice into the aft section which had wooden seating running around the inside of the stern.

Clay put back his head and shouted, 'You know what this craft's called?' He gave another of his one-note laughs. 'It's named *Clay Pigeon*.' The one-note laugh again. 'A joke. My own private launch with plenty of firepower to shoot at any pigeon who wants to take on Brutus Clay. Enrico, man the aft gun!' As he gave the command, and Enrico stepped into position, settling himself into the swivel housing of the MG3, Clay started the motors which, in the confined space, sounded like a bad day at the Monaco Grand Prix. The launch slipped her moorings and turned neatly, pointing out towards the lake as the General operated the automatic doors to the boathouse, then piled on power and allowed the craft to shoot away very fast out into the lake, leaving a twin rooster tail of water behind it.

Enrico was testing the mounting on his gun, while Tomaso looked steadily towards the villa, uttering a short curse as he saw part of the large house was in flames. Bond flashed a look at Beatrice, showing that both his hands were free. She nodded, looking up at Enrico who had stuffed his pistol inside the left of his waistband.

The launch turned almost parallel with the shore, and now it was the General's turn to curse. Not only was the house on fire, but the fighting was almost over. Men who had seemed undaunted at the briefing were being lined up and shackled together by the sinister-looking black shapes of the Leatherheads in their dark fighting uniforms and ski masks.

Bond made out the Tempesta brothers and the men from COLD under heavy guard being marched away from the buildings by men armed with what appeared to be H&K automatic weapons. He smiled, then, above the engine noise and the slipstream, he heard another roar and saw the two police launches bearing down on their starboard side, streaking in from around a mile's distance.

Clay had also seen them, for he turned the launch so that its bows were facing the oncoming craft, and as they came within rage, he fired several bursts from the for'ard guns, the noise like someone ripping the very sky apart. A long rattle of fire came from one of the police launches, and woodwork was chopped away from the deck above the bow.

'Enrico! Get them!' Brutus Clay swung the wheel so that they came side on to the two launches and the rear weapon stuttered out, a stream of tracer going wide as Enrico tried to bring the weapon to bear.

'James!' Beatrice shouted.

He looked towards her to see that she had snatched the pistol from Enrico's belt and thrown it towards him. For a second the weapon seemed to levitate in the air then curved down towards his outstretched hands.

'General, the . . .' Tomaso began as his hand went for his own gun, but he did not even finish shouting the warning as Bond's two fast shots found homes in the man's throat. He was hardly down before Beatrice was on him, scrabbling for the keys to the handcuffs and pulling the pistol from him.

Clay heard none of this, for his whole concentration was on the two launches moving in for the kill. He took *Clay Pigeon* around in a long sweeping turn, trying to bring the for'ard guns to bear, and in that movement, Enrico swung back hard against the mounting at the rear of the boat.

'Jump, Enrico,' Bond shouted at the man. 'Over the side or I'll send you to join Tomaso!'

Enrico hesitated only for a moment, saw the carnage that had once been his partner and heaved himself into the spray and churning wake.

'General Clay!' Bond shouted above the engine din. 'General Clay. Stop engines and back away from the wheel.'

The General either did not hear, or pretended not to hear the order. Bond raised the pistol and was about to fire when there was a sharp crack to his right, and he saw a clump of fabric, bone and blood come flying off Brutus Clay's right shoulder.

'That'll get his attention,' Beatrice called out.

Clay spun around, his ravaged and monstrous face showing something of the shock, his right arm hanging useless at his side.

The launch, still at full power, had nobody at the wheel. It leaped forward out of control, swinging the wounded Clay against one side of the cockpit, then backwards so that he lost his footing, coming down the steps in a series of little stuttering movements, and sending him spinning and twisting as he hit the port side of the craft, going head first into the water.

'I'm wid you Mr Bond,' Roberto shouted, jumping towards the cockpit, closing the throttles and taking control of the craft. Bond wondered if Rhabb could make use of Roberto back in the States. The man certainly deserved a break.

As the engine noise died, the only thing they could hear was the cry from Brutus Clay— 'Help! Help me! I can't swim! Help!'

'Don't do a thing,' Bond yelled, watching the man bobbing up and down like a buoy, thrashing out ineffectively with his prosthetic legs.

They watched him go down several times, still screaming for help, and then disappear with a huge air bubble coming to the surface.

The two police launches came close and Roberto turned the wheel of the *Clay Pigeon*, allowing Brutus Clay's vessel to be escorted in towards the Villa Tempesta.

Eddie Rhabb was waiting for them at the pier. After he had helped Beatrice ashore, he reached out and pumped Bond's hand. 'Gee, James, how can we ever thank you?'

'Thank me? For what?'

'Getting that crazy General for one thing.'

'He isn't crazy. In fact, he's very effective: good planner; sound strategist; has an excellent tactical mind . . .'

'Had.' Rhabb raised an eyebrow.

'I thought the launches picked him up.'

'Well, they kinda did, but they threw him back in again. There would have been a lot of paperwork. You can understand that.'

'Ah,' Bond nodded. 'Anyway, it was Beatrice who really got him.'

'Could never have done it without you, James.'

'Oh, I don't know.'

'I do,' Beatrice said softly. 'That man could have changed the history of the Western world, and you know it.'

Bond raised his head, feeling that someone was looking at him. There, up near the house, Luigi and Angelo Tempesta were ringed with guards, but they stared with utter hatred at Bond.

'What's going to happen to them?' He inclined his head towards the brothers.

'Like I told you. We're giving them to the Italians. They'll keep them for a hundred years and then have a trial. The paperwork for those two'll take a very long time to sort out. I can't thank you enough, James. How can we really show our appreciation?'

'I'll think of something, Eddie. Maybe you should write to the Queen. Maybe you'll have to.'

The air was filled with the smell of explosives and smoke, but through it, he caught the sweet aroma of Beatrice's scent. He put his arm around her and they walked slowly up towards the aftermath of the battle.

26

Facing the Music

THEY FLEW INTO Dublin, using what Bond called 'the soft route'. From there they took the last available flight into Heathrow, which was quiet at this time of night. Nobody bothered them and he used a public telephone to call Sanusi.

'Everyone's going crazy looking for you,' the perky doctor told him. 'You're wanted for about two million contraventions of standing orders. You know M's retired, and the new M's a woman? She's out for blood, it seems. Anyone who lays eyes on you is to bring you in.' He gave a little chuckle. 'I fear she'll give you the worst wigging you've ever experienced.'

'She can only fire me.'

'From a cannon probably. No, James, I somehow don't think she's going to get rid of you. She knows better than that.'

'Then she really cannot be as bad as the old M.'

'They say she can curse like a deck-hand.'

'Heard it all before: seen it; done it. Have you got Freddie's ashes, doc?'

'Yes, they're here, at the clinic. You want me to bring them to you?'

'I'll drop in on the way home.'

'You'll be okay. There's nobody else here. I can't say the

275

same for your flat. They're probably watching it round the clock.'

'We'll see about that. I'm coming straight over.' He felt tired, dazed and now terribly sad that M had at last retired. It was like some old and familiar building of beauty being destroyed and turned into a carpark, or left as a wasteland. Hollow men, he thought. It's all changed now. Straw men.

They took a taxi to the clinic where he picked up the little brass urn. Sanusi again told him to be careful, but he had gone past the point of caring about anything – except Beatrice, of course. He had no regrets.

When they reached his flat in that side road lined with plane trees he saw a van with three aerials parked two doors down. He knew what *that* meant.

Beatrice went straight into the kitchen and made coffee while he sifted through the mail. Nothing there except bills, junk and two official-looking envelopes. One was an invitation to M's retirement party. The other a direct order, under the new M's signature. He was to report to her immediately he returned to London. She had ended by saying there were certain serious matters that needed discussing . . . Time is of the essence, she had put. Damn that for a game of soldiers, he thought, sipping his coffee.

The message light was blinking on the answering machine, so he wound back the tape and played it – 'James, my boy. You'll have heard that I've retired,' M's voice, nostalgic. 'The question is did I fall or was I pushed? Nobody seems to know where you've got to, and, of course, I couldn't give them any help with that. Nip over to see me when you've got a minute, will you, there's a good chap. As for my successor, in confidence her bark is worse than her bite.'

Beatrice was certainly his kind of woman. She could see that several things were bothering him, so she left him alone.

He went through to the front of the house and suddenly saw them coming for him. He knew them by sight. One tall, muscular, in a pair of slacks and a sports coat with leather patches at the elbows. The other much shorter, fat, a little pompous, walking with the roll of a sailor on leave and wearing a grey lightweight suit. They were both hired thugs, but he had, at one time or another, worked with them.

'We might have to deal with Freddie's ashes next week.' He took Beatrice in his arms and kissed her. 'I think I have an appointment with my new boss.'

The front doorbell rang.

'That'll be my car now. If you wouldn't mind waiting for an hour or so.'

She nodded and pulled him close. 'I'll wait as long as it takes. Where shall I put Freddie?'

He felt a small pang of pain: guilt for her death; sadness over the whole business. He knew where she wanted the ashes scattering, but until then . . .?

'Look,' Beatrice had one hand on his arm. 'Why don't I put her in the bedroom. She's from your past and I don't mind sharing you with her. I know how badly you must feel.'

He nodded, gave her another quick kiss. 'Be back soon,' he smiled and devoured her with his eyes.

Yes, of course, he would be back.

'Captain Bond,' the taller one said, putting a foot inside the door.

'I know, I know,' he said. 'Madam wants to see me yesterday. Got to face the music.'

He climbed into the back of the waiting Rover, shaking the man's hand from his arm. One drove and the other sat with him in the back.

'A shade chilly for this time of the year,' Bond said, but neither man answered. Their job was to bring him in for a dressing-down from the new boss.

He smiled to himself, suddenly remembering the Winston Churchill speech he had memorized at school. 'This is not the end. It is not even the beginning of the end. But it is, perhaps, the end of the beginning.'

Under his breath he said. 'Good with words, Churchill. Very good with words.'

JOHN GARDNER

GOLDENEYE

She is beautiful. She is Russian.
And she is very dangerous.

Once Xenia worked for the KGB. But her new master is
Janus, a powerful and ambitious Russian leader who no
longer cares about ideology. Janus's ambitions are
money and power: his normal business methods include
theft and murder. And he has just acquired GoldenEye, a
piece of high-tech space technology with the power to
destroy or corrupt the West's financial markets.

But Janus has underestimated his most determined
enemy.

JAMES BOND

Based on a screenplay by
Michael France and Jeffrey Caine

HODDER & STOUGHTON PAPERBACKS

JOHN GARDNER

SEAFIRE

JAMES BOND 007

is back in action, with the stunning Flicka von Grüsse at his side and his licence to kill renewed once more. His target is Sir Maxwell Tarn: a businessman whose legitimate empire spans the globe, whose wealth is uncountable, who also deals in illegal weapons on a breathtaking scale.

But even Bond is unprepared for the speed of events, as a sting operation in a Cambridge hotel leads rapidly to an assassination in Spain, a fugitive in Israel and neo-Nazi plotters in Germany.

Bond finally catches up with Tarn in Puerto Rico, where his prey becomes is captor. Can he escape in time to stop Tarn?

HODDER & STOUGHTON PAPERBACKS